BEN McQUEEN—The her...
endary patriot Dan McQueen, ...
tween a noble legacy, allegiance to his country—and
the smoldering Mexican beauty whose raging obses-
sion for revenge could destroy them both.

DOÑA ANABEL CORDERO DE TOSTA—She is the
fiery daughter of the infamous bandit El Tigre de
Coahuila, whose brutal death at the hands of Texas
Rangers cries vengeance from the grave. Sworn to
carry on his legacy of hate and violence, she plots to
lead his men in battle against the despised Ameri-
cans—but she cannot forget the heroic lieutenant
who saved her life, a man she has grown to love.

SPOTTED CALF—The Commanche's fiercest warri-
or, he has seen his people and way of life destroyed
by the conquering white man. Now a prisoner of the
hated Texas Rangers, he lives only for the day he
will escape—and gather his tribal forces against his
enemies to right a terrible wrong.

SNAKE EYE GANDY—A rugged, one-eyed Texas
Ranger driven by a savage lust for battle, he's no
friend to the Indians—or Mexicans. He's the man
who once slew a great warrior chief's brother, en-
dured a scalping—and lived to tell about it. But
now that great warrior chief is his prisoner—and
one day he will take his revenge.

THE WARRIORS OF THE NIGHT—Servants of the
blood-eating god, they are a tribe of swift, silent,
and cunning killers who strike under cover of darkness. When day ends, the terror begins.

Bantam Books by Kerry Newcomb

The Medal
GUNS OF LIBERTY
SWORD OF VENGEANCE
ONLY THE GALLANT
WARRIORS OF THE NIGHT

MORNING STAR
SACRED IS THE WIND
IN THE SEASON OF THE SUN
SCALPDANCERS

★ THE MEDAL ★
Book 4

WARRIORS
OF
THE NIGHT

Kerry Newcomb

BANTAM BOOKS
NEW YORK · TORONTO · LONDON · SYDNEY · AUCKLAND

WARRIORS OF THE NIGHT

A Bantam Domain Book / December 1991

ISBN 0-553-29370-2

Published simultaneously in the United States and Canada

PRINTED IN THE UNITED STATES OF AMERICA

RAD   0 9 8 7 6 5 4 3 2 1

For Patty, Amy Rose, P.J., and now Emily

As ever, my thanks to the good folks at Bantam, with a special tip of my coonskin cap to my editor, Greg Tobin, and publisher, Linda Grey. I am deeply grateful for the unwavering faith of my agent and friend, Aaron Priest.

Chapter One

The scent of blood drew the big cat to the sunbaked ridge overlooking the Rio Grande. The mountain lion moved with swift, sure grace, a fleeting, tawny shadow among the stark, upthrust layers of volcanic rock. With a body as long as a man was tall and armed with fang and claw and powerful muscles capable of ripping an enemy to shreds, the panther of the Big Bend country had never known fear—until now.

The mountain lion leaped from boulder to boulder and alighted atop a ledge of compressed ash. With calm, patient resolve, the predator waited. His keen eyes surveyed the dry wash where, in the past, flash floods had scrubbed the smooth-worn limestone walls of the arroyo and littered the floor with palm-sized pebbles in a variety of earthen colors, dark shades of red and gray, white, brown, and black. There had not been a spring shower in the past week, so the arroyo should have been bone dry. But today, in the mid-morning heat, a rivulet of blood traced a crimson path along the watercourse. The "headwaters" of this grisly stream were the mutilated remains of a mestizo goatherd and his son. Man and boy lay stretched across a flat outcropping of table rock, their chest cavities slit open and their hearts ripped out.

The stench in the watercourse was no stranger to the lion; nor were the buzzing flies and the shadows that swept across the corpses and the spattered rocks as the vultures located the kill and began to circle in ever-tightening spirals against the hard blue dome of sky.

In another time or place, the lion might have hurried to the feast. But something old and dark and terrible had passed this way and left a trail of death that even a prince of predators was loath to follow. As if warned by some deep-rooted instinct against an evil as ancient as these weathered hills and wind-sculpted peaks, the big cat did not enter the arroyo, but turned its back upon this place and crept away.

A gust of wind sighed among the desert mountains, like some final, faint, agonizing cry, stirred the dust, and then, like the panther, departed in silence.

Three hundred miles away, Dona Anabel Cordero de Tosta had problems of her own. She was a slim, dark-eyed young woman with raven hair pinned back; she wore a flat-brimmed sombrero. Anabel was dusty and tired and certainly not looking for trouble. But trouble she'd found. Or rather, it had found her, in the menacing form of a Quahadi Comanche war party. Though the Comanches were an ever-present danger in the Chisos Mountains of the Big Bend, it was highly unusual for the braves to be raiding so close to San Antonio now that a company of Texas Rangers had set up quarters in town. But here they were, eight fierce-looking warriors, and Anabel in the thick of them.

Carmelita had warned her against going alone to visit the grave of her father. "At least if you will not wait for your vaqueros, take your brother," she had said. Ah, but Anabel was impatient, and as for her brother Esteban, of what use a priest in her present situation? Beneath her lap blanket, her hand coupled around the trigger of a sawed-off shotgun that had belonged to Don Luis, her father, a stubborn, hard-bitten bandit who had fought the Anglos until his death a few weeks past. He had been laid to rest near the ruins of a mission ten miles north of San Antonio on land that had once belonged to the Corderos and was now considered part of the Texas Republic. Don Luis Cordero de Tosta had never recognized Texas's independence, but considered the republic to be part of Mexico. From his lair in the Chisos Mountains, El Tigre—the tiger of Coahuila—had fought to the bitter end to drive these Anglo invaders from his country's sacred soil. He had hoped to restore his family's wealth and influence in the process. His dreams were worm food now, and he had left his unfinished business as a legacy for his daughter.

On this second day of May in 1845, Anabel was more concerned with living through the next five minutes than with the weight of her inherited responsibilities. She had gone to her father's grave site searching for answers, a quest that might well, it seemed now, prove fatal. However, she wasn't dead yet. There still might be a way out. Anabel knew the lead brave, Spotted Calf. During a visit last year to her father's retreat in the desert mountains, she had watched Don Luis conduct trade with the Comanches. If the chief remembered her, Anabel might be able to reason with him.

One of the Comanches struck the brown gelding hitched to her carriage with his war lance in an attempt to startle her horse. Several of the braves followed his example. They ringed the carriage, whooping and waving their weapons as Anabel fought to keep the gelding under control. Gripping the reins in her left hand, she refused to give in to panic. The shotgun beneath the blanket was some assurance, but she'd need more than buckshot to survive the day. Don Luis Cordero, her father, had established a formidable reputation among the Quahadi Comanches in the mountain country. They had respected his strength. Don Luis had many vaqueros riding for him, men skilled with the gun and knife, each man an experienced Indian fighter. Unfortunately those vaqueros were miles away.

Outnumbered by a contingent of Texas Rangers, Don Luis's men had scattered after the running fight that had claimed the life of El Tigre himself. Anabel knew they'd find some way to return to San Antonio and contact her. For a fleeting second she even entertained the hope that they might come riding down out of the hills, guns blazing as they charged past thickets of mesquite and mountain cedar. But the howling savages surrounding her knew she was alone.

The Comanches, eight lean and wiry warriors, were painted for war. Their coppery features were hidden behind masks of red and yellow war paint.

The rumps of their sturdy mountain-bred ponies bore the mark of the snake, the sign of the Comanche.

Spotted Calf led them, but there was little in the way of attire to indicate his leadership, save for three turkey feathers fastened to a topknot of shiny black hair.

He wore a brown brocaded vest, no doubt the prize of some raid, that hung open to reveal his naked chest. A blue breechclout and long-fringed buckskin leggings covered his lower limbs. His calf-high moccasins were decorated with tiny glass beads and elk's teeth.

Some of the warriors were armed with muskets, some with war lances. All of them carried the short, highly lethal orangewood bow prized by every Comanche. The war party continued to circle the carriage. Men rode up and counted coup, striking the frightened gelding with their bows. And still Anabel kept the horse under control.

Impressed, Spotted Calf broke from the ranks of the taunting braves and walked his mount up to the carriage to confront what he believed to be a helpless young woman.

"The daughter of my enemy is foolish to come alone among these hills," said Spotted Calf. He was close enough now for Anabel to see the bear-claw necklace the brave wore around his neck and to smell the dried bear grease on his buckskin leggings.

"Enemy?" The woman made a show of her surprise. "The Quahadi have always traded in peace with Don Luis Cordero." If the Comanche didn't know of her father's death, the señorita wasn't about to tell him.

"In the time of the new calf moon, your father

came with many men and stole my horses," Spotted Calf told her. "And killed Whistler, the dream walker."

Anabel refused to be cowed by the warrior. She remembered the incident well. "El Tigre de Coahuila only took back the horses your braves stole from him."

The brave ignored her reply. He would not hear the truth in her words.

"It was a bad thing, to kill the dream walker. Only Whistler could see beyond seeing. His magic was strong. But now his voice is silent. His songs no longer hold back the dark spirits of the old ones." Spotted Calf turned to the braves surrounding the carriage and raised the rifle gripped in his strong right hand. At his signal his followers quieted and ceased their failed efforts to spook the señorita's horse. Then the war chief leaned forward and peered into the carriage.

"I will take you with us."

"My father is close by. He will bring his vaqueros and hunt you down and kill you," Anabel warned.

"I do not think so." Spotted Calf seemed wholly unconcerned. "Because then I will kill his daughter. No. I think you will be worth many horses and guns." Spotted Calf reached for the reins she held. The time for talking was finished. Anabel steadied herself, and with a quick flick of her wrist, tossed her lap blanket over Spotted Calf's head, then struck him square in the face with the twin-barreled shotgun.

The Comanche howled in pain and lashed out at the blanket covering his head. His horse reared, and the war chief lost his purchase and landed on his backside in a thicket of prickly pear. Anabel slapped the rump of her horse with the reins as the braves in front of her tried to block her path and bring their muskets to bear. Other warriors notched arrows to their bowstrings. All of them were unprepared for what happened next. The shotgun roared and buckshot toppled from horseback the three braves blocking her path. The shotgun's recoil knocked Anabel back against the leather walls of the carriage. The gelding bolted forward, carrying the woman through the powder smoke and racing away from the startled Comanches. A couple of shots rang out. An arrow glanced off one wheel as the carriage rolled up and over a rise and dipped out of sight. In its wake, one brave lay dead on the side of the road. Two others sporting flesh wounds struggled to bring their skittish ponies under control and to remount. Spotted Calf, his broken nose a gory fountain of crimson, exhorted his warriors to pursue the carriage as it disappeared from view, leaving a trail of white dust to settle on the wheel-rutted road. The braves responded slowly. The momentary loss of their chief and the death of one of their number had left them benumbed. Spotted Calf regaled his companions with every insult he could think of, calling them helpless women and the offspring of camp dogs. He caught up the reins of his horse from Little Coyote, who had kept the animal from running off. Spotted Calf leaped astride the animal. Then he winced and, reaching beneath himself, plucked nettles from his buttocks.

"Dancing Horse is dead," said Sees the Turtle, the stern-featured older brother of Little Coyote. Spotted Calf listened as he probed his nose. Pain seemed about to split his head in two. He sucked air through his mouth and struggled to will the pain into submission. The death of his companion, Dancing Horse, only added to the anger he was feeling.

Spotted Calf wrapped a strip of buckskin around his face and covered his nose in an attempt to staunch the flow of blood. Once that was accomplished he grabbed a war lance from Sees the Turtle. The weapon, fashioned of bois d'arc wood, was seven feet in length, tipped with an iron lance head bound to the shaft with sinew. A half dozen turkey feathers were attached near the butt of the lance.

"I will have her scalp," said Spotted Calf.

"We are too close to the village of the white eyes," Sees the Turtle cautioned. "The Rangers are camped there."

"My vision has led us," Spotted Calf replied. "Our band has been driven from the mountains by the dark ones. Now we tremble before these Rangers? Have we become old women afraid to leave our lodges?" The war chief glanced past Sees the Turtle and addressed himself to the other dispirited braves.

"Are there no men to follow me?"

"I will follow," Little Coyote spoke up. He was bold and brash and eager to fight. He met his brother's disapproving gaze and refused to be swayed. Full of a young man's pride, Little Coyote wanted to prove himself the equal of those he rode with. The remainder of the war party raised their weapons and shouted war cries. Spotted Calf grinned and looked at Sees the Turtle, who shrugged and nodded his willingness to continue the pursuit.

"Our horses are swift. She will not escape us," Spotted Calf reassured his rival. The blood had ceased to flow from his flattened nose, but he left the makeshift compress in place just to be safe. "She will not escape...me." He struck his horse with the butt of the lance; the animal lunged forward and in a matter of seconds was galloping full out. Galvanized once more, and despite the bad omen of their initial loss, Sees the Turtle, Little Coyote, and the rest of the war party joined in the hunt. Like a pack of coppery-skinned wolves, they would not close the chase until they'd made their kill.

Minutes later and a mile and a half down the road, Anabel Cordero met Lt. Ben McQueen. It happened without warning, as is the way of that coyote trickster—fate—who turns a man's or woman's life inside out on a whim.

Every gulley she crossed, every hill she passed brought Anabel closer to San Antonio. The carriage lurched from side to side like a storm-tossed ship in the violent embrace of the sea. Her pursuers were slowly gaining on her. Once she cleared the hills, though, the Comanches might abandon the chase rather than risk a run-in with the well-armed Rangers. For once, Anabel was almost thankful for their presence in the town.

She clung to the carriage as the wheels jumped from rut to rock and somehow kept herself from being thrown from the seat. The gelding was galloping full out now. Anabel began to figure she had the edge when she dashed around a chalky white outcropping of stone, rode a precipitous incline across a dry creek bed, and began a climb between two scantily wooded knolls. Just then, a long-limbed, red-haired horseman in a dusty blue uniform dashed from a cedar break and in a matter of seconds brought his sleek brown mare up alongside the gelding.

The officer in blue leaned from the saddle and, with the practiced ease of a natural-born horseman, caught the gelding's harness and forced the animal to a swift stop. The gelding stood with sides heaving, nostrils flared in the rising heat, as the sun continued to climb toward noon.

Ben McQueen turned and flashed a broad smile at the woman he thought he had rescued. "There you go, ma'am. I believe that's got him under control. Snake spook your horse? I heard a gunshot and—"

Her buggy whip cut him short. He reacted with a hawklike quickness that was surprising in a large man and managed to shield his square-jawed features from the stinging kiss of the whip.

"*Imbecil! Idiota!*" Anabel was furious. He had cost her precious moments.

"You've got one hell of a way of thanking a man who has just saved you from a broken neck. A runaway horse on a road like this—"

"Not runaway. Running away!" She pointed back along the road toward the rise she had just crossed. "From them!" In an example of perfect timing, the war party swept over the rise and, without breaking stride, loosed a volley at the couple on the incline ahead.

Ben McQueen had envisioned himself the gallant rescuer. Indeed he'd been enjoying the role of hero, especially after the señorita proved to be as pretty as a summer sunrise. Alas, with the arrival of the Comanches, his fall from grace was brutal and complete. Hero one moment, *idiota* the next. Ben's sun-bronzed features paled and his green eyes grew round and wide.

A bullet nicked the leather frame of the carriage; feathered arrows sprouted from the rubble underfoot. Ben slapped his cap across the gelding's rump and the horse bolted forward. "I'll lead them away," he shouted. "They won't catch me!" His words were no sooner spoken than his brown mare staggered and swung halfway around as a lead slug plowed into the animal's side and punctured a lung. Ben kicked free and slid from the saddle as the mare went down. The soldier looked over his shoulder and saw that the señorita had once more halted the carriage. Ben turned toward the howling Comanches. Well, he could stay and die or run like hell. A whirling arrow missed him by inches. Another buried itself in the road at his feet. Ben was armed with an army-issue carbine, a saber, and a pair of .36-caliber single-shot percussion pistols. He ought to be able to make a heroic stand lasting all of thirty seconds. The hell with it! Ben turned and dodged another volley of flint-tipped arrows all the way to the carriage.

Anabel used her whip on the gelding as Ben crowded onto the seat. The gelding responded, sprang into action, and climbed the rise ahead, while back along the road Spotted Calf led his braves across the dry wash and started up after his quarry. Once again the carriage momentarily disappeared from view. Spotted Calf raised his war lance over his head and called to his braves to double their efforts. His surefooted stallion climbed the last few yards. The carriage was just ahead. He had closed the gap. He didn't know who the white man was or where he had come from, but it had been plain to see the man was alone. And that made him fair game for a Comanche lance.

The carriage churned a thick cloud of dust in its wake. Spotted Calf and his warriors ignored the grit, which stung their eyes and burned their lungs. It was time for the kill, before the carriage cleared the foothills and reached the grazing lands along the San Antonio River. This was the moment; now was the time. Thirty yards became twenty, then ten, as the Quahadi war party closed in for the kill. Muskets were loaded by braves who rode at a gallop. Arrows were notched and loosed with such velocity they pierced the carriage's folding cover. Muskets blasted holes in the back and sides. Spotted Calf rode up alongside the carriage and jabbed his spear in a killing thrust that sawed at the empty air above the riderless seat. The rest of the war party swarmed over the carriage and brought the gelding to a halt.

Little Coyote had his arrow ready to make a kill. He eased the sinew string and stared at the carriage. Sees the Turtle spat a rifle ball down the barrel of his musket and tamped it in place by striking the gun butt against his thigh. Spotted Calf raged and shoved his war lance into the leather walls, hacking through the sides and back in a series of savage attacks until the folding cover lay broken and shredded in the road.

"What trickery is this?" asked Little Coyote. "What spirit has carried them off?"

"This is a bad thing," one of the wounded braves said. Spotted Calf studied the winding road as a sudden gust of wind swept away the settling dust revealing the hill behind them, fringed with post oaks and cedar. The war chief ignored the superstitious complaints of the braves around him. His attention remained riveted on the wooded slope. The war party fell silent. Even Sees the Turtle ceased his complaining. He waited like the others and watched the hills.

"I think we've lost them," Ben said, peering over the jumble of limestone rocks and cacti that formed a natural barricade among the deep green scattering of cedars halfway up the slope.

"You don't know Comanches," the young woman beside him coldly remarked.

"No, I don't," he admitted. "Lieutenant Ben McQueen, at your service." He touched the leather brim of his cap and smiled, hoping to thaw her chilled reserve.

"I don't want you at my service."

"So I noticed. You just about took my ear off with that buggy whip."

Anabel sighed, unable to cling to anger. She did not trust these Anglos. Yet this man had placed himself in harm's way for her sake. And his idea of abandoning the carriage once out of sight of the Comanches had bought them a little extra time. She softened, and with guarded emotions introduced herself.

"I am Anabel...Obregon." No one in San Antonio, save her brother and Carmelita, knew her real identity, knew that Anabel was the daughter of Don Luis Cordero de Tosta, the tiger of Coahuila, whose death cried vengeance from the grave.

"Pleased to meet you," Ben said. He removed his cap and wiped the perspiration from his forehead. He thick red mane was plastered to his skull. His blue flannel uniform was unbearably hot, and the spiny thickets that dotted every hillside and choked the gulleys had played havoc with his trouser legs.

Ben McQueen scrunched his big-boned, six-foot-four-inch frame down behind the rocks and tried to take stock of the situation. He knew Choctaw, Cherokee, and Creek, the legacy of a youth spent in the Indian territory. But of the Comanches he had only heard rumor and tall tales since disembarking in Galveston. The squat, leathery warriors gathered in the road below were providing his first encounter. If only the soldiers he had left to escort retired Gen. Matthew Abbot into San Antonio were here ... No, of what use was blame? Flights of fantasy weren't going to see him through this. It would take powder and shot and cold steel, not to mention nerve and a wagonload of luck. He felt a hollow pit form in his stomach and struggled to ignore the sensation. He concentrated on seeing that his weapons were loaded and primed. He couldn't help but notice the practiced ease with which Anabel bit open the paper cartridges and loaded the twin barrels of her shotgun. She sensed his interest and shifted her dark-eyed gaze.

"What is it?"

Ben's square-jawed features split with a grin. He wiped a hand across his stubbled jaw and with a wry look told her.

"There's some ladies in Philadelphia that would be most impressed by your talents."

"A woman must be able to do more than braid her hair and wear silk dresses to live here," Anabel remarked with disdain. She worked a metal ramrod down each barrel, tamping the loads in place. Her riding skirt was torn at the hem and her black boots were scuffed. The boulder felt warm against her back. The hill rose gradually for another twenty-five feet before playing out beneath a sheer wall of limestone too steep to climb. To reach the crest they'd have to follow the contour of the hill around to where the cliff had eroded and broken off into rubble. The hill was slowly being reclaimed by mesquite trees, whose twisted roots and branches seemed able to thrive in even the most arid of soils and most precipitous conditions. Unfortunately, any attempt to climb the remaining slope would require crossing open ground.

Ben removed his blue cap and slowly eased himself onto his knees. He set aside his saber and carbine and edged around the barricade that nature had provided for them and, once in place, studied the war party. The warriors in the distance were framed by the spiny pads of a prickly pear cactus. The Comanches had started to backtrack, but had yet to pick up any sign of their prey. The ground was so hard-packed and broken, Ben doubted he and the señorita had left any tracks for the war party to follow. His hopes began to rise. He crawled back behind the rocks and crouched alongside Anabel.

"I think we're safe here," he whispered with confidence.

Then he saw the rattler.

It was a big diamondback, six feet of cold-blooded nightmare thick as Ben's forearm, and devil-nasty. The rattlesnake had been sunning itself on a ledge above them. Something had disturbed the reptile and caused it to retreat downhill. Ben didn't care about the creature's reasons, only its immediacy. The rattlesnake noticed the two intruders blocking its path and coiled itself within striking distance. Charcoal-gray and black, with black and white bands at its buzzing tail, the rattler continued to warn the humans in an attempt to drive them away. The rattler's mouth opened once to reveal a pair of poison-drenched fangs as Ben tossed a handful of pebbles in its direction, hoping to force it to retreat.

"Don't move," Anabel whispered. "Maybe it will go away."

"Good Christ, señorita," Ben hoarsely replied. The rattler looked like it had no intention whatsoever of going away. Ben eased his hand toward the hilt of his saber. A gunshot would alert the war party below, but Ben figured if he could just free his sword, silent steel might save the day. He gripped the scabbard in his left hand and, with his right hand curled around the hilt, began to slowly slide the blade out to where it would do some good. Sweat beaded on Ben's forehead and rolled down into his eyes, with stinging effect. The buzzing of the rattles seemed deafening in the confines between the jumble of rocks and underbrush and the base of the limestone cliff. Anabel started to caution the lieutenant, then reconsidered; she did not want to run the risk of distracting him. The rattler's head wavered between the man and woman as if uncertain which to kill first. Then it struck.

Even expecting the attack, the savage swiftness with which it came so startled Ben that he leaped to his feet. He parried those gaping fangs with the length of his scabbard and struck with the saber, slashing again and again at the writhing creature. The tip of the sword shattered against stone. Ben didn't care. He continued to hack at the rattler until it lay dead upon the blood-smeared rocks. Then, with the adrenaline still pumping through his veins, he slowly turned. The hairs rose on the back of his neck. He was standing completely in the open! He looked downslope and found himself staring into the upturned faces of the Comanches, who had seen the flash of his saber as sunlight glinted off the blade.

Spotted Calf raised his war lance and loosed a savage cry. "See, my brothers? The All-Father has shown us our enemies!" Then he charged the hiding place along with the war party, who sensed an easy kill. Ben kicked the rattler's carcass downhill in disgust and tossed his saber on the ground. He took up his carbine, cocked it, and looked at Anabel.

"Work your way around to the top. Find another place to hole up. I'll hold them as long as I can," Ben said.

"No,'" Anabel flatly replied, cradling the shotgun in the crook of her arm. "The daughter of Don..." She caught herself in mid-sentence, shrugged, and lamely said, "I will not run."

Ben stared down at the Comanches as they swept across the broken terrain at a dead run. He had never seen finer horsemen; however, two of the braves were having trouble keeping up and appeared to be wounded. Ben took stock of his own weapons, the two single-shot pistols in his belt and a muzzle-loading carbine. He and the señorita would have to make every shot count. He caught Anabel staring at him.

"You are from Philadelphia?" she asked.

"Well, yes—sort of." There wasn't time to give an account of his past.

Anabel sighed. Philadelphia? She did not expect much help from the easterner.

Ben stiffened as the war cries filled the air. The braves were almost in range, coming full on in a ragged frontal attack. Ben shouldered the carbine and sighted on the brave in the lead, the one holding the feathered lance. Ben swallowed. His mouth was dry. He did not think of dying. The words of his father, Kit McQueen, sounded in his mind: "Pick your target. Let your air out. Squeeze gentle." Ben concentrated on the Comanche in his sights, exhaled slowly as the brave started up the slope. Ben curled his finger around the trigger.

A gun boomed, and Spotted Calf clutched at his shoulder and tumbled from horseback. Ben McQueen blinked and stared in disbelief at the carbine in his hands. The barrel was still cold, its load unfired. Gunshots filled the air, fired methodically and with deadly accuracy. Ben whirled and looked up to see a buckskin-clad Texas Ranger. Black smoke curled from the twelve-inch gun barrels of his Patterson Colt revolvers. He raised and fired with his left hand, then his right.

"C'mon, my heathen brothers. You ain't forgot ol' Snake Eye Gandy, have you now?" Ben stood motionless, mouth agape. Anabel, too, seemed spellbound by the man's sudden and miraculous appearance on the hilltop.

"Watch your fool head, pilgrim," Gandy shouted.

Ben instinctively ducked. He caught a blurred glimpse of an arrow flash between him and Anabel and glance off the limestone cliff. Ben swung around with his carbine, but once again the man on the cliff beat him to the punch. The Patterson Colts continued to blast away. A Comanche brave, thrice wounded, dropped his bow and rolled down the hillside. Blood smeared his shattered bone and shell breastplate. Another of the attackers clutched at his belly and doubled over but managed to cling to his stallion's mane as he rode clear of the fight. The two remaining braves had lost their taste for battle and retreated out of range of the white man's guns. In a few minutes all that remained of the war party was a trail of dust dissipating against the distant hills.

Ben ruefully lowered his eyes to the carbine in his hands. Color crept into his cheeks. The fighting was over and he hadn't even fired a shot.

Chapter Two

In all his twenty-four years, Ben McQueen had never met a man quite like Snake Eye Gandy. He cut an imposing figure, despite the fact that the bandy-legged Ranger stood half a foot shorter than McQueen. Gandy's arms were unusually long and ended in large, strong hands that had a grip like a vise. His shoulders were corded with muscle. He seemed older than thirty. His hair was already streaked with silver and his ugly, wrinkled features were as weathered as the Texas hills. Years ago, Gandy had survived a scalping, one of the few men to ever do so. Gandy had killed his attacker and salvaged what he could of his scalp. And area the size of a man's fist had been peeled back from his forehead. It had healed into a livid patch of scar tissue. Gandy had braided the scalp and wore it like a Mongol's top-knot, long enough to dangle down the side of his face to his neck.

Gandy's glass left eye completed his grim vis-age. In place of pupil and cornea, Gandy had paid some craftsman to paint a coiled rattlesnake on the orb's surface. The effect was disconcerting, to say the least. Ben doubted there was a man alive who could stare Gandy down.

"Lieutenant, eh?" Gandy said after introductions had been made on the hillside. The Ranger gave McQueen a swift appraisal. "You must be one of those soldier boys escorting that general fella around the Republic." Gandy reloaded his Colts as he spoke. He wore his guns waist-high. A bowie knife was sheathed beneath his left arm, bone handle jutting forward. "Looks as though you bluecoats are gonna need looking after while you're busy protecting the general. That is, unless you learn to shoot a little faster." He dropped his gaze to the unfired carbine.

"It's retired General Matthew Abbott," Ben corrected. "We were clear of the hills when we heard a gunshot. He asked me to investigate while he continued on to San Antonio with the escort." Ben looked at Anabel. "I intercepted the señorita's carriage. The war party was something of a surprise."

Snake Eye Gandy finished loading his revolvers, holstered one, and turned his attention to the woman standing close by.

"Afternoon, Señorita Obregon. Funny thing, a woman riding out here by her lonesome. Wonder what brings a woman to do such a fool thing."

"I was visiting a family for my brother," Anabel lied smoothly. Her eyes never wavered as she told a story of how her brother, Father Esteban, had been unable to leave San Antonio to visit a farmer in the hills whose wife was ill. Like a good Christian sister, Anabel had agreed to go and care for the woman in her brother's stead. "Of course, I would never have made the trip alone had I known the Comanches were raiding so close to town."

Gandy nodded. "We heard rumors that Comanches had been seen crossing upriver. Captain Pepper sent me to track 'em."

"One man?" Ben asked.

It was plain the Ranger had little regard for the lieutenant, but the one-eyed rascal sure held himself in high esteem. "There was only one war party," Gandy replied.

He snapped up the .36-caliber Patterson Colt in his right hand, thumbed back the hammer, and fired. Anabel and Ben both jumped, startled by the Ranger's sudden action.

A geyser of dirt exploded six inches from the head of one of the corpses downslope. Gandy cocked the pistol and centered the octagonal barrel directly on his target.

"Spotted Calf. You speak English as good as any white man, so I know you understand. I aim to part your war feathers with my next shot, less you stand up and show me the palms of your hands."

Ben had to give Snake Eye Gandy his due. One of the "corpses" stirred, then rose from the ground, reincarnated by the Ranger's threat.

Spotted Calf held out his hands to demonstrate that he held no weapon. Blood seeped from a flesh wound in his right arm. His nose was broken and obviously hurt like hell, but defeat was the worst calamity that had befallen the brave. Spotted Calf noticed the bullet-riddled body of Sees the Turtle where he had fallen alongside his rival and friend. The warrior had died fighting. Spotted Calf was envious of his companion's fate. Better to die in battle than suffer the humiliation of capture and the white man's justice. He turned and glared at the Texas Ranger.

"Here I am, Snake Eye. Here is my heart. Kill me while you can or I will yet wear your hair on my belt!"

Gandy chuckled at the threat and glanced around at Ben. The Ranger tugged the topknot braided in his hair. "Spotted Calf and I go way back. I managed to kill his brother when the red devil took a trade knife to my scalp. This here Comanch has been looking to finish the job ever since."

He shrugged, placed two fingers in his mouth, and gave a shrill whistle that echoed across the hills. A couple of minutes passed, then a nimble-footed buckskin Appaloosa mare came trotting from behind the hill. The animal neighed and tossed its head and proceeded up to Gandy's outstretched hand. The Ranger actually exhibited a moment of tenderness as he scratched beneath the mare's jaw.

"If you think you can manage to keep Spotted Calf from lighting a shuck and skedaddling, I'll fetch the carriage," Gandy said, looking over his shoulder.

"I'll do my best," Ben said in mock earnestness. He was beginning to seriously dislike Mister Snake Eye Gandy, even if the Ranger had made a timely entrance.

Gandy seemed to take no notice of the younger man's tone of voice. He swung up astride his horse and rode on down the hill. Once the Ranger was safely out of earshot, Anabel removed a scarf from around her neck and started over to the wounded brave.

"Hey...?" Ben raised the carbine and followed her. He kept the Comanche covered while Anabel proceeded to bandage the warrior's arm wound. The brave glared sullenly at McQueen and then spoke in his native tongue to the woman ministering to him.

"Help me to escape these white eyes or I will tell the Ranger that you are the daughter of Don Luis." Spotted Calf looked after the figure on horseback heading down the road to the carriage. "I do not think you wish the Rangers to know such a thing."

"If I help you, then there must be peace between us," Anabel said, stalling for time. She had begun to formulate her own plans upon hearing that Ben McQueen was part of the American general's entourage. If Spotted Calf revealed her identity, it would spoil everything. She had to keep him quiet, at least for a few days.

"There will be peace," Spotted Calf said.

"I will help you," she told him. "But not now. Let Gandy take you to San Antonio. I will come with my father's vaqueros and set you free, and together we will kill many Rangers."

"You speak for the tiger of Coahuila, your father?"

"I speak for him," Anabel replied flatly.

"You two are carrying on like old friends," Ben interrupted. He could speak Choctaw and Cherokee and a smattering of Creek, but the quick, clipped phrases of Comanche were just so much gibberish.

"I am merely assuring him that I mean him no harm, that I intend to bind his wound and nothing more," Anabel said.

"Well, he meant us plenty harm a few minutes ago, señorita, or have you forgotten?"

"It is not Christian to dwell on the sins of the past. I wish to demonstrate the mercy of our heavenly father to this poor savage."

"Fine," Ben said. "But don't get in my line of

fire, because if he so much as breathes wrong I'll douse his lights, as sure as I am standing here."

Anabel sighed. "Now you sound like that awful one-eyed man. I liked you better as the gallant young lieutenant who saved my life."

"You did—I did—uh—you do?" Ben stammered, caught off guard by her remarks. Her tone of voice was downright inviting.

He had heard that Mexican women were passionate and volatile by nature. He could add mercurial as well.

She had finished bandaging the Comanche's arm by the time Gandy arrived back with the carriage. He had managed to round up one of the horses the war party had left behind. Spotted Calf recognized the stallion that had belonged to Sees the Turtle. He walked over to the animal and, with pained effort, climbed astride the animal's back. To the warrior's horror, Gandy dropped a loop over Spotted Calf's head and tightened it around his neck.

"You get any fancy notions on our way into town and I'll drag you through the cactus by your neck. Savvy?" The brave's features were etched in stone, but he nodded.

"Is that necessary?" Ben asked. The Comanche was his enemy, but he didn't see any need to be cruel. "I can keep my carbine trained on him all the way into town."

"A Comanche ain't afraid of dying," the Ranger explained. "It's how he goes about it that's important. If he took a notion, he'd take your bullet and slit your throat as he dies. But hanging or being choked by a rope keeps his soul from reaching the happy hereafter." Gandy jiggled the horsehair rope.

"This lariat will keep him honest. I make straight talk, don't I, Spotted Calf?"

The Comanche warrior stared impassively at the road ahead. The Ranger chuckled. "Get to your carriage, Brass Buttons, and ol' Snake Eye Gandy will see you get safely home."

"I am an officer in the army of the United States. And as this Republic is seeking annexation and hopes to become the twenty-eighth state, you'd do well to show some respect for this uniform, its rank, and the nation it represents." Ben drew himself up and with all the dignity he could muster started down the hill to the señorita's carriage. He took one step and heard his trouser leg tear as the spiny branch of an ocotillo seemed to clutch at him with a life of its own.

"Mighty fine speechifying, Brass Buttons. But it takes more than fancy talk to walk this land." Gandy folded his rough hands on the pommel of his saddle, winked, and turned his horse back toward the road. Spotted Calf obediently fell in behind the Ranger.

Ben managed to extricate himself from the cactus, but left a patch of blue on the thorns. Texas had the last word after all.

Chapter Three

"Fastest-growing town in Texas," Gandy bragged, looking back at Ben in the señorita's carriage. "No place finer. Can't see how them folks in Houston stand it. They got skeeters in swarms so thick a man has to take an axe and hack his way from street to street."

Ben grinned at the Ranger's tall story. He'd heard plenty of similar ones since disembarking in Galveston. But he could see that Gandy spoke the truth about San Antonio. Over a century ago, the town had sprung up around a horseshoe bend in the San Antonio River. On the edge of the Texas frontier, its population had swelled to more than five thousand, who were attracted to the area by its arid climate and the rich beauty of the surrounding countryside. Wild figs and pomegranates grew here, as well as sugarcane and corn. There was grazing for cattle. Missionaries had seen to the construction of aqueducts that carried water to every major section of town. To the northwest, groves of ash and elm, oak and cottonwood hid springs of cold, clear water from hillside seeps to shaded pools frequented by deer, coyote, bobcat, and other creatures of the wild, including man.

Civilization had come to the San Antonio River, but it had yet to cross over, at least to any degree.

"You have chosen a good time to visit San Antonio," Anabel said. "In three days we will have fiesta. It is a time of much celebration."

Ben nodded as they turned onto the Calle de Soledad, the Street of Solitude. Or loneliness. Ben had known both over the past months.

The town itself, for the most part, was an orderly arranged collection of flat-roofed, one-story houses, thick-walled and constructed of mortar, stone, or adobe brick. The riverbanks were lined with lofty cottonwoods and elms and formed a border on three sides of the town, whose expansion had sprawled westward.

"That is my brother's church, San Fernando," Anabel said. Ben glanced down a side street and noted a whitewashed adobe bell tower rising above the row of shops and homes. "It lies between the Plaza de los Islos and the Plaza de Aroros—Military Plaza, as you would call it. The plazas are the heartbeat of my town. There the children play, there young lovers may meet and walk together, and the old may sit, dreaming and remembering sunlit days and nights of fire."

Ben had started to comment that the woman beside him had the heart of a poet, when she turned toward the plazas and headed west along the Calle Dolorosa, the Street of Sorrow. By now the entourage had picked up quite a following. Children had become distracted from their play by the strange procession and now scampered along, peeking into the carriage at the blue-clad officer, then hurrying up ahead to pelt the captured Comanche with pebbles. Spotted Calf rode stiffly erect and would not deign to even so much as flinch at the abuse. Snake Eye managed to at last drive them off with a few well-placed slaps of his quirt upon the posteriors of the troublemakers. The children fell back to a respectful distance. But the townspeople continued to gawk as the Ranger, his prisoner, and the carriage rolled past.

The storefronts and walkways, roof lines and walls surrounding the plazas were in the process of being decorated, and when Ben inquired, Anabel told him about the fiesta coming up on the fifth of May. The whole town would be one big carnival. Everyone was excited and looking forward to the event. Farmers from the outlying area and people from the smaller settlements to the north and south would be coming to San Antonio to take part in the celebration.

"There will be much music, much dancing, much laughter, and the food..." Anabel closed her eyes a moment and then smiled. "Breathe in."

The air was already heavy with the scent of baking bread and pies, spice cakes, and sugary preserves. As the day drew closer, nearly every street would be filled with mouth-watering aromas.

"Perhaps I might see you at the fiesta," Ben suggested.

"Or sooner," Anabel replied.

Before Ben could further pursue the topic, the carriage turned yet again and followed Snake Eye Gandy and his prisoner along the western edge of

Military Plaza. They followed the street up to an impressive-looking rock house that had once served as the governor's palace, before Texas became a republic. The single-story sandstone building housed the Ranger headquarters, as well as providing room for visiting dignitaries like Matthew Abbot.

Ben immediately recognized the retired general and Abbot's son, Peter, standing with a lean, tough-looking individual whom Anabel identified as Capt. Amadeus T. Pepper, the commandant of San Antonio's Texas Rangers. Ben noticed with some amusement how the half dozen blue-coated soldiers acting as Abbot's personal guard stood opposite a few of Pepper's Rangers. Each faction eyed the other with suspicion and cool disregard in the heat of the afternoon sun. To the soldiers under Ben's command, these Rangers appeared to be no more than rabble. They were dressed like Indians, and smelled like them too. Of course, from the viewpoint of Pepper's men, these bluecoats were about as fierce as puppies. The Rangers doubted there was one among the soldiers who could acquit himself in a running battle with war-painted hostiles.

A long, wide veranda, covered by a low roof of cane and dry grass, ran the length of the governor's palace. Two *ollas*, clay cisterns containing cool water, were suspended from the roof poles in netting of braided hemp. A dipper had been hung by each of them. Honeybees and mud daubers were drawn to the puddles that collected on the sandstone flooring below each cistern.

The arriving procession soon became the object of everyone's attention. The three Rangers, a rough-looking bunch armed with Colt revolvers and bowie knives, sauntered forward to greet Snake Eye Gandy and good-naturedly rib him about his traveling companions.

"Snake Eye, you always were the one could be counted on to bring in strays," one said.

"Better'n sitting around here dusting flies from the sugar bowls," Gandy retorted. "You know, Virge, if you ever eased your tired ass up out of a chair once in while, you might find there's all kind of things a man can get into." Gandy winked at the two men standing behind Virgil Washburn. "Things like chasing bandits and capturing renegade Comanches and rescuing pretty gals and brass-button toy soldiers." Gandy tossed the rope to Washburn. "Better lock Spotted Calf here around back. I'll see to him after I cut the dust." He smacked his lips and dry swallowed.

Ben bristled at Gandy's insult, but let it pass. Now wasn't the time or place for a confrontation. He climbed out of the carriage and walked up alongside Spotted Calf.

"This man has a wound that needs dressing," Ben said. "I assume there is a physician we can send around to check on him?"

"Doctor up a Comanche?" Virge Washburn exclaimed. He was a man of average height, solidly built, with that perpetual squint a man develops when he has spent most of his life outside beneath a western sky. Washburn glanced at Gandy as if debating Ben's order.

Another voice spoke up. Captain A. T. Pepper walked around the horses. "See that our prisoner is cared for. I want some answers from him."

"You'll get them," Gandy said in a matter-of-fact manner. He dismounted as the brave was led away. The Ranger fixed Ben in his glass-eyed stare, then snorted in disgust and helped himself to a dipper of water.

"I will want a full report from you later," Pepper said. His upper lip was hidden by a thick, bushy brown mustache. He tended to tug and twist the ends when deliberating.

"Yes, sir," Gandy replied. His features were shaded by a battered hat that he immediately tilted back until it hung down his back by a leather thong. The scarred, scalped part of his skull looked sunburned and made him appear even uglier than usual. "Just as soon as you finish playing nursemaid to these here bluecoats."

"Nursemaid? Indeed, my good sir," Matthew Abbot objected. He was short and stocky, white-haired and bull-necked. He had fought the British at the Battle of New Orleans and crossed swords with pirates on the Carolina shores. Sweat beaded his creased features and glistened in his close-cropped white beard. The retired officer didn't like Gandy's attitude and was determined to make his position known. Behind him, Peter Abbot, a slim, bespectacled man who seemed elegant despite his dusty garb, studied Anabel with keen interest. For the first time since arriving in this interminable wilderness, Peter Abbot was actually happy his father had insisted he accompany him to Texas.

But before Peter could approach the carriage and introduce himself to the señorita, Matthew Abbot blocked his path in order to confront the Ranger.

"See here, Mister... what is it? Gandy? I have undertaken this appraisal of the Republic's military preparedness at the request of both your own president, Anson Jones, and James Polk, President of the United States. No less than Sam Houston has blessed my efforts. If Texas is annexed as the twenty-eighth state, there will no doubt be war with Mexico. The United States Army is extremely interested in how you Texicans handle yourselves. Well, sir, if rudeness was a crown you'd be king!"

Gandy seemed nonplussed by Abbot's outburst. He hooked a thumb in his gun belt and glanced over at his captain.

"I believe you owe our guest an apology, Ranger," Captain Pepper suggested, tugging at his mustache. "General Abbot has come to us in an official capacity. These are delicate times. I expect you to show the general the same respect you show—uh—" Pepper stammered, and his voice trailed off. Damn, he couldn't think of anyone Gandy showed much respect for. He was a quarrelsome individualist, a man who went his own way and asked nothing of anyone. Sometimes he could be downright infuriating. But the vast country west of San Antonio was ugly, mean, and ruthless, and it required those same qualities in the men who dared to ride its lost and lonely places. "Well...just show him some respect."

Gandy shrugged and kicked at the dirt. Then the wiry Indian fighter smiled, though no one was fooled by the pretense. "Beggin' your pardon, Mister Abbot. But if you want to know how a Texican handles himself in a fight, just ask Spotted Calf...or maybe Brass Buttons over there." Gandy made a halfhearted attempt at a salute, then turned and ducked through the door.

Color crept into Ben's stubbled cheeks as Matthew Abbot, Captain Pepper, and the soldiers nearby focused their attention on him. He didn't appreciate being put on the spot. Fortunately, Anabel came to his aid. She left the carriage and approached the porch.

"Excuse me, *Capitan*. May I say something?"

Amadeus Pepper quickly doffed his hat. The unmarried sister of San Antonio's own Father Esteban had been the center of speculation since her arrival from Mexico City, and talk hadn't stopped. She was one of the most sought after young women in the town.

"Why, certainly, Señorita Obregon."

"I foolishly went alone to visit a family north of town. The Comanches tried to capture me. The lieutenant saved my life and with Mr. Gandy fought off an entire war party. Both men behaved gallantly."

Ben looked at her in disbelief. She never ceased to amaze him. What exactly was she up to? Then again, what did it matter? He was beginning to enjoy her surprises. It sure kept things from getting dull. And by heaven, he certainly liked her version of the incident better than his own.

"I thank you for your candor, my dear," Matthew Abbot said. He took her hand and patted it, then bowed slightly before releasing her into Ben's good graces. "Lieutenant McQueen, please escort this young woman safely to her home."

"My pleasure, sir," Ben replied.

"I assure you I am perfectly safe here in town," Anabel said. "And we are practically neighbors, for I live with my brother there in the hacienda alongside the church, just across the plaza." Anabel noticed a look of disappointment cross Ben's face. That was just what she wanted. "However, I suppose a soldier ought to obey the orders of his *commandant, si?*"

"Absolutely." Ben offered her his arm and proceeded to escort her back to her carriage. Peter Abbot hurried to catch up to the officer. Anabel looked at him, her eyes filled with curiosity. She saw some resemblance between Peter and the general.

"Ben, if you will do me the honors." He flashed a handsome smile at the dark-haired beauty who was arm in arm with Lieutenant McQueen.

"Señorita Anabel Obregon...I regret to introduce you to Peter Abbot, General Abbot's son and, by reputation, the scourge of young ladies from Boston to Baltimore."

"Pay no attention to my friend," Peter countered as he glared at the officer with mock hostility. They had been good-natured rivals throughout their friendship of the past three years. Peter was older by five years, but it was Ben who always seemed to be extricating General Abbot's prodigal son from one predicament after another. "He does me an injustice. A sin for which our heavenly father will no doubt punish him." And pointedly ignoring Ben's look of displeasure, Peter fell into step alongside the señorita.

"I doubt the three of us can fit in the carriage," Ben said, trying a new tactic.

Peter caught up the reins to the mare as they walked past. "No problem. We can walk. A few extra minutes will help us all get better acquainted, don't you agree, señorita?"

Even Anabel seemed a little flustered. But she smiled graciously. "Of course." The plaza was nearly devoid of townspeople. It was as if everyone in town was holding back, waiting for the day of fiesta before they would reappear in force. Some farmers had come in with baskets of dried peppers and fresh onions and sacks of dried corn to be ground into meal.

Still, they kept to the street and rounded Military Plaza. Those merchants decorating their shopfronts nodded in greeting as the attractive young woman walked past with the tall, rawboned young officer on her right and the proud, dapper gentleman on her left. A pair of matronly women intercepted Anabel and her escorts on the north side of the plaza. Anabel stopped and exchanged pleasantries and introduced Ben and Peter to Aurelia Moreno and Hilda Grummond, two of San Antonio's leading citizens. Come next morning, Anabel had no doubt that the news of her adventures and arrival arm in arm with the *norteamericanos* would have spread throughout the town, embellished no doubt by the fertile imaginations of the town's two gossips.

"I am Father Esteban Obregon, Anabel's brother," the priest said as he met them in the courtyard of the house that served as his rectory and home to his sister and her devoted woman servant. The padre was a man of average height, with narrow shoulders and a thickening girth that he kept firmly circled with a braided cord. He wore the coarse brown robes of a Franciscan. His eyes were kindly though deep set in a face burned brown by the sun. His black hair was thinning, but he kept his bald spot covered by a brown cap. His hands were covered with mud, his fingernails caked with dirt. Behind him the courtyard wall had been recently patched with adobe mud. A trowel lay beside a clay jug of water. The padre's robes were mud-spattered and his knuckles were scraped. Before he could invite Ben and Peter into the house, the front door flew open and Carmelita, a round-figured woman in a black cotton dress and black blouse trimmed with scarlet stitchery, came waddling out into the courtyard and hurried through the cactus garden to embrace Anabel. The woman started to sob and carry on, as if Ben had brought her a corpse instead of a young woman, safe and sound.

"I heard stories that the Comanches had been sighted back in the hills. A thousand times I blamed myself for letting you go. A thousand times I prayed for your safety," the woman exclaimed. Her cheeks were smudged with masa meal. The aroma of peppers and beans and corn tortillas clung to her like a cloak.

Anabel hugged the woman who had all but raised her. In Carmelita's warm embraces, in the tucking into bed and the lazy afternoon stories, the moments of closeness in the kitchen, in the shoulder to cry on and the softly spoken words of comfort, Anabel had found the love a cold and distant mother had failed to provide. Her father had loved her, but his hatred of the Texans overshadowed his affections for his daughter. She had watched Don Luis become consumed with bitterness. And yet, his resolve had never wavered. When Santa Anna took Maria de Tosta to wife, the fortune and destiny of the Corderos became irrevocably linked to that of Antonio Lopez de Santa Anna, now languishing in Havana with his bride, Anabel's cousin.

"I suppose we had better allow you to get

some rest," Ben said. He shook hands with the padre, who seemed relieved at the officer's suggestion.

"But you must return," Anabel said. "Join us for dinner tomorrow. At sunset. Yes, that will do. Allow us to give you and the good general a proper welcome. Carmelita and I will prepare a magnificent meal." She ignored her brother's look of alarm. "It is the least we can do to honor the American general and his son. And Señor McQueen, you risked your life for me today. I insist you allow me to show my gratitude."

"I couldn't impose..." Ben said.

"But I could," Peter Abbot interrupted. He swept his hat before him as he bowed and kissed the señorita's hand. He had already decided to avoid mentioning the invitation to his father. Ben McQueen saw through his friend's plan.

"We accept your kind offer. I am sure the general will be delighted," Ben pointedly interjected. He took pleasure in seeing Peter Abbot's crestfallen features. Abbot grumbled and started back toward the street, his romantic ambitions momentarily thwarted.

"Until tomorrow." Ben nodded farewell to the padre and Carmelita, then turned to Anabel. The dark-eyed beauty extended a graceful hand, which he took and kissed as he bowed. Was that interest in her guarded gaze? Ben scolded himself for being a fool. Months ago, he had welcomed the chance to come to Texas, in hopes of escaping the painful memories of one he had loved well but not wisely. Now here he was, like some giddy youth, diving blindly into the fray once again. This was crazy.

Oh hell, this was Texas.

He'd fought Comanches and rescued a beautiful woman and kissed her hand and been invited to her house. Who could ask for a better day? Maybe he had yet to see a fiesta, but Ben McQueen already felt like celebrating.

Chapter Four

Father Esteban shook his head in exasperation and slumped into the chair nearest the fireplace in the sitting room. The hacienda was large enough to hold three bedrooms, the sitting room, and a kitchen, all of which opened onto the shaded confines of the cactus garden where Anabel, Carmelita, and the priest had just bid farewell to Ben McQueen and Peter Abbot.

Anabel weathered her older brother's displeasure, accustomed as she was to such reactions. She'd spent a childhood chasing trouble, then watching as her older brother hurried to the rescue, complaining every step of the way. But he always came.

"Are you mad, inviting a general of the American army into this house?" Father Esteban asked.

"What are you afraid of?" Anabel replied. She hugged Carmelita, then removed her hat and gloves as the housekeeper hurried off to the kitchen to bring the young woman a cup of hot tea. "There is no one to tell them our name is Cordero and that *El*

Tigre de Coahuila was our father. Don't worry, Esteban, you are safe in your pulpit."

"Maybe there is someone else the priest fears will be discovered," said a voice from the kitchen doorway. A handsome young vaquero with dark skin, flashing eyes, and black hair shiny as a pelt stepped into the room. Miguel Ybarbo had a temper as short as a two-inch fuse, and it didn't take much for one to strike a match to it. He wore brown canvas trousers and knee-high boots, a ruffled shirt, and a short brown jacket trimmed with wine-colored stitching. A twin-barreled percussion pistol was tucked in the broad leather belt circling his waist. A dagger jutted from the top of each boot. Pearl-inlaid hilts flashed in the firelight as he swaggered into the room.

Anabel cast a furtive glance toward the shuttered windows. She hadn't expected to discover one of Don Luis's vaqueros in San Antonio. "You should not have come here."

"Tell me, do you worry for me or for yourself?" Miguel said. He reached out and, with his fingertips beneath her chin, tilted her head until he could look into her eyes. His own features smouldered with jealous desire. "I see the gringo kiss your hand. I see you smile at this soldier and laugh and I hear you invite him to your house, your father's killers."

"Enough," Anabel retorted. "He did not kill my father." She did not like being scolded, especially by Miguel Ybarbo. "You presume too much. I will not be spoken to in such a manner." She turned to her brother. "I have my reasons for inviting the general. Are you not here to serve all the people of San Antonio?"

"Of course I am," Esteban replied.

"Good," Anabel said. "Then you can 'serve' them supper." She grinned and patted his shoulder, then headed into the kitchen, where Carmelita had already filled two stoneware cups with hot tea. She'd added a few drops of brandy to each cup to give it substance. She noticed Anabel and patted the space beside her on the bench seat.

"Come sit." Carmelita placed a platter of *pan dulce* within easy reach and helped herself to one of the crusty bread rolls she had glazed with honey and dusted with cinnamon. "Naughty child. You must have left at first light."

"Before you had awakened, else you would have tried to stop me," Anabel said, sitting beside the woman who had been her housekeeper, nurse, confidante, and friend since Anabel's earliest recollections. "Carmelita, I had to visit Papa one last time. Alone. With no one to tell me what I must feel or do from now on. I needed to be able to listen."

"To who, child?"

"Papa," Anabel replied. Carmelita blessed herself. Don Luis Cordero de Tosta speaking from the grave—that was all she needed to hear.

"Am I so foolish, mamacita, for I did hear him," Anabel said. She touched a fingertip to her forehead. "Here." She placed the palm of her hand over her heart. "And here."

Carmelita watched her. The old woman's mind wandered in memories of a winsome, dark-haired child, a baby she had nursed, a child with whom she had watched the seasons change, a child to be nurtured along the winding path of time. In her mind's eye, Carmelita relived a moment stolen from the stream of passing years—a child cups a small scarlet-winged bird and holds the fragile, captured creature up to the sky and releases that fluttering miracle, returning the gift of life to a barren blue heaven.

The child had become a woman. Perhaps her wings were stronger than Carmelita knew. The older woman could no longer shelter one who was determined to stand—or fly—alone.

"Foolish? No, my dear one," Carmelita said. "You are your father's daughter." The buxom housekeeper stood and walked over to a bin of dried corn. She lifted the lid and thrust her hand down into the cool, dry kernels. When she straightened, she was holding a ring that Anabel immediately recognized. It consisted of a smooth, irregularly shaped chunk of obsidian roughly an inch and a half in diameter and set in gold. It had belonged to Anabel's father, something he wore as a symbol of his authority. He had never revealed how he came by the ring, saying only that he had found it in the mountains many years ago.

Carmelita placed the ring on the table before Anabel. "Don Luis asked me to keep this. For you. Don Luis told me that you must choose for yourself whether or not to wear it." Carmelita looked down at the glassy, black surface.

Anabel stared down into the smoky facets of the hand-chiseled stone. *Madre de Dios.* Was that the image of her father, etched upon the eerie surface, staring back at her from the stone's black heart? She reached out and caught up the ring. She shuddered and slid the ring over the middle finger of her right hand. Anabel gasped as fire coursed through her limbs and played along her spine. Then the sensation subsided, her muscles relaxed. She had made her choice.

"No!" Miguel said from the doorway. He hurried into the kitchen, brushed against a string of dried chilies, and sent them clattering to the floor. "The ring should be mine. Your father wanted us to be together. He told me so the day he died at the hands of the Rangers."

"I was not there to hear his words," Anabel replied. Miguel Ybarbo was handsome and dashing and no woman was completely immune to his charms, least of all Anabel. But there was more on her mind now than Miguel's jealous fancies.

He reached to snatch the ring from her finger. Anabel caught up a carving knife from the table and turned on the vaquero with such ferocity that he stopped in his tracks and retreated against the adobe wall that Carmelita had hung with iron cookpots. He struck a shelf lined with neatly arranged clay jars of spices and honey and salt. An orange-colored jar crashed to the stone floor, raising a small cloud of cinnamon-scented dust. Miguel studied the woman, his eyes wide with alarm. When she refrained from attacking him, his cheeks reddened with embarrassment. A log in the fireplace popped and splintered in half in a shower of sparks. The sound startled Anabel, but she kept her fingers tightly clenched around the hilt of the carving knife. The black ring reflected the dancing flames upon its somber surface and leeched the warmth from the captured firelight.

"My father is dead," the daughter of Don Luis Cordero said in a quiet voice. "But the tiger of Coahuila remains." Anabel tilted her hand and peered into the ring's smoky depths, and this time she saw herself.

*   *   *

Ben McQueen's thoughts lingered on the pretty señorita he'd left at Father Esteban's house as the lieutenant crossed Military Plaza.

"You weren't much help to me," Peter Abbot scowled, walking alongside his lucky friend in blue.

"I didn't plan to be," Ben replied with a grin.

"We'll see who has the last laugh," Peter retorted. "What's this?" Abbot found himself distracted by a comely young woman in a swirling green skirt and cotton blouse who waved to him from the balcony above the Alameda Hotel's front entrance. The hotel was located on the south side of the plaza and frequently housed San Antonio's more illustrious guests. Matt Abbot had insisted on staying at the Ranger barracks.

"You go on and look after my father," Peter said. "I'll look after me." He headed for the cantina, ignoring Ben's warning. The lieutenant continued on to the governor's palace. General Abbot and Captain Pepper had disappeared inside, while the remainder of the general's escort left to unload their bedrolls in the barracks, a long, wide, adobe structure furnished with elmwood cots and straw-filled mattresses, along with a scattering of tables and ladder-backed chairs. The soldiers had seen better, but they'd seen worse too. They had been given leave to explore the town and were anxious to begin. Ben McQueen saw no point in delaying them and ordered his sergeant, stern old Hezekiah Palmer, to keep an eye on the command.

The governor's palace made an impressive sight, with its nearly three-feet-thick stone walls and massive double doors of carved walnut. The palace itself had seen its moments of glory come and go with the Spanish rulers and Mexican commandants who had housed themselves within these walls. The Texas rebellion had brought war to San Antonio and looters to the palace. With many of its rooms stripped of finery, the ballroom and living room, which dominated the center of the hacienda, were used for storage. Where ladies in silk finery had waltzed across tile-inlaid floors, rifles and grain, sacks of shot and barrels of salt pork, dried beans, flour and apples were now stored.

Ben continued down the hall, passing a chapel on his right and a dining room where the general and Captain Pepper were trading lies over a freshly uncorked bottle of Irish whisky Abbot had retrieved from his belongings.

"There you are, Lieutenant. Come and join us, that's a god lad," the blustery, good-natured general exclaimed. "I trust you escorted that pretty little girl home without incident."

"Yes, sir," Ben said, remaining in the doorway. "She invited us to dine with her tomorrow night. I took the liberty of accepting."

"Excellent," Matt replied. He cocked an eyebrow and glanced at the Ranger captain. "That's the ticket. Win over the locals to our side."

"Our side, sir?" Ben asked.

A. T. Pepper nodded. "A rider came in yesterday and brought word from President Jones in Austin that the Mexican government has offered to recognize the sovereignty of the Texas Republic. They'll sign a treaty to that effect, recognizing the Rio Grande as the boundary, giving us everything we ever wanted from them just so long as Texas doesn't decide to join the United States. I was just telling Matt that folks hereabouts figure such a treaty is mighty tempting." Pepper helped himself to the general's whisky.

"A decision to remain a republic would be certain folly," Abbot dryly observed. He was not about to allow the Ranger to bait him into an argument. The news had unsettled him and made his mission as an ambassador of goodwill as important as his assessment of the quality of the Republic's military capabilities.

"Join us in a libation, Ben," the captain said. "You'll find we don't stand on ceremony here in Texas. Or for that matter, rank—leastways most of the time."

Ben noted that Gandy wasn't in the room and he began to hazard a guess that the man was up to no good. "Perhaps later, Captain Pepper. I thought I might try and find a horse for myself, as the Comanches killed mine."

"We keep our mounts in the corral just beyond the courtyard. The barn and the calaboose are back there as well." Pepper gulped his drink, sucked in a lungful of air, and nodded his appreciation to the general. "When you're fixing to leave, just help yourself."

"I'll look over the stock, just the same," Ben said, and after saluting both men he continued down the hall to the kitchen. A middle-aged black woman glanced up as Ben entered. A boy who looked to be about nine or ten years old sat near the woman, his skin darkly similar to hers, as was the set of his eyes and the broad, flat shape of his nose. He was grinding chili peppers in an earthenware bowl while the woman kneaded dough, a sheen of flour dust upon her ebony hands.

"Pardon me. Just passing through, ma'am."

The boy looked up at Ben. "Ma don't talk. She did afore the Comanches took her. Not anymore." The boy shrugged. "My name's Toby. My ma's name is Stacia." The boy scratched the tip of his nose with his forearm.

"Pleased to meet you, Toby. I'm Ben McQueen."

"You a Ranger, too?"

"No," Ben grinned.

"I'm gonna be a Ranger when I git growed." The boy spoke with the conviction of youth as he crushed chili peppers in the warm interior of the kitchen. Charcoal pulsed with orange-red heat in an open stove brazier against the wall. Coals in the hearth supplied heat to an oven set outside the kitchen door. Ben continued on through the kitchen and out into the courtyard. The Negro cook watched him every step of the way. Toby followed the lieutenant and stood in the doorway.

"You stayin' here?"

"For a little while."

The boy nodded sagely. "You need anything, I know this ol' house inside and out. There's a apple jar in the pantry and I can slip into the wine cellar through a crack in the door anytime I wants." Toby flashed a broad grin.

"I'll keep that in mind," Ben said, smiling back. Then he started across the courtyard. He had no time to admire the stone fountain in the center of the patio. The fountain was bone dry, the water lilies a thing of the past. The dry, dead stalks of flowers sprouted from uncared-for beds. Only one herb garden near the kitchen showed tending, no doubt by Toby and his mother.

Ben might have lingered to explore the detritus of so many yesterdays, but a premonition kept him moving toward the back gate and the confrontation that waited beyond.

Spotted Calf balanced on his tiptoes, the noose tight around his neck. He was having visions of his ancestors dancing in the glare of a campfire, with the sky behind them splitting into scarlet streaks, as the oxygen slowly left his brain.

"You'll talk now, you red butcher, or by heaven I'll stretch your scrawny neck," Snake Eye Gandy said, keeping a tight grip on the hemp rope he'd tossed over the limb of a cottonwood tree out behind the governor's palace. He hadn't wasted any time in making his way to the calaboose. He'd come to interrogate the Comanche the only way he knew how. And that's where Ben McQueen found him.

Squint-eyed Virge Washburn was there, looking a might uncomfortable, though not near as much as Spotted Calf. And leaning against the front of the ten-by-ten adobe jail was a stocky, hard-bitten Ranger who abandoned his position and swaggered forward to plant himself firmly between Ben and the cottonwood.

"The name is Clay Poole," the man said. He cocked a thumb toward the scene being played out over his shoulder. "This ain't none of your look-to." Poole was bald, with a fringe of brown hair around his head. His bushy brown beard looked thick enough to conceal a bird's nest. A Patterson Colt rode high on his left hip. He kept a tomahawk thrust through his gun belt on his right. The black iron blade was honed sharp enough for a man to shave by. Poole's tone of voice was firm but nonthreatening. Though

Ben towered over him, both men knew that height wasn't the measure of a man.

Ben saw no reason to waste time trying to face the man down. Besides, Clay Poole probably had as much give in him as forged steel. The lieutenant stepped around the Ranger and headed straight for Gandy and Spotted Calf, who was indeed at the end of his rope. Clay Poole quickened his pace and fell in step alongside the soldier in blue.

"Now see here, younker, maybe I didn't make myself clear," Poole said, still hoping to avoid a confrontation. Snake Eye Gandy was in a particularly dangerous mood and no man to be trifled with or to brook an interference.

Gandy slowly and inevitably hauled the warrior up on his tiptoes. The Comanche's hands were securely bound behind his back and there was nothing he could do to prevent his strangulation.

"Just give the nod and I'll ease off. I want to know what brings the Quahadi down from your mountain haunts. Are you just out for blood? Is the whole tribe on the move?" Snake Eye thumbed the taut rope strung between the brave and the cottonwood. "Talk or die. Either way don't make me no never mind."

Spotted Calf groaned. His legs were cramping. He could no longer balance. He dreaded the white man's hanging death but he refused to give his old enemy the satisfaction of seeing a warrior disgrace himself. It was ended. He must die and there would be no life for him among the spirits. He would never join his grandfather and father on the last great hunt and dance in the circle of the All-Father or hold again his first child, the son whom the spirits had taken away in the seventh month of his life.

The noose tightened about his neck, reducing his air intake to a trickle. Gandy seemed to be speaking to him from far off. Spotted Calf ceased to resist and dropped.

Ben McQueen's hand was a blur as he reached to his left and snatched the tomahawk from Clay Poole's belt and hurled it with uncanny accuracy. With a whisper rush of air, the iron blade bit deep into the cottonwood tree, severing the rope that circled the trunk. Spotted Calf collapsed to earth, pulling the frayed end of the rope over the branch and down on top of his back. He rose up on his knees, surprised to find he was still alive and even more shocked to discover that his rescuer was none other than the soldier he had tried to kill earlier in the day.

Snake Eye stared at the length of rope remaining in his hands. He stared at the Comanche. He lifted his gaze and stared at Ben, and still couldn't believe what had happened. Clay Poole, standing behind the lieutenant, grimaced and shook his head, and his features flashed an unspoken communication to Virge Washburn. The wiry, bowlegged Ranger recognized the warning and braced himself for the coming storm.

"Lawd, Lawd, Lawd. Ummm-mmmm," another voice called out. It was young Toby. He stood with his forearms crooked through the wrought-iron gate, black as the iron tracery that framed his face. The nine-year-old shifted his stance and waited. He pitied the lieutenant.

Ben ignored Gandy and slipped the noose off the Comanche brave. Spotted Calf climbed unsteadily to his feet, leery of his benefactor. The Comanche had another surprise coming to him. Ben loosened the slipknot binding the brave's wrists. With his hands free, Spotted Calf gingerly rubbed his neck. Now he glanced at Snake Eye, wondering if the Ranger was up to some new trick. He saw at a glance that Gandy was dumbstruck. No one had ever interfered with him before. His ugly features turned uglier. His frown wrinkled the livid white scar tissue where the scalp had been sliced away. The rattlesnake in his eye socket seemed ablaze, a trick of reflected sunlight, but effective all the same.

"Come with me," Ben told the brave, and steered him toward the calaboose.

"The hell!" Gandy muttered. He drew his long-barreled Colt and pointed the revolver at Ben's chest.

Ben experienced a flash of fear but brought it under control and kept his expression free of concern.

"You won't shoot. If you did, the general and no doubt Captain Pepper would have you dancing from the end of a rope all to yourself."

"Might be worth it," Gandy dryly observed. He kept the octagonal barrel trained on Ben for what seemed an eternity but couldn't have been more than a minute. Then he lowered the gun and returned it to his holster.

"I am your enemy. Why you do this thing?" Spotted Calf asked in his halting English.

Ben looked from Gandy to the brave and shrugged. "I doubt either of you would understand." He gestured once more toward the jail. Spotted Calf started down the path, then stopped and faced the white man.

"My people have fled the mountains. Evil is there."

"What could be worse than you red devils?" Virgil Washburn said, drawing up alongside Gandy.

Spotted Calf took them in at a glance, then focused on Ben. "The warriors of the night." The Comanche continued on back to the jail with Ben keeping a respectful distance, a hand on his gun.

The Rangers gathered at the cottonwood while from the gate, young Toby cried out, "Oo-eee, Mister Bluebelly sure is somethin'. Yes, sir."

Gandy fumed and gnawed at his lower lip while Clay Poole retrieved his tomahawk. Poole had to give the "hawk" a sharp tug to free it from the tree trunk. He examined the blade, spit on the metal edge, and then scratched at his bushy brown beard.

"Best watch yourself, Snake Eye," said Poole with renewed respect for the Easterner. "Appears there's more to that younker than Philadelphia." He returned the weapon to his belt. Virge Washburn silently concurred with a nod of his head.

"Oh, shut up," Gandy scowled, and stalked off, trailing the short end of the severed rope.

Chapter Five

Fire Giver suffered for his people. He suffered so that Tezcatlipoca, the god of darkness, would bring him a vision of what he must do, a vision of where Fire Giver must lead his warriors. Already they had traveled far from the mountains of home, on a pilgrimage whose goal had yet to be revealed. Tezcatlipoca, the blood-eating god, was angry. By opposing him Fire Giver hoped to put an end to the spotted sickness that had crept across the ancient ridges and found the People in their place of solitude, the Valley of Eagles. Home lay many walks behind them—still the warriors followed the high priest, because they trusted his vision. Weeks ago, Tezcatlipoca had whispered in his ear and told Fire Giver to follow the rising sun. The high priest had obeyed. And he would continue to do so. But now he sought direction, the purpose of his journey, that revelation which all men seek.

And so Fire Giver sat alone among the weathered rocks on the lonely summit of a thirsty peak and stared into the flames of the ceremonial fire before him while the warriors watched from below. Like the soldiers who had followed him, Fire Giver was small of stature, wiry as whipcord. His chest and shoulders rippled with red muscle and his eyes were the same color as the caked blood that matted his waist-length black hair. He was covered from head to toe with a sootlike paste denoting his station as a high priest, the reflection of the dark god, and wielder of the sacrificial knife. Suddenly he rose and stood completely naked, his hands held palm outward in an attitude of submission. Blood already trickled down his back and chest and forearms where thorns of the maguey cactus pierced his flesh. Now he waited, trembling as two of the warriors from farther down the slope left their vantage points and climbed the dozen yards separating them from the priest. The two men wore eagle-head helmets made of hide and feathers that hid their blue and yellow painted features behind beaklike visors. Body armor of quilted cotton soaked in brine covered their hardened torsos.

Striker, the closest warrior, was covered with battle scars and brandished an enormous wooden club studded with razor-sharp obsidian chips. An obsidian dagger was thrust through the woven belt at his waist. Young Serpent followed close behind Striker and carried an atlatl (a spear thrower favored by the elite warriors) and several obsidian-tipped javelins. Young Serpent had recently buried his wife, a silky-skinned maiden who, like many others, had succumbed to the spotted sickness. This night the two men knew what was expected of them and they quickly set down their weapons beside the great axe wielded by Fire Giver when in battle. Its serrated obsidian edge had split the skulls of count-less foes.

Fire Giver's limbs were already crisscrossed with tiny crimson rivulets. Another pile of thorns wrapped in a tanned elkskin had been placed upon the ground at his feet. These cruel slivers of the maguey were capable of inflicting extreme pain. Striker and Young Serpent began to chant softly as they went to work, inserting the thorns in the high priest's thighs, calves, and scrotum.

"God of darkness, ancient killer, see how your shadow embraces his suffering. Drink of the blood of your shadow, accept his gift, and grant him what he seeks. Open his eyes that he may see."

They sang this song until the last of the thorns had pierced the flesh of Fire Giver. Then Young Serpent and Striker reverently gathered their weapons and dipped the stone blades in Fire Giver's blood. The other elite soldiers in their eagle helmets and war-painted faces climbed the hillside to join them. Barbed javelins, axes, stone swords and knives, war clubs both curved and straight were baptized in the blood of the high priest. No sound did he make as he stood unmoving—eyes glazed with pain, his breath ragged. He stood searching—waiting.

Images rushed to him in waves of white-hot pain. The night seemed ablaze with searing fire and an incandescent light that flickered on the periphery of his vision, then stabbed toward the center of his sight.

He saw himself, suffering, wrapped in the crimson ribbons of his own life's fluids. He saw a great eagle, with wings that blotted out the sky, swoop down and clutch him in its golden talons and bear him aloft. The world lay before him like an unrolled blanket: a vista of dry hills and craggy, windswept peaks dotted with ocotillo cactus and the sacred maguey whose roots could be pounded to a mash and fermented into pulque.

Fire Giver saw every hidden spring and every shaded tinaja where bees hovered above pools of collected rainwater. Down through the shimmering light the eagle soared until it alighted upon a peculiar mountain whose eroded slopes had been sculpted to resemble a crouched jaguar. In the folds of the mountain's front paws, beneath the volcanic stone head, burned a pyre beside an altar, a place of final sacrifice.

And when the last weapon had been pressed to his tortured flesh the high priest cried out and collapsed. Striker and Young Serpent caught him and lowered him to the ground and began to remove the thorns.

Fire Giver did not stir until the morning sun climbed above the weathered mountains to the north. Then the high priest opened his eyes, rose, and walked along the ridge until he came to a pool of rainwater that filled a cavity in the stone beneath an overhanging ledge of eroded rock. He lowered his face into the cool shallows and drank till his belly felt about to burst. When he straightened, Young Serpent and Striker were standing behind him. Striker carried the high priest's robes and Young Serpent the priest's quilted armor. Both men appeared anxious to learn, yet were loath to pressure the high priest or ask an unseemly question of one who was the shadow of a god.

"I saw a mountain like a sleeping jaguar. It waits there." The high priest pointed to the north. "We must go and find the sleeping jaguar. There we will feed Tezcatlipoca what he most desires. And when the Smoking Glass tells us, we will return to our people. And the spotted sickness will be no more." Fire Giver gingerly slipped into his robes and armor and led the way back along the ridge to the place of his suffering. Another couple of warriors waited, holding a young Comanche brave between them. He struggled, to no avail, in their grasp. He moaned and pleaded, for the brave knew what was coming. There had been others before him. He was the last of the captives.

The two warriors forced the Comanche over on his back and stretched him across the smoothest slab of rock they could find. Striker and Young Serpent immediately stepped forward and grabbed their victim's arms, while the other two men held his legs. The remaining warriors began to drum their clubs and axes upon feather-decorated wicker shields covered with toughened hide. Striker and the other three soldiers bent their victim backward, bowing his chest outward from the pressure. His eyes wide with terror, the hapless brave watched as Fire Giver drew the tecpatl from his corded belt. This was the sacrificial knife. Its blade was eight inches of serrated obsidian, the hilt inlaid with gold in the form of a warrior with shield, atlatl, and spears. The warrior's features were an animalistic caricature peering through the jaws of his jaguar headdress.

It was the arch sorcerer, the shaper of the world,

the god of darkness. Fire Giver placed the tip of the blade over the chest of the Comanche and, with a strength and skill born of gruesome practice, hammered the blade downward and ripped open the chest cavity. He reached in and plucked out the still-beating heart of the dying man and held it aloft as an offering to the savage deity of this ancient race.

Then the drumming ceased.

The ground beneath the makeshift altar was dark with blood.

It was only the beginning.

Chapter Six

Ben McQueen woke that same morning haunted by dream images that clung to him like the webs of a spider. Entangled and yet defiant, he fought his way out of the nightmare and sat upright. Sweat was streaming from his face and body and soaking the cotton sheet beneath him. He sat on the edge of the bed, put his bare feet on the tile floor, cradled his head in his hands, and began to breathe slowly and deeply. He hadn't had the dream since leaving his father's farm in the Indian Territory. Why now? Perhaps it was the devil's way of plaguing him, of ruining whatever happiness he had begun to feel. He was attracted to Señorita Obregon, the first woman he had noticed since the annullment of his marriage eight months ago.

Anabel Obregon was charming and fiery and even intriguing. What harm was there in enjoying her company during his brief stay in San Antonio? *None at all*, his father would say. Ben had to smile at the thought of Kit McQueen. "Never had any use for guilt," his father had told him. "At least not for very long. Comes a time man has to quit watching the ghosts behind him and get on with life." It was advice Ben had tried to take to heart.

So the tall, rangy young lieutenant lingered on the bed and gathered his thoughts and allowed the aftereffects of a troubled rest to slowly subside. He reached for a boot and started to pull it on.

"Wouldn't do that if'n I were you," Toby said, craning his neck to clear the bedroom door he had eased open. His bright black features radiated good cheer. He pointed at the boots. "Best you knock 'em out first."

Ben tilted his boots sole up and whacked them together. A wriggling brown scorpion dropped to the floor and scuttled toward the far wall, its curved, venomous tail poised in the air, ready to strike. Ben nodded his thanks to the boy.

"Appears I had a visitor last night," he observed. He glanced toward the shuttered window. Sunlight poured through the slats and dust motes danced through patterns of golden light and sandy shadow.

"Ma fixed eggs this morning. You best hurry if'n you want your share," Toby said.

"I appreciate the concern."

"Oh it ain't nothin'." Toby flashed a grin. "You only been here a half a day and things already got plumb exciting. No telling what trouble you gonna step into today." He ducked behind the doorway and hurried toward the rear of the house.

"Always glad to be of service," Ben muttered. He pulled on his trousers and boots and took a moment to survey his surroundings. General Abbot had a room to himself, but Ben and the general's son were to share a room. Ben looked across the bare tile floor at the bed opposite his. It was obvious Peter Abbot had spent the night elsewhere, no doubt in the arms of a beautiful woman. Ben sighed and shook his head, then straightened. A look of alarm crossed his features. Anabel? No... impossible. Then he remembered the girl on the balcony of the Alameda Hotel. She was a surer bet. Now if only she wasn't somebody's wife.

The bedroom, like much of the house, had been stripped of any finery it might have enjoyed in an earlier era. Two beds and a trunk that was set on its side and held a washbasin and earthenware pitcher were the only articles of furniture in the room.

Ben quickly dressed, pausing once as he began to fasten the brass buttons of his blue tunic. Gandy was certainly right about one thing. The uniform was out of place here and ill-suited to this crazy, semiarid, violent land. And he wondered if the same were true of the man who wore it.

Captain Pepper had already eaten, but was having a second cup of coffee. From the look of the empty cups and plates Stacia was clearing away, the captain hadn't eaten alone. Pepper was busily entering some names in a ledger. He glanced up as Ben entered from the hall.

"Morning, Ben. C'mon in and help yourself. I just sent out a couple of men to see if they can cut the trail of the Quahadi village, seeing as they're on the move." He finished making his notations and closed the book. "Seems kinda simple, but this way I know where my men are. And so will the next captain should anything happen to me." He eased back in his chair and wiped the drops of coffee from his mustache with the back of his hand. "Of course, I don't foresee biting the dust anytime soon. Spotted Calf's in the calaboose. And that bandit Cordero hasn't been seen or heard from since our last run-in." Stacia appeared in the doorway carrying a platter of eggs, chorizo (spicy sausage), and tortillas to the table. She left as quietly as she came.

"Cordero?" Ben repeated. The captain was an easy man to talk to. He briefly recounted the notorious career of El Tigre de Coahuila while the lieutenant poured a cup for himself and topped off the captain's. He spooned a helping of eggs and chorizo onto a tortilla, rolled it up, and, pinching one end shut, prepared to eat.

"We ambushed Cordero's men a couple of weeks back. Caught him and his bunch in an arroyo and put them under. A few of his vaqueros escaped. But we emptied the saddles that day. Gandy said he dusted Cordero twice, but we never found the body."

"Gandy again," Ben grumbled. "Always there when you need him." He took a bite of the tortilla. His cheeks turned red and his eyes began to water.

"Well, you don't need to worry about him, Lieutenant. I sent Snake Eye on an errand out of town. He won't be back until tomorrow at the earliest... Chorizo's a might on the spicy side." A glimmer of a smile touched the corner of his mouth. "I heard about your run-in with Snake Eye yesterday afternoon. There aren't many men who'd face him down, but I figured the son of Kit McQueen would be one of the few."

"You know my father?"

"Only by reputation. Fought the Creeks and the British back in the last war. Married a Choctaw medicine woman, so the story goes."

"My mother, Raven O'Keefe McQueen," Ben said after drowning the fire in his mouth with a gulp of black coffee. "She's half Irish, but it only shows when she's angry."

"I had a notion there was more to you than Eastern gewgaws and polite society."

"I was raised among the Choctaws," Ben admitted. "But I've got an Aunt Esther that's never been west of Pennsylvania, and she can outshoot most men. Told me she wanted to be ready in case the British tried one last time to take back the colonies."

Captain Pepper chuckled. He pursed his lips a moment and rubbed at his jaw. "I'll make you a deal—I won't judge your Yankee cousins if you'll keep an open mind about Gandy."

"That *will* be a challenge."

"But worth the effort. He's a good man," Pepper said. "With just a bit of bark still on."

"Hell, Captain, he's wearing the whole damn tree."

Pepper stared down at the grounds sloshing at the bottom of his coffee, then set the cup aside.

"Ben, if you and the general want to understand us, I can tell you where to start."

"I'm listening," the lieutenant said.

"Go to the place all good Texicans hold dear. Kind of a holy ground."

"A church?"

"A shrine," the Ranger replied. "On the northeast side of town; follow the Calle de Mission. You'll find where Texas was born, where a hundred and eighty brave, glorious Texican fools made a stand against Santa Anna's whole blame army, five thousand strong. Travis, Bowie, Crockett, Dickinson, and all the rest, they died to a man and took half the Mexican army with 'em ... at San Antonio de Valero." Capt. Amadeus T. Pepper, whose father had been one of those gallant defenders, looked up from his folded hands. "Most folks just call it the Alamo."

Silence filled the room, a warm and lazy quiet. Captain Pepper had momentarily run out of steam. In fact, he almost seemed in pain. A man's life was like a river, and memories the mud at the bottom that were scooped up from time to time and clouded the waters, for better or ill.

"I hope I'm not interrupting anything," Retired Gen. Matt Abbot said as he filled the doorway with his short, stocky physique. He wore a black frock coat and trousers, a gray vest, and a ruffled white shirt, and looked for all the world like a bantam cock preened and ready to fight. Indeed, Abbot had never run from a battle.

But his arrival jarred Ben into remembering the unslept-in bed and Peter's absence.

"You are a late riser, Ben," Abbot said, clapping him on the shoulder. "It's probably just as well— you might have protested my actions. However, it's too late now."

"Sir?" Ben was puzzled and a little alarmed. Matthew Abbot was by nature wholly unpredictable.

"Captain Pepper has informed me that Sam Houston will be attending the fiesta and is due in any day now. And after the festivities we can return to the capital with Houston and a guard of Texas Rangers. Makes for good politics." Matt Abbot swelled with pride at his own brilliance. "There should have been a Texas escort all along."

"What of my men?" Ben asked.

"I sent them back to Galveston under the command of Sergeant Hezekiah Palmer."

"Sir..." Ben went from puzzled to speechless. "You had no authority..."

"Oh, hell, Lieutenant. I was commanding men while you were still in knee pants," the former general replied.

"Not these men," Ben said, taken completely off guard. "Your welfare is my responsibility."

"And I appreciate your efforts," Abbot replied in his most conciliatory tone. "But Captain Pepper has graciously offered to assign a few of his Rangers to us. They will be under your command, of course."

Captain Pepper nodded in accord with the former officer. "My men will have no problem with following your orders. I'll personally see to it."

Ben rose from the table and crossed around to the window that looked out on the few rows of corn Stacia had managed to coax from the arid ground behind the barracks.

It was plain to see what Abbot had in mind: to placate the Texans' injured pride by having the Republic's own military act as his honor guard. The plan made sense. And from what he had seen of Snake Eye Gandy, these Rangers were more than capable of insuring Matthew Abbot's safety. Still, it galled him the way the ex-general had exceeded his authority. Well, if it smoothed some ruffled feathers in the Texas legislature, Ben decided he'd put up with it. And as his men had already left, what other choice was there?

"Whatever you say," Ben at last conceded. "But your words better carry some weight around here, Captain. I'd have an easier time commanding a troop of Comanches than the likes of Snake Eye Gandy."

Father Esteban emerged from the sanctuary and carried the two-foot-tall solid gold crucifix to the altar, where he placed it alongside the tabernacle. He lit a votive candle housed in a red glass holder and placed it at the foot of the crucifix, which reflected the flickering candle flame along the burnished metal legs of a suffering Christ. Father Esteban Cordero de Tosta, who longed for peace and prayed every day that his true identity would remain undiscovered, ran a velvet cloth over the base of the crucifix and wiped it clean of fingerprints. He had noticed the peon kneeling before the statue of the Virgin in the alcove set in the south wall of the church. This was the church of the common people; the poor were always welcome here. From another pew, two girls in faded white dresses approached with their mother, who was dressed in homespun clothes, a coarse woven shawl covering her head. Though the woman had been kneeling at prayer, she had other motives for being in church today.

"Padre, we come to see you," one of the girls said, dark eyes warm with affection. Esteban hugged them both. He knew the family's situation. The woman's husband sold firewood and frequently squandered his meager earnings in the cantinas surrounding the Main Plaza, east of the church.

"Ah, my dear Señora Flores. It is good you come to visit our Lord today, for our Saviour has recently blessed me with an abundance of fat, noisy chickens. You must stop by and see Carmelita and tell her to choose a couple for you."

"You are very good to us," Señora Flores replied, bowing to kiss his hand. Esteban embraced her. "I wish that I could repay your kindness." The woman lifted her narrow, tear-streaked face.

"Repay God, dear woman. Be generous with prayer, eh? God uses me. The glory is His."

"Still, yours is a kind heart."

"Go on now." Esteban shushed her along. "I think Carmelita may even have some *pan dulce* for the children."

The little girls clapped their hands and hurried back down the aisle of the church to the front doors, their footsteps clattering on the tile. When they and the señora were gone, the peon kneeling before the statue of the Virgin stood and faced the priest.

"Such a good and gentle man to be the son of a bloodthirsty bandit like the tiger of Coahuila."

The voice was hoarse and strikingly familiar. Father Esteban gasped and spun around, half expecting to see his father standing in the shadows. Indeed the man in the shadows even looked like Don Luis. He had roughly the same build—tough, solid, thick-waisted, with short, well-muscled arms. His black hair was streaked with silver. In his forty-ninth year, the man's features were crinkled and leathery from a life spent chasing Comanches and raiding the homesteads and settlements of families both light-skinned and dark who dared to call themselves Texans.

As the man stepped forward out of the alcove, Esteban sighed with relief. He had not encountered an apparition of his father, after all.

The priest's happiness was short-lived, however, for the bandit disguised as a humble peon was none other than Jorge Tenorio. If Don Luis Cordero had been El Tigre, Jorge Tenorio had been the claws. A man of striking contradictions, Tenorio could bounce a child on his knee, cooing and playing, and in the next instant shoot the father of the child stone-cold dead. It was not that Tenorio was a brutal man, but years of living with a gun in his hand had taken their toll. To his compadres, no man was more steadfast and loyal, but his enemies called him a ruthless butcher. Somewhere in between was the man who had bounced young Esteban Cordero on his lap and taught him to ride.

"Tenorio . . ." Esteban said. "*Madre de Dios*, how many more survived the battle with the Rangers?"

The old cutthroat shrugged and smiled as he sauntered forward, his spurs clinking with every step.

"Tomas, Chico, and Miguel, who I sent on to see you and Señorita Cordero. And Miguel's brother Hector. The man does not live who can outshoot or outride Hector Ybarbo." Tenorio grinned and patted the bulge of a gun butt beneath his blousy cotton shirt. "Except me." He scratched at the week-old stubble prickling his jaw. If he'd let his beard grow it would have come in mostly silvery-white, with just a smattering of black. Tenorio was sensitive about his age. He wanted a shave more than anything. He knew a barber across the river in La Villita, the oldest section of town, and was anxious to pay the man a visit.

"What do you want here?" Esteban asked.

"Sanctuary, what else?" Tenorio said, his eyes wide with innocence.

"And you shall have it," Anabel interjected, entering the church from a side door that opened onto a thatch-covered walk connecting the church to the priest's house. Anabel was followed by Miguel Ybarbo and his brother Hector, who was older than Miguel by a few years and wiser by twenty, or so it seemed. Where Miguel was headstrong and vengeful and too quick to act, Hector was a calming influence. He wore the loose-fitting cotton shirt and trousers of a field hand, but he kept a pistol tucked in his boot top just to be on the safe side. His black hair was close-cropped though ragged-looking; his mustache was a shaggy black scrawl that hid his upper lip and hung to his chin.

Esteban shifted and looked past his sister, expecting to see the remainder of his father's stern-faced henchmen file into the church. Sanctuary was one thing, but they were transforming the house of God into a den of thieves and cutthroats.

Anabel told her brother, "Don't worry, Chico and Tomas are waiting outside of town. No more surprises for you, dear brother." The young woman patted Esteban's arm. Then she glanced over her shoulder at Miguel. The vaquero was still angry at being spurned by the daughter of Don Luis Cordero.

"Miguel, bolt the door. We cannot afford interruptions. We have more enemies in San Antonio than friends."

The vaquero hesitated, and Hector gave him a

shove. Miguel turned on his brother with fists clenched.

"Ah, little one, you forget your place. We ride for Cordero. Now do as you are told."

"Maybe I no longer choose to follow," Miguel suggested.

"If you are not one of us, then you are our enemy," Tenorio said. The old one's lips curled back and his hand reached beneath his shirt for the gun hidden there. "You are my enemy." Miguel fidgeted nervously. His brash pride drained away with his courage.

"I said maybe," he clarified, then stepped around Anabel and the priest, gave Tenorio a wide berth, and hurried up the aisle to the front doors.

Jorge Tenorio turned to Anabel. He lifted her hand and looked at the obsidian ring that had belonged to Don Luis. He nodded sagely and cupped her hand in his.

"It is right for you to wear the ring. But it is a heavy responsibility. I wonder, señorita, if your shoulders are strong enough to carry such a burden." Tenorio lifted his gaze to Father Esteban. "A son's duty is to avenge his father's death. But in this case..." He wagged his head in despair.

"Do not seek to pass judgment on me, Jorge," Esteban said. "I wish Carmelita had buried the damn stone."

"And I wish Don Luis had never allowed your mother to carry you back to Mexico City to raise in the company of women until you were old enough to be sent off to that seminary in Spain." Tenorio held his hands up in despair. "But Doña Isabell was determined to have at least one saint in the family. And here you are."

Father Esteban swallowed his anger, though he trembled from the effort. At last he turned to his sister, but even then he had to struggle to contain himself. Words failed him. His brown robe flared as he turned and headed for the side door.

"Make your plans. I do not want to know anything, not so much as a hint." He looked around at Tenorio. "And take off those damn...uh...those spurs. The first Ranger you pass will spy that silver work and know immediately you are no poor farmer." Esteban enjoyed catching Tenorio's mistake. It enabled him to leave with the last word and a smattering of dignity.

Anabel granted his request: After her brother left, she asked Jorge Tenorio to remove his silver spurs. Alone at last in the serenity of the church, beneath the shadow of the golden cross and the prince of peace, Anabel Cordero gathered the vaqueros to her side and revealed to them her plans for war.

Chapter Seven

"Mother McQueen," Peter Abbot remarked as Ben took the seat across from him in the Red Bull Cantina. "You found me."

"It wasn't difficult," Ben said. "The clerk at the Alameda told me the name of the girl on the balcony and where she could be found—Cecilia from the Red Bull Cantina."

"A winsome lass," Peter sighed, pushing his spectacles up on the bridge of his nose. "We promised to always be faithful. We shared secrets. Then someone came along with a deeper purse." Peter's slender hand raised a cup of pulque in salute to his friend. Sheets of scrap paper littered the tabletop. Several of them bore hastily rendered charcoal sketches of patrons who had come and gone through the Red Bull's swinging doors the night before. Many of the drawings were quite good and revealed the artist's keen sense of observation, as well as his considerable talent. Peter was seldom without the packet of charcoal sticks he kept in his coat pocket.

Ben reached out and caught Peter's arm and forced him to set the fired-clay cup back on the table. A short, squat man of Mexican descent entered from a back room and noticed with disapproval that not only had the Anglo with the eyeglasses not left, he had been joined by another, and this one a soldier.

"We are closed. Comprende? The women sleep. I must sleep too. Come back in the afternoon."

"Bring us coffee. Then we will go."

"No, we are closed. Leave now."

"Coffee first," Ben said, and flipped a coin in the air that the barkeep snatched in mid-flight. The Mexican glanced down at the money in his hand. Too much for coffee, but enough for the inconvenience of serving it. He shrugged and disappeared through a back doorway that led into the kitchen. Unlike Military Plaza with its shops and hotels, church and governor's palace, Main Plaza was home to the noisy underbelly of town life. The Red Bull held a dominant place among the assorted saloons and brothels surrounding the plaza. The cantina was a single storied adobe building with a roof of red-clay tiles and a deep porch that shaded the front. Within its thick stucco walls, round hardwood tables and hand-hewn, straight-backed chairs were placed around the room for the convenience of the rowdy patrons. The thirty-foot walnut bar ran the length of the south wall. On the north wall, the likeness of an enormous red bull had been painted upon the faded whitewashed surface. The painting was framed by a pair of bullfighter's capes tacked to the wall and spread like fans.

The cantina smelled of tobacco smoke and stale pulque. Behind the bar were a number of brown glass bottles marked "Whisky," "Bourbon," "Rye," and "Brandy." Ben suspected they all came out of the same keg beneath the bar.

"Still looking after me, eh?" Peter said, scratching at the brown stubble shading his features. He leaned back and studied his friend. "I figured you'd have tired of the task by now." He dropped his gaze to the clay cup of milky-white liquid set before him. "It's awful stuff, really. Bitter as gall, but it packs a wallop like a nine-pounder cannon."

"Then it's time you called a truce," Ben said.

"Well put," Peter replied. "I'll make an artist of you yet."

"No. That's not my calling." Ben glanced around the cantina. At a table in the corner, another of last night's customers sat hunched forward, head resting on folded arms, pouchy face turned toward them. The man was wrapped in a serape and snored in loud, harsh, rumbling tones.

"Too bad. You are cursed with a sense of responsibility. More's the pity." Peter reached for the pulque, hoping to catch the lieutenant in a moment of reverie. Ben was not so easily fooled and slid the drink out of reach. "Hmmm . . . Well, anyway," Peter added, "it seems I am cursed with your sense of responsibility." He rubbed his forehead and tried to will away his headache. Maybe McQueen was right, he thought.

The barkeeper returned with a blue-enamel tin coffeepot and two cups. He placed them on the table, poured, and said, "Please, señors. I am tired. Not too long, por favor." He started to leave, then remembered Peter's outstanding account.

"How will you pay for the last pulque, señor?"

Peter searched through the drawings until he came to a likeness of the barkeeper, who beamed with happiness as the artist handed him the sketch.

"Gracias, Señor Abbot," the round-faced barkeep said. He noticed a second drawing, this one of the señorita Peter had accompanied from the Alameda Hotel. The buxom young prostitute lay upon a narrow bed, naked, her legs provocatively crossed, her breasts dark and sumptuous. "And maybe one other. Ah, the *puta*. She makes an old man's blood flow hot."

"Your pulque is expensive," Peter dryly noted.

"Yes, it is," the barkeeper admitted, and licked his lips as he held out a pudgy hand for the second drawing. Peter scrawled his signature and handed it over. As the man hurried off with his two prizes, Ben examined the other sketches. Some were quite hastily rendered and had little detail. Others revealed the artist's greater interest in his subject.

The backs of posters and irregularly torn fragments of brown wrapping paper were adorned with a variety of faces: four men huddled around a table; a flush-faced German immigrant out for a night on the town; two peons, one of whom wore fancy roweled silver spurs, standing at the bar; a prostitute whose tired, painted features stared back at Ben with sad eyes and an inviting smile; a drunkard propped in the corner whose puzzled countenance looked like a wooden mask; three frock-coated merchants gambling in earnest. A second sketch of the señorita from the Alameda showed her dressed this time and seated upon the lap of a handsome vaquero. They were laughing and the vaquero's shirt was open and the señorita had her hand on his chest.

"A woman's fancies," Peter sighed. He gulped coffee and shuddered. The hammering in his head— too much pulque, too much cheap whisky, and not enough love. He sifted through the sketches and pointed to the drawing of the four men seated at a table. Three of them wore buckskins and formed a grizzled, hard-looking bunch. The fourth figure was older and nattily attired in frock coat and flat-crowned beaver hat. Hook-nosed and with close-set eyes, this was a singularly unattractive man.

"Now here was an intriguing bunch," Peter said, lifting the sketch into the light. "It was difficult to understand what they were saying, but from what I could discern Mr. Ashworth—the man in the coat—is a gun merchant and has come to San Antonio with a crate of Colt revolvers to sell to whoever meets his price. He also intends to exact retribution against someone in town. The unsavory characters at the table with him are his hirelings." Peter handed the drawing to Ben, who examined it with interest. Although this was none of his affair, he didn't like the looks of this Ashworth fellow. The gun merchant meant trouble and ought to be stopped. "I daresay someone is in for quite a thrashing," Peter added. His hand still trembled. He gulped more of the black coffee.

Ben frowned and tapped the drawing. "A fair fight is one thing, but a merciless beating is quite another. Where is Mr. Ashworth now?"

"Gone on the wings of the wind," Peter said, shrugging. "Who can say?" He scrutinized his friend. "I see that look again. Ben McQueen, the proud and gallant soldier. I salute you." Peter unsteadily stood and brought his right hand to his forehead.

"Sit down, you drunken fool," Ben growled. "And I don't appreciate your ridicule."

"No, no," Peter said, easing down into the chair. "You misjudge me. I do respect you, Ben. No man holds you in higher esteem. You are everything my father wants me to be, everything I am too weak to become." The general's son paused, uncertain as to his train of thought.

"Now you're talking nonsense," Ben said. "C'mon, I'll sneak you into the governor's palace. I left the shutters open to our room. For heaven's sake, get some rest before you run into the general."

Peter nodded and managed to stand. He closed his eyes and rubbed his forehead.

"You leaving? Good. Gracias, señor. Come again to the Red Bull Cantina," the barkeeper said from the doorway of his kitchen.

"Tell Cecilia I shall expect to see her tonight, my good man, *all* night," Peter said with a wave of his hand.

"We're guests of Señorita Obregon this evening," Ben reminded his friend.

"Then you are a most fortunate man," Peter said, and clapped Ben on the shoulder. "For now I am in love with Cecilia: I give the Señorita Obregon to you."

"You are most kind," Ben said, leading his friend out into the hazy noonday heat. They skirted Main Plaza and entered Military Plaza, one block over. The vendors were out in force today. Stalls had been erected overnight where men and women hawked their wares. There were baskets for sale, pottery, firewood, spicy enchiladas, and hot tortillas cooked upon flatiron griddles set over open fires. A man offered an assortment of caged birds; a woman arrayed herself in a half dozen brightly stitched shawls and busily haggled with a prospective customer. One enterprising man composed love letters on the spot and for a fee inserted the appropriate name of the beloved. A pair of shy young men lingered near the scribe as if gathering the courage to approach him. Stalls were hung with corn and chili peppers and freshly killed rabbits, squirrels, and chickens.

Ben noticed Carmelita threading her way among the vendors. She carried a reed basket that already bulged with vegetables, a bolt of cloth, and a string of sausages. Ben looked for Anabel, but she was nowhere to be seen. The lieutenant told Peter to stay put and started forward to bid Carmelita good day. The buxom servant recognized Ben and for a brief moment looked alarmed at his presence.

"Señora, it is a fine day to visit the plaza. Perhaps you are not alone and the señorita is nearby?" He once again searched the faces of the people around him.

"She is not here, señor," Carmelita said. "Señorita Obregon is with her brother, in the church." Carmelita glanced past the soldier and saw two men coming toward her. The men were dressed as peons, but she recognized them instantly, for one was her son, Chico Raza, and the other was his friend Tomas Zavala.

Ben noted the change in the woman's expression and turned, hoping to discover Anabel behind him. Instead he caught a glimpse of the bandits.

Chico Raza was burly and bearded, with a livid white scar across the bridge of his nose. Tomas Zavala was a smaller man, barely five and a half feet tall. His short, bowed legs and flat face betrayed his Apache bloodline. A sombrero shaded his features. Both men noticed Ben's blue uniform and immediately turned on their heels and started back through the crowd.

Ben looked back at Carmelita. The servant was busily inspecting an array of hearth-baked breads, none of which she intended to purchase. He saw that Peter had reached the corner of the governor's palace. Ben returned his attention to the two men, who had already made their way across the plaza. Perhaps he had imagined Carmelita's reaction—but not the behavior of the two peons.

He started through the crowd as the two men reached the mouth of an alley on the north side of the plaza. They paused to check for any sign of pursuit and spotted Ben coming toward them. The lieutenant was impossible to miss, with his blue uniform, and the fact that he towered over the people around him, his red hair gleaming in contrast to the darker heads of the townspeople in the plaza.

Chico scratched at his scarred nose and nudged his smaller companion.

"I don't know this man."

"He is a *norteamericano*," Tomas replied. He ran a hand across his mouth. "I warned you against coming into town."

"Enough. The Rangers do not look for us in town. And I wanted to see my mother. No one cooks better, eh?"

"But you found a *norteamericano* soldier instead. Your empty belly is our misfortune."

"You have the courage of an old woman," Chico scoffed. "*Vamanos.*" He tugged Tomas's shirtsleeve and the two men dashed down the alley toward the Camino Real.

Ben quickened his pace, more intrigued than ever by the men's unusual behavior. The Choctaw blood flowing through his veins gave him a keen instinct for trouble. The voices of the merchants and shopkeepers mingled with those of the browsing townsfolk and became an indistinguishable noise that Ben no longer heeded. His attention was focused on the alley. Children scampered past unnoticed; a dog nipped and barked at his heels, then darted off after a couple of little girls eating tortillas fresh from the cook fire. An old man offered to sell Ben one of half a dozen goats, a woman wanted to show him the necklaces she had made from shells, another man tried to interest him in rattlesnake skins.

But the lieutenant never wavered, and at last reached the mouth of the alley and started down a narrow passage that was bordered on either side by the thick adobe walls of a hacienda and its court-yard and the two-story outer wall of the Ridenour House, the hotel recently acquired by a German immigrant.

The noise of the plaza faded behind him as Ben continued on toward the Camino Real. Sunlight shone on the upper floor of the hotel and hacienda but left the alley in shadow. After the commotion of the marketplace, the stillness in the alley seemed almost oppressive.

A footstep behind him! Ben whirled as his right hand dropped to a pistol grip. Toby jumped back, alarm in his eyes.

"Lordy, Mister Ben, you plumb scared the bejesus out of me," the nine-year-old said.

"What are you doing?" Ben asked, loosing a breath. He eased the single-shot percussion pistol back in its holster.

"I seen you from across the plaza. Figured you must be lost. Ain't nothing down this ol' alley 'cept trash." Toby hooked a thumb through his suspenders. "I been all over San Antone. I can help you find just about anything, and that's a fact." The boy's eyes twinkled as he fished in his pocket a moment and produced a pair of *cigarillos*, the slim, hard-packed cigars favored by the vaqueros who drove cattle into San Antone and worked some of the outlying *ranchos*.

"You're a little young for those, aren't you?" Ben asked.

"Not if my ma don't see me," Toby replied with a wink. Then his attitude suddenly changed as two horsemen entered the alley from Camino Real. Two mountain-bred stallions—whipped into a mad gallop by their riders, the "peons" Ben had followed—bore down on the soldier and the boy.

"Son of a bitch!" Toby shouted. Ben heard the clatter of hooves, glanced over his shoulder, saw the pair of stallions about to trample him, and reacted on instinct. He hooked Toby in the crook of his right arm and dove for the wall of the hotel, flattening himself and the startled boy against the adobe. Chico and Tomas missed them by inches. Chico slapped down with his braided rawhide quirt and struck Ben on the back of the neck. Ben winced and raised an arm to ward off another blow, but the riders swept past in a shower of rocks and pebbles and flashing hooves. By the time Ben freed his pistol, the bandits had cut to the left and vanished past the corner of the hotel. Ben ran back toward the plaza, but the few seconds it took him to retrace his steps were all Chico and Tomas needed. Ben dashed out into the plaza, gun in hand, only to find that the horsemen had eluded him and vanished down another side street on the opposite side of the hotel, leaving only a sandy cloud of settling dust to mark their passing.

People were staring at him and the gun in his hand. The lieutenant grudgingly returned the weapon to his belt. Whoever the two men were, they certainly didn't ride like farmers.

Toby trotted up and stood beside the tall soldier. The black youth stared with regret at the crushed remnants of the cigarillos in the palm of his hand.

"Lawd have mercy," he said, still gasping for breath.

Ben searched the plaza and spied Carmelita as she ascended the steps to San Fernando Cathedral. She paused before the heavy oak doors and turned, hesitated as if aware she was being watched, then quickly entered.

"Yeah," Ben replied. "Have mercy." It appeared his stay in San Antonio was going to be anything but dull.

Chapter Eight

Night...

Miguel Ybarbo centered the rifle sights on Ben McQueen and curled his finger around the trigger. Even in the filmy moonlight, where clouds trailed across the sky like bridal veils, he could make the shot. It wasn't all that far from the bell tower to the roof of the padre's house below. Minutes ago Miguel had watched as Ben and Anabel climbed the outside stairway to the flat roof of the house, where they now stood together overlooking the lantern-lit plaza. On this soft spring night, guitar music filled the air with romantic ballads, and would-be suitors, rich and poor alike, came to Military Plaza. It was a custom the Anglo residents of San Antonio had adopted from their Spanish-speaking neighbors. Young women were not only allowed to visit the plaza, but under the watchful eye of mother or guardian were permitted the company of whichever man the family found acceptable. The couple might then excuse themselves and walk arm in arm around the plaza, chaperoned from afar, yet enjoying a moment of privacy.

Miguel's finger tightened on the trigger. He trusted his marksmanship. Just a few seconds more and this gringo soldier would be out of his hair. Miguel's jealousy ran deep. Anabel was his woman whether she knew it or not, and he did not like the game she was playing. There was something in her eyes when she talked about the lieutenant, a spark of interest Miguel intended to keep from bursting into flame.

"Put the rifle down, brother." A voice drifted up from the trapdoor in the floor of the bell tower. Hector Ybarbo scrambled up through the doorway and gingerly maneuvered his way around the bell to stand on the narrow walkway alongside Miguel.

"Leave me," Miguel hissed back.

"Put down the rifle," his older brother repeated. Hector had practically raised Miguel after the death of their mother, and often addressed him like a father.

"Look at her. See how close she stands? Next she will allow him to put his hands on her."

"The Señorita Cordero will do what needs to be done. She has a plan." Hector tried to remain calm. The confines of the bell tower were too restrictive to risk trouble. "Come down with me. Carmelita has brought news. She learned today there is a gringo in town who has guns to sell. Colt revolvers like the Rangers carry."

Miguel lowered the rifle. It was a .52-caliber muzzle loader, capable of blowing a fist-size hole in a man; a trusty firearm, but no match for six-shot pistols in a running battle. With such guns the Rangers, though outnumbered, had attacked the bandits and driven off Comanche war parties.

"We will find him later," Miguel said.

"Not if you kill this gringo and alert the whole town to our presence," Hector said, stroking his mustache as he tried to think of a way to defuse his jealous brother. "The señorita wears the ring of El Tigre. She has ordered us to find the gun merchant."

"So she can be alone with the *norteamericano*," Miguel bitterly retorted.

"You are a fool. Have your vengeance another day." Hector sighed. His brother was too proud. The boneyards were full of men like Miguel who acted without thinking. Hector tried a different tactic. "I watch with you, then. Wait. Nothing will happen. The señorita talks to the gringo. Nothing more, eh? You'll see."

Ben wasn't certain as to the names of everything he'd eaten for dinner. Anabel and Carmelita had set a feast suitable for royalty. The heavy oaken dinner table in the padre's dining room had been crowded with platters of chicken roasted in pepper sauce, tortillas, beans, squash, and large green chili peppers stuffed with sausage and rice and covered with a fiery red sauce that brought tears to his eyes.

"What are you thinking now?" Anabel said, standing close to the adobe wall that bordered the roof. Ben had suggested they take the night air. She had led him from the cactus garden to this roof. "You were so quiet at dinner." She listened to the strains of a distant guitar accompanying the solitary tenor voice of some lovesick vaquero.

"Had to let my tongue cool off before I could speak," Ben replied good-naturedly. He moved nearer the woman. She wore a loose, frilly blouse, a purple shawl, and a wine-colored skirt. A white cactus flower tucked over her right ear made a vibrant contrast to her long black tresses.

"You did not like what we prepared?"

"Yes. Most assuredly. I have never enjoyed a meal more." Ben found himself groping for an explanation. His mind had indeed wandered during dinner. Was he so obvious? And was she really interested? He hardly knew the young señorita, yet he felt he could confide in her. Maybe he was simply being deluded by the warm breezes, the melancholy guitar, and the shadows of the lovers passing in the night beyond the walls. "I owe you an apology, señorita."

"I do not understand.

"My mind has been elsewhere throughout the evening. Such behavior dishonors you and your hospitality. Forgive me if I have offended you."

Anabel paused a moment, mulling over his unusual behavior and puzzled by his reply. "I will forgive you only if you explain. Have we not become friends? We have much in common, sí? We fought Comanches together and we both dislike Señor Gandy."

Ben laughed and lost himself in her dark eyes and nodded. "Yes, we do have much in common." He watched the couples strolling through the plaza. "I was thinking of my children. One day I would like for them to see Texas." He noticed her stiffen. "My wife left me," he added. "It happened almost a year ago. Jesse and Daniel, my boys, are staying with my parents."

He leaned upon the wall and looked directly into the small courtyard and the path leading to the iron gate. Lamplight flooded the walk as the front door opened and Peter left the house. He rounded the corner and climbed the steps to the roof, where he joined Ben and Anabel.

"I hope I am disturbing something," Peter said. He hurried over to Anabel and bowed, kissing her hand. "Thank you for the wonderful meal and your charming and gracious hospitality."

"We did not mean to sneak off...." Ben said.

"Of course you did and I don't blame you," Peter replied. "I had all I could take. Father is trying to recruit the padre into helping promote the cause of annexation among the Mexicans." Peter sighed and shook his head. "He never stops being a general."

Anabel remained impassive. "And what does my brother say to all this?"

Peter chuckled. "The padre is just about con vinced. Matthew Abbot can be very persuasive." He patted the wrinkles from his frock coat and returned his flat-crowned hat to his head. He had a leather bag draped over his shoulder. It contained sketch paper and charcoal.

"Where are you off to?" Ben asked. He could sense the tension in Peter's voice. His friend had a talent for self-destructive excesses.

"Now, Mother McQueen, have no fear," Peter said. "I'll keep a clear head. After all, I have my father's reputation to uphold."

Ben made no attempt to hide his doubts. An hour before they had left for dinner, Ben had overheard a muted argument in the general's room. Afterward, Peter had come storming out of his father's quarters. Such clashes were frequently over Peter's determination to shape his own destiny.

The general's errant son made his farewell and then headed back toward the stairway. However, he couldn't resist one parting salvo at Ben.

"Señorita, I must admit you've a prize lunkhead there. McQueen's as stubborn as any full-blood Scot. And when it comes to women, he's a babe in the woods. So if you want a kiss before the night is through you'll have to claim it yourself." Peter touched the brim of his hat, bowed, dashed down the steps, and without breaking stride trotted down the walk and darted through the iron gate, leaving Ben to smoulder and plot a variety of painful deaths for his friend.

"Anabel, please excuse Señor Abbot," Ben said. "He often speaks without thinking." The lieutenant was grateful for the darkness that hid his flustered expression.

"There are times when such talk makes the most sense." Anabel was amused at his discomfort, and touched by his earlier admission of loss. Those feelings startled her and caught her off guard. This Ben McQueen was a big, good-natured, handsome and likeable man. The kind of man Anabel might have opened up to, but she had secrets better kept locked away. Anabel focused herself on the plans she had set in motion. The ring on her hand fractured the moon's reflection and transformed the image into a pale and ghostly eye that seemed to peer from the center of the stone's glossy depths.

"The general, at dinner, spoke of a medal you carry..."

Ben nodded. Matthew Abbot had regaled Father Esteban with a capsule history of the United States in hopes of impressing on the padre how beneficial it would be for the Texas Republic to become part of the Union. Abbot had bragged about the quality of men and women who had carved a nation out of the wilderness and won freedom from England. Ben's own grandfather, Daniel McQueen, had played a significant role in that heroic struggle.

"Yes," Ben said. "It's really just a coin. But it's been passed from my grandfather to my father and now to me."

"The general said it bore the mark of the great man, Washington? May I see this medal?"

Ben shrugged, opened his shirt at the throat, and pulled out a shiny silver coin affixed to a chain. It was an English crown, and scrawled across the features on one side of the coin were the initials "G.W." Anabel held the coin in her fingertips. It was indeed only a coin, like the ring on her hand was but a rock set in a band of metal, yet both carried responsibilities and duties that shaped the life of their bearers.

"You keep it with you always?"

"Yes," Ben said, tucking it back inside his shirt.

His memory conjured a moment from the past, a leave-taking. It was January. On a brisk winter's morning. A gleaming frost had settled on the buffalo grass that surrounded the farmhouse like an amber sea. Jesse and Daniel had already hugged him good-bye. His departure was easier for them to accept because they were so young. And Raven had made pancakes this morning and left a jug of sorghum syrup on the table for the boys to have as much as they wanted. No, leaving was harder for their father. But he was a soldier. And he had a job to do.

Kit McQueen waited alongside his son's horse. At fifty-nine, Ben's father looked to be in his forties. His hair was white and hung to his shoulders. A small, compact, solidly built man, Kit McQueen cast a long shadow. His features were dark from the sun and chiseled by the passage of time. His eyes could be hard and cold as death at times, but today they mirrored the love he felt for his only son.

He shielded his gaze and glanced up at a lone formation of geese, winging southward across the harsh blue sky.

"Glad to see you aren't leaving alone," he said. It had been a relatively mild winter, but a norther must have been on the way. Ben heard the cries and watched for a moment, taking time to enjoy a spectacle that never failed to fill his soul with happiness. The flight of geese was a reassuring constant in an all-too-changing world.

Kit exhaled slowly and nodded, as if nature had whispered a secret in his ear. "Nothing lives long except the sky," he said.

"And the mountains," Ben replied.

"And the mystery between," Kit added, finishing the Choctaw prayer his wife Raven had taught him. Then Kit reached under his buckskin shirt and removed the medal he had worn for more than thirty years. It was time. Ben realized what was happening and, speechless, lowered his head to allow his father to drape the chain around his throat. He straightened and looked down at the gleaming coin.

"It doesn't weigh much," Kit said, "But it can get awful heavy sometimes." Then he embraced his son and whispered, "Be well."

"Ben...?"

Anabel's voice brought him back, and the lieutenant stammered his apology.

"I'm sorry...uh...I...guess that glass of wine

was one too many." A warm May breeze tugged at his wavy red hair and caressed his cheek. His mind was clear now, as was the reason he had suggested Anabel accompany him outside, away from the dining room and the older woman who had brought them food from the padre's kitchen.

"Señorita Obregon..."

"You may call me Anabel."

"Gracias," Ben said. "How long have you known Carmelita?"

The question caught Anabel off guard. Her pulse quickened and she became instantly wary of the man at her side.

"All my life. Why do you ask?"

"I met her in the plaza. There were two men... she seemed to know them," Ben said. "In fact, I thought she was even...frightened."

Anabel shrugged and tried to appear nonchalant. She reached out and took Ben's hand in hers.

"Carmelita is much like a farmer—always afraid. It will not rain enough, the crops will dry up. It will rain too much, the crops will drown. Every shadow hides a Comanche, beneath every sombrero waits a murdering bandit," the señorita lightheartedly explained.

She was impossible to resist. Ben saw no reason to doubt her. Carmelita certainly struck him as a fussy, overprotective old woman. She probably found menace in Ben's own blue uniform.

"But enough of mamacita and your wandering thoughts and sad memories. I will give you something else to think about." Anabel stepped forward, pressed against him, and found his lips with hers. A rush of fire swept through his veins and stole his breath away.

The bell in the tower of San Fernando Cathedral began to clang, startling the couple on the roof. Anabel skipped back and spun around, eyes wide with alarm. The ringing ceased as quickly as it had begun. But it had done its damage. The moment was lost. The young woman turned and lowered her gaze.

"Perhaps we had better rejoin the general and my brother, sí?"

My God, was he dreaming...had she kissed him? Yes—the taste of her lingered on his lips like sweet nectar.

"I—suppose—so," Ben grudgingly conceded and followed her to the stairs. He paused and glowered at the tower. *Damn bell*, he thought. *Funny thing, it ringing like that.*

Hector crouched below the wall and waited for his hearing to return. His brother, Miguel, lay unconscious on the wooden decking. The kiss had enraged him. Mad with jealousy, he had snapped up the rifle, determined to avenge himself on the lieutenant. Only Hector's fast reflexes had salvaged the moment and the life of the *norteamericano*.

A hand thrust between the hammer and percussion cap had kept the rifle from firing. With his other hand, Hector had swung the brass bell against Miguel's skull, knocking him senseless.

"Ah, Miguel, it is for the best," Hector said as he wrapped a piece of cloth torn from his shirt around his bleeding knuckles. "One shot and we all die. For what?" He leaned against the wall. "Another day, Miguel. *Por nada*. There will come another day. You kill him then."

In the plaza below, after being startled by the church bell, a singer in the shadows began to play his guitar again and resumed his melancholy song of love.

Chapter Nine

It was near midnight, but Ben felt alive and too damned aroused to try and sleep. What kind of place was this San Antonio, with its dry, clear nights and soft breezes, distant music and utterly perplexing señoritas?

He stood in the courtyard behind the governor's palace and allowed his vision to readjust to the darkness. He glanced over his shoulder and noticed Matt Abbot through the window. Abbot leaned over the kitchen table, a clay mug of coffee in one hand. He found a cold biscuit with the other. Steam rose past the rim of his cup as the former officer chanced a taste of the bitter brew. Rangers liked their coffee black as sin, thick as mud, and strong enough to float a horseshoe, Captain Pepper had boasted.

Ben grinned. These Texicans were almighty sure of themselves, especially Snake Eye Gandy and the other Rangers in town. With Pepper's men stationed in San Antonio, the town marshal was seldom called upon to settle disputes. Folks just naturally showed up at the captain's door. This night, Clay Poole had been sent to make the rounds and let the rowdies of Main Plaza see the presence of law. Ben had no doubt but that the bearded, gruff-looking Ranger with his six-gun and well-honed tomahawk would have a taming effect on San Antonio's more notorious populace.

Ben knew that Matt wanted him to sit a spell and listen to the worried old man's fears for his son's well-being. But it was a conversation they had had before. Peter Abbot, like every man, would find his own way. He just thought too much; like a grocer, he weighed everything. That was his problem. Ben chuckled and chided himself, Who's thinking too much now?

He turned his back to the light and headed off down the walk, across the courtyard, past the fountain, dry and empty as last year's dreams, and on through the rear gate to the path that led toward the calaboose and the barn. He glanced toward the tree where he had confronted Snake Eye Gandy. Nothing stirred by the cottonwood but the tree's own pattern of shadows as the pale moonlight filtered through the twisted branches overhead.

Ben continued on to the barn. Chanting, faintly heard, caused him to detour and follow the song to its source, the thick-walled *jacales* that served as a jail. Within the dim interior of the calaboose, the singer sensed Ben's approach and ceased his chanting. Ben stood outside the door. A barred window set in the middle of the door provided the only avenue for fresh air and daylight, except for another slit cut high in the back wall and covered with iron bars. The meager windows permitted a cross breeze but offered no chance for escape. Whatever Spotted Calf's transgressions, Ben couldn't help but feel a tinge of sympathy for the Comanche. As for all riders of the wild, free places, imprisonment was a living hell for the warrior.

Ben heard a rustling sound and sensed movement. Half a second later Spotted Calf's broad, ugly face filled the window in the door. He'd sweated most of the war paint from his battered features. His shoulder was wrapped with a fresh bandage, evidence that Captain Pepper had been true to his word and sent San Antinio's only doctor to tend the brave's wound.

"The white eyes want to kill me," the brave said. "It is good to have enemies." He seemed to take pride in the fact that his life was in danger. "But this slow death is not good." Spotted Calf's fingers curled around the iron bars in the window. There was desperation in his voice. He was no longer impassive. "I am Quahadi, not an animal to be caged. I have killed this many men"—he held up the fingers of both hands—"all of them in battle." His breath smelled of chili and beans as it fanned Ben's face. The warrior's eyes were like two dull coins. The life in him was being throttled as surely as if the hangman's noose still circled his throat. He shook the bolted door. "What kind of men are these?"

"Civilized," Ben said.

"Then it is a bad thing," Spotted Calf said. The brave studied the soldier a moment. "Why do you come here?"

"I heard your death song."

Spotted Calf appeared surprised. He also had assumed Ben McQueen was a mere tenderfoot and nothing more.

"You speak the language of my people?"

"No," Ben replied, his voice low. "But my mother is a medicine woman. And she has taught me the ways. Among her people I am called Bitter Creek. As for the chant, the songs for dying are always the same."

Spotted Calf nodded. "You have spoken truth. Your uniform is blue, but you have a red heart."

"Maybe a divided heart," Ben corrected. Fireflies illuminated the patches of shadows, burning for brief seconds, self-extinguishing, flaring again elsewhere in the darkness. "Who are the Warriors of the Night?"

Spotted Calf's expression changed. He retreated from the door and vanished into the confines of the jail. "Children of the blood-eating god. Some say they are dead. Some say they never will be."

The hairs rose on the back of Ben's neck at Spotted Calf's explanation. With perfect timing, beyond the cottonwoods in the Arroyo de San Pedro, a great horned owl made its kill and rose into the air carrying its struggling prey in ironlike talons. A prairie dog had been caught outside its burrow. The hapless creature loosed a high-pitched shriek as the horned owl crushed its spine and bore the animal away on wings of darkness.

Ben nearly leaped out of his boots at the sudden noise. He retreated a step and turned toward the arroyo, his hand reaching to his side. Then he remembered he had left his pistols in his room rather than carry them to Father Esteban's dinner table. He proceeded along the path until he reached the barn. He eased the door open and stepped inside. A lantern glowed where it hung from a wooden peg in one of the support beams. Virge

Washburn reclined in a mound of hay piled between two stalls. The Texas Ranger was studiously whittling a chunk of oak into the bust of a Comanche chief, war bonnet and all. Slowly, features were taking shape. Virge's outstretched legs and the front of his serape were sprinkled with curled wood chips. He squinted through the slatted sides of the stall as Ben made his way down the center aisle toward the circle of light.

"Evening, Lieutenant. Ya'll finished over at the padre's?"

"Yes. His sister sets a fine table."

"I'll just bet she does, though with a looker like Señorita Obregon, I wouldn't care if she couldn't carry a plate." The Ranger grinned.

"My sentiments exactly," Ben conceded. He glanced around the barn and spied half a dozen saddles draped across the gates of various stalls. One of the saddles was his. It looked out of place among the high-pommeled Mexican saddles favored by the Rangers.

"Mind if I borrow a horse?"

Virge interrupted his whittling. He gestured toward the bridle and Mexican saddle closest to him, his short-bladed knife gleaming in the firelight.

"Better take Poole's gear. Our horses are kinda particular. I'll drop a rope over the roan; she'll carry your weight." He set the carving aside, scrambled to his feet, and dusted off his faded serape, front and back. Ben noticed carvings of a horse and a mountain lion among Washburn's gear. The Texan could work miracles with a pocketknife.

"Mister Poole won't mind?" Ben asked, remembering yesterday's encounter with the burly, tomahawk-wielding Texas Ranger. The man was obviously

not one to trifle with. Gandy was trouble enough—
Ben McQueen didn't need a run-in with Clay Poole.

"Hell, Clay's got another rig. This here's just
collecting dust. Either way, he won't be missing it."
Virge chuckled softly. "Cap'n Pepper's got him playing
nursemaid to General Abbot's son over in Main
Plaza." Virge fished a *cigarillo* from his belt pouch,
lifted the glass chimney on the lantern, and lit the
tobacco from the dancing yellow flame. Gray smoke
curled around him like a shroud that unwound as
he led the way out of the barn and to the corral.

The horses reacted to the approaching visitors
by trotting to the far side of the corral. A brown
stallion pawed the earth, shook his mane, and neighed
a challenge. Most of the mares bunched together,
made skittish by the strangers in the moonlight.
Virge set his *cigarillo* on top of a fence post and
reached for the lariat that was hung over the gate.

"See the roan mare yonder. She's a head taller
than most and built strong in the chest. Anxious as
a widow at a hoedown. Maybe you better wait till
sunup. Night ain't no time...hey." Virge stepped
back as Ben tossed his rig onto the top rail and
climbed over the gate. He took the hemp rope out of
the Ranger's hands and stalked off across the packed
earth. Virge watched, thumbs hooked in his gun
belt, legs bowed, his hat tilted back, and a look of
curiosity on his face. He was convinced the soldier
in blue was fixing to get himself trampled.

Ben McQueen swung the lasso over his head.
When he reached the center of the corral, the rope
snaked out and the loop settled over the mare.
Then, with a firm hand Ben guided the roan away
from the other horses and brought the nervous animal to the gate. Virge heard a soft, sibilant chanting

as Ben approached, and for a brief second the Ranger glanced around to see if there was an Indian close by. Then he realized the chanting was coming from Ben. The Ranger had seen Comanches calm their mounts in the same manner, singing softly to them, using their red magic to calm even the wildest stallion.

"Well, I declare," Virge said while Ben saddled the mare and slipped the bridle into place. "You're about as much a Yankee blueblood as I'm the King of England." Virge blew a cloud of tobacco smoke. The burning tip of the *cigarillo* glowed like a miniature caldron each time the Ranger inhaled. "Never seen the roan handled so easy. What did you say to her?"

Ben shrugged, unlatched the gate, and led the animal out of the corral. "I gave her a choice—she could come with me or I'd leave her for Snake Eye." Ben stroked the roan's neck and rubbed her behind the ears.

Virge chuckled and didn't press this newcomer for any further information about himself. Virge might be curious, but it wasn't his way to pry. However, what he had seen served notice that Gandy had yet to take the measure of the man he called "Brass Buttons."

"Lightning off to the west," Virge mentioned. "There's an abandoned mission just off the south road. Be a place to hole up and wait out a storm. Nothin' but open country and mesquite everywhere else." The Ranger stroked his jaw in thought. Then he pulled off the serape, taking care not to ignite the fabric with the glowing end of the *cigarillo*. He draped the serape behind Ben's saddle.

"You might need this," Virge muttered as Ben swung up astride the horse. The Ranger looked out at the night. From afar came the rumble of thunder. It reminded Virge Washburn of the buffalo he had seen up in the panhandle. Herds from sunup to sundown, the sound of their hooves a thunder on the land. He had hunted hides upon the staked plains and battled his share of Comanches and Kiowa before joining up with Amadeus T. Pepper's command. A crack shot with a Hawken rifle and dangerous in a scrape, Virge possessed all the necessary qualities Captain Pepper expected in the men of his command: honesty, skill, and not an ounce of "quit." The Ranger reached out and caught the bit before Ben could turn the mare aside.

The lieutenant looked down as Virge offered one thing more, his Patterson Colt revolver. "Might need this too."

"I can't take your gun," Ben protested.

Virge reached behind the small of his back and produced a second revolver identical to the first, which he promptly dropped into his holster. "You can return the other with the horse. And ride clear of La Villita. It ain't a place for an Anglo soldier boy to venture in come nightfall. Them narrow alleys is best seen at noon, not midnight."

"Thanks," Ben replied, and tucked the long-barreled weapon through his belt, butt forward and within easy reach of his right hand. Then the lieutenant pointed the mare east toward the Calle Dolorosa, the Street of Sorrow. Ben didn't intend to ride it for very long.

He kept to an easy pace and took his time leaving the city. He skirted the Main Plaza, with its noisy crowd. The din of voices, strumming guitars, and occasional gunshots carried to him from a couple of blocks away. He turned south on the Calle del

Paso and crossed a wooden bridge over the San Antonio River. To his left, the adobe buildings of La Villita, the Old Town, huddled cheek to jowl with thatched-roof *jacales*. He considered ignoring Virge Washburn's warning concerning the settlement, then decided to press on. He was looking for solitude, not confrontation. and what he intended to do required privacy. He rode south, leaving the town in his dust and heading into the rolling countryside. The western sky shimmered with sheet lightning and Ben hoped he'd find shelter from the storm before it hit. A breeze kicked up and the wind bore the scene of rain. Ben McQueen rode on. The mare had an easy canter, a distance-eating pace, easy on man and beast. The moon ducked behind the clouds. The darkness prevented Ben from leaving the wheel-rutted road. He would not chance crippling his horse by stumbling blindly into a prairie dog mound or cluster of spiny cactus. He kept the river to his right and a wary eye on the approaching storm. Lightning draped the clouds with its bone-white glare and outlined the twin limestone towers of a mission in the distance.

Ben quickened the mare's pace to a gallop, and twenty minutes later, by the time the first drops began to spatter the thirsty earth, he had reached the mission's outer buildings and the crumbling ruins of what had once been a defensive wall. Ben rode beneath a limestone arch and guided his horse into the nearest ruins, a granary consisting of three walls and half a roof. At least it afforded shelter. Ben dismounted and tethered his horse to the remains of a broken beam. Fortunately there was enough debris to start a fire. Soon the mission's solitary visitor was drying himself by the flames while rain dripped from the ragged edges of the roof.

Lightning flashed and outlined the lieutenant's deserted surroundings. He found no threat in the empty facade of the abandoned church. And if there were ghosts of those the mission had served, well, they were welcome at his fire. Alone now and free from the threat of discovery, Ben removed a buckskin bag he had tucked inside his coat, then the carved stem and bowl of a sacred pipe given to him by his mother, Raven O'Keefe McQueen. He filled the Choctaw ceremonial pipe with a mixture of cherry bark, wild roots, and tobacco, tamped it into the bowl, and lit it with a shard of burning timber.

It made an incongruous sight, an officer wearing the dark blue uniform of the United States Army, seated on his haunches in the glare of a campfire, enacting a ritual taught to him by his mother's people, the Choctaws. He raised the pipe to north, south, east, and west. A gust of wind fanned the embers in the bowl. His prayers rode the sacred smoke up beyond the edge of the roof to the black sky.

> "Grandfather
> I walk a path between
> Red Truth and White Truth.
> Guide my steps.
> Hear the words I speak,
> And those I do not know how to speak.
> Find them in my heart."

He paused in his chant and puffed on the pipe, blowing four clouds of smoke that swirled and trailed out into the storm. Ben thought of his sons and ached to see them, to hold them in his arms. Jesse and Daniel. They, too, would one day walk the path of their father, between two truths. Like Ben, the boys would have to decide for themselves and cut their own trail.

Ben set the pipe on the ground and, reaching beneath his shirt, palmed the medal. Duty...honor ...the legacy of the McQueens had cost him dearly. It had been a storm worse than this one, a driving downpour that lashed the roof and shutters of the Hound and Hare Tavern and pounded the hard-packed clay surface of the Trenton Pike.

Eleanor McQueen was used to having her own way. Young and prideful, with porcelain-white skin and hair fine as corn silk, her pretty face was a mask of suppressed anger as Ben revealed his decision to accept a position in the army with the rank of first lieutenant. As far as Eleanor was concerned, her husband had betrayed her. She had never planned to be a soldier's wife, not when he could have found a place managing her father's iron mines north of Philadelphia. But Ben had a different calling. The same voice that had whispered in the ears of his Highland forebears, warriors all, had called him by name.

An ember crackled in the campfire, and Ben added fuel to the fire. The memories came, one upon the other, like misfortunes, unbidden. He did not try to avoid them. The past had to be faced.

In her fury, Eleanor had abandoned the children—unannounced to Ben or his Aunt Esther—and fled into the night, returning to Philadelphia.

Ben followed Eleanor to her father's estate but the gates remained closed to him. Wealth and prestige and power were insurmountable adversaries.

*Within the month, the marriage was dissolved and
Eleanor was spirited away to stay with a relative in
the south of France, well beyond the reach of the likes
of Benjamin Bitter Creek McQueen.*

Movement in the weathered rafters overhead
distracted him and the memories of his wife's death
drifted away with the smoke from the Choctaw pipe.
He wasn't sorry to see them go. He looked up and
saw a patch of blackness like a dark angel move
along the length of a darkened beam.

Ben lifted a burning brand from the flames and
held it aloft. In the dancing light a raven preened its
glossy black wings and eyed the man with unsettling
familiarity. Tendrils of smoke wreathed its talons
and feathers. The bird seemed wholly unafraid of
Ben or the storm. It belonged here. Man was the
intruder. Nature was in the process of reclaiming
the mission. The raven was the harbinger of that
change.

Memories again, behind veils of medicine smoke.
*He was a child of ten and seated by his mother,
watching her as she scraped a deerskin pelt, making it smooth and pliable. Soon she would make
him a shirt to wear when he joined the other boys
as they ranged the rolling hills, eager to prove their
hunting prowess.*

*"I will have the finest shirt," Ben proudly
proclaimed.*

*"It will do for now," Raven said. She was lithe
and strong and the dark cascade of her unbraided
hair spilled forward across her shoulders as she
worked. Raven paused and adjusted the hide upon
the tanning rack, then looked aside at her only
child. "But the day will come when you shall walk
among your father's people and need more than a*

shirt of buckskin, my darlin' boy," she added, her speech touched with the brogue of her Irish father.

"I don't understand."

"The world of your father is like a great forest. The true paths are harder to find." The ten-year-old started to interrupt, but Raven waved his unspoken question aside. The words she spoke had to remain with him all his life.

"You have been given two names. You are Ben McQueen and you are Bitter Creek. When one is lost, the other will know the way."

Chapter Ten

Snake Eye Gandy knew better, but he couldn't bring himself to ride away from a fight. It was a weakness of character he hoped to correct one day. But not this day, with Cal Ashworth sitting astride a horse before the ruins of the powder house on the Camino Viejo. Gandy recognized trouble and altered his course to ride toward it.

"Hello, Ashworth. Ain't seen you since Austin," Gandy said. The information he'd gathered on the Comanches had him worried. He'd circled the town and twice cut sign indicating whole villages were on the move. Whatever or whoever had chased them out of the mountains, he figured, must be bad medicine indeed.

"I'm honored you remember me," Ashworth said. His flat-brimmed beaver hat shaded his pinched features. "I, too, have found your unwarranted attack on me impossible to forget." He patted a wrinkle from his frock coat.

"You got all the airs of a gentleman right enough,"

Gandy said. "But with a belly full of rum, you've all the sweet disposition of a rattler."

Ashworth's gaze darkened. He remembered only too well how this disreputable Ranger had interfered when Ashworth had attempted to discipline a lady friend. Gandy had wrested Ashworth's cane from the gun merchant's grasp, soundly thrashed him, and left him lying senseless in the middle of an Austin Street.

"There is unfinished business between us," Ashworth said. Tracking Gandy to San Antonio had been part luck, part educated guess. "This time I'm stone-cold sober."

Snake Eye grinned. His glass eye gleamed in the morning light. He considered Cal Ashworth a pompous, arrogant fortune hunter without scruples. He had a mean vicious streak and could be cruel simply for the sake of cruelty. These were qualities Snake Eye Gandy had no tolerance for.

"Lead on."

Ashworth jabbed a thumb in the direction of the Alamo's shattered, broken walls. "I've camped by the old church. We won't be disturbed there."

The gun merchant turned and walked his mount across the mud-soaked street. Gandy bristled at the man's choice of campsites. The likes of Cal Ashworth had no business being within those hallowed walls.

It was mid-morning on the fourth of May. After waiting out another cloudburst that struck at sun-up, Ben had left the abandoned granary to its ghosts and the spectral raven who had kept him company through the night. Cutting across country to intersect the mission road, Ben skirted the bend of the San Antonio River east of town. The clouds covered the sky like a quilt, a patchwork of light and dark gray textured by the wind at the upper levels of the atmosphere. The temperature wouldn't climb much past sixty today, a cool day for late May, but then Texas weather was as fickle as a spring bride, so no one was particularly surprised. Coats weren't usually stored away until well into June.

Ben reached the Calle de La Mission and followed it north, keeping a greenbelt of cottonwoods and elms on his left, cactus and open ground on his right. The Calle de La Mission, despite its hard-packed appearance, was wheel-rutted and dotted with brown, silty puddles, and the roan's shod hooves became caked with the yellow-brown clay as the mare carried Ben up to the ruined battlements and broken walls of the Alamo. Ten years ago, this same ramshackle mission fortress had been the scene of vicious fighting. Ben knew the story: After thirteen days of glory, a hundred and eighty valiant defenders gave their lives for Texas liberty, maiming Santa Anna's army and leaving a legacy of courage for an entire nation to remember.

Ben McQueen headed for a breach in the south wall as voices carried to him across the rain-heavy air. There came a crash of pots and pans and the muffled curses of struggling men. Curiosity got the better of him, and Ben urged his horse to a brisk trot that covered the remaining few yards in a matter of seconds. He entered the breach, and the entire court-yard before the pocked facade of the church opened up to him. A hundred feet away, in the muddy environs of a peddler's makeshift camp, four men were locked in mortal combat.

It was an uneven contest, waged in a campsite consisting of several loosely tethered horses, a cook fire and coffeepot, and a heavy freight wagon. Ben groaned as even from across the yard it was impossible to mistake Snake Eye Gandy. Fierce as a bantam fighting cock, the Texas Ranger struggled against overwhelming odds. He hit and gouged and twisted. His long reach landed blow after blow in a losing effort against two serape-clad Mexicans and a wiry, hook-nosed gentleman brandishing a stout hickory cane. The two Mexicans had finally succeeded in pinning Gandy's shoulders to the side of the canvas-covered wagon.

Ben recognized the hook-nosed man with the cane from Peter Abbot's sketches. It was Ashworth, the gun merchant. Ben hadn't liked Ashworth on paper, and he didn't much care for him in real life.

As Ben looked on, the gun merchant prepared to administer a vicious caning to Snake Eye Gandy. Not even the Ranger deserved such treatment. Against his own better judgment, Ben knew he was going to interfere. The lieutenant drove his boot heels into the roan's flanks. The mare leaped forward, crossed one puddle, and splashed through another, dousing Ben with a fine spray of muddy water. Ben never slowed, but gave the animal plenty of rein and charged the wagon. Ashworth paused, cane in hand, arm raised. He struck Gandy a nasty blow to the collarbone. The Ranger sagged.

Before Ashworth could strike again, a squat, muscular hide hunter came lumbering through the arched doorway of the abandoned church. He was

hitching up his pants when he noticed Ben Mc-
Queen. The hide hunter called out to Ashworth.
Too late, the men by the wagon turned to face this
threat. The mare leaped the campfire and crashed
into one of Ashworth's cohorts, pinning him to the
side of the wagon. The Mexican dropped, the wind
knocked out of him. The other released his hold
on Gandy.

The Ranger seized the opportunity to free himself. He grabbed Ashworth and wrestled him to the
ground. Ben kicked out and the toe of his boot
caught the other hireling in the forehead and put
him momentarily out of action. But Ben's elation
was short-lived, as the man from the church leaped
up and caught him in a powerful bear hug and
dragged him out of the saddle.

"Watch your backside, Brass Buttons," Gandy
shouted, clambering to his feet. He sounded jubi-
lant, as if he was enjoying himself. The bear hug
tightened around Ben's midsection, driving the air
from his lungs. Ben's opponent, though smaller, had
immense upper body strength; his arms felt as if
they were made of iron, and the pressure he exerted
was nigh unbearable.

The roan bolted out into the courtyard, away
from the combatants. Ben decided his horse had
showed remarkable good sense; if only he had done
the same. Yet despite his own desperate circum-
stances, Ben found something to cheer about. Through
pain-glazed eyes, he watched as Ashworth rose up
behind Gandy. The Ranger was absorbed in Ben's
predicament. Gandy might have offered to help, but
he was curious to see if the lieutenant could handle
himself in a tight situation.

"You've got him now," Gandy chuckled. He

assumed Ashworth was unconscious. But the merchant in the mud-spattered frock coat knotted his fist and struck Gandy in the back. He'd been aiming for the base of Gandy's neck, but mud in his eyes caused him to misjudge the angle of the blow. Nevertheless, Snake Eye howled in pain and stumbled forward.

"Watch your backside, you ugly son of a bitch," Ben gasped through clenched teeth. If his ribs weren't about to be crushed, he'd have enjoyed the last laugh even more.

Gandy stumbled forward, spun on his heels, and dove forward, burying his head in the pit of Cal Ashworth's stomach. Both men lost their footing and tumbled into a shallow puddle of muddy water. Locked in a violent embrace, the two men disappeared beneath the wagon.

"I don't know who you be, soldier blue, but I'll learn you to mind your own business from now on," the hide hunter growled in Ben's ear. "Ain't nobody ever broke loose of Lester Harlan."

Ben McQueen could believe it. He grabbed at Harlan's wrists and tried to break his hold, but the hide hunter's ironlike hands were clasped together as if they'd been forged that way. Without oxygen, Ben's strength was fading. He was losing consciousness, but he had one last chance. He doubled over and lifted Harlan onto his back. The hide hunter refused to break his bear hug even when his feet left the ground. With no way for Harlan to gain leverage, Ben turned and worked his way over to the campfire, then fell forward while rolling onto his right shoulder. Ben landed on his back, smack-dab in the middle of the campfire, with Lester Harlan between him and the flames. Ben spread his legs to help pin Harlan to the flames. He wrinkled his nose at the stench of burning buckskin. Harlan began to struggle and curse, while Ben resisted losing consciousness. Suddenly, Harlan had had enough. As the flames reached his backside, he released his rib-crushing embrace and shoved Ben aside.

Harlan bellowed. Streaming smoke from his blackened buckskin shirt and breeches and singed hair, he scrambled toward the nearest mud puddle and plopped down into it. He groaned, then sighed in relief.

Ben rolled to his knees and sensed movement behind him. The three years he'd spent back East had dulled those rough-and-tumble fighting skills developed during a childhood spent among Choctaw, Cherokee, and Creek playmates. But it was coming back to him. One of the Mexican hirelings had left the fight. The man staggered off across the courtyard, clutching his sides. The man Ben had kicked was still in the picture, though. Momentarily stunned, the Mexican gathered his strength and slid a knife from a boot sheath. Ben reached for his revolver. It was no longer tucked in his belt. He must have lost it when Harlan dragged him from horseback.

The Mexican grinned and darted forward. He was a dark-skinned, boyish-faced rogue with the haughty air of youth about him. The knife gleamed wickedly as he feinted, then attacked. Ben scooped up a handful of horse droppings and threw it in the young man's face, catching him wide-eyed and openmouthed.

The Mexican halted in his tracks, dropped his knife, and clawed at his features. He spat excrement, doubled over, and retched. He had to cling to the side of the wagon for support, and when his spasms subsided, Ben grabbed him by the scruff of his coarsely woven shirt and cocked a right fist, ready to flatten his attacker's nose.

"No, señor. Por favor..." the young man weakly pleaded. "Not in the face. Think of the señoritas. Have pity on the señoritas who love me."

Ben paused, his fist ready. Then he muttered, "Oh hell," and, with his left hand, slammed the hireling's head against a wheel rim. The Mexican slid down the spokes and came to rest, senseless, his head pillowed on the iron hub, legs doubled beneath him.

"You're a real hellion when you get riled, Brass Buttons," Snake Eye said. He rose up at the end of the wagon and stepped over a singletree, dragging Cal Ashworth in his wake. He draped the unconscious gun merchant over the singletree. "Story has it, Crockett died over yonder, fighting to the end. I wasn't about to leave this bastard lying there." Snake Eye was soaked head to foot. His glass eye and its coiled snake peered ominously through a mask of mud. "You're a pitiful sight, Lieutenant."

Ben stared down at his uniform. One sleeve was torn. His coat and trousers were matted with mud. He shrugged. "You aren't exactly the belle of the ball."

"No. Reckon I ain't," Snake Eye admitted. He shifted his gaze. "Lester Harlan, is that you?"

The hide hunter struggled to stand in the puddle. The seat of his pants had been burned away and his coat was black, and patches of skin showed through the holes in his clothing. Harlan wiped the silt from his eyes. Recognition came instantly. "Gandy," he muttered.

"What the hell are you doing with the likes of Cal Ashworth?" Gandy asked.

"Ashworth never told me it was you we was after," Harlan replied, eyes lowered.

"You're a lying dog, Lester Harlan," Gandy retorted.

The crestfallen rogue seemed to sag, as if gravity itself were pulling him into the earth. "I got robbed by Mescans over in Taos. Took my packhorses and half a year's worth of pelts and buffalo hides." He stared glumly at his benefactor, belly-down across the singletree. "Reckon it was a bad call," he muttered. He glanced at Ben. "You'd've never broke free if you hadn't tripped me in the fire."

Ben shrugged. He felt no need to trade brags with the man. The hide hunter looked the worse for wear, and that was enough for McQueen.

"What now?" asked Harlan.

"If the lieutenant here ain't got any druthers, you can skedaddle." Gandy cocked an eye toward Ben, who had to admit that Texans were a peculiar lot. Ben had the feeling he was being tested one more time. He couldn't shake the sensation. He walked over to the hide hunter and looked him straight in the eyes. Ben's ribs ached from the bear hug, but knowing he had bested the man left him elated. The altercation had served a useful purpose after all. It had given him a glimpse of his true self. Beneath the air of civility he had acquired back East lurked the mixed-blood Choctaw whose ferocity no formal education would ever tame. Part of him would forever heed the call of a raven.

Ben leaned toward Harlan and spoke in a quiet, ominous tone of voice.

"I don't ever want to see you again."

Anger flared in the hide hunter's eyes, but he held himself in check. There was something unsettling about the lieutenant. Ben's breath fanned Harlan's cheek like the kiss of death. Menace seemed to crackle from McQueen like lightning. Harlan, once struck, wasn't about to chance trouble a second time. He gulped and nodded in agreement and lumbered over to the tethered horses. He saddled the first nag he came to and rode off toward Old Town.

Ben and Snake Eye retrieved their mounts. The lieutenant recovered Virge Washburn's Patterson Colt and wiped the mud from the cylinder as best he could. The gun needed to be broken down and given a good cleaning. He tucked it in his belt and swung up astride the roan.

The man draped over the singletree moaned and rolled into the dirt. Gandy rode up alongside the lieutenant.

"Leave him lie. I reckon he's been paid for damn near busting my shoulder with that cane," the Ranger said. Gandy brushed back his topknot and settled his sombrero on his head.

"He'll probably try again sometime," Ben remarked.

"Yeah." Gandy rubbed his knuckles, winced, and then chuckled. "I can hardly wait." He studied the old and crumbling walls surrounding them. Gandy took on an almost wistful expression and grew silent. Perhaps he was hearing the bugles of yesteryear. Then Gandy returned to the present and studied the lieutenant, who patiently waited at his side. "How come you dove into this fracas? There ain't been love lost betwixt us. I'd have been tempted to ride on and let a proud, troublesome son of a bitch like myself get what's coming to me.''

"Maybe I was tempted," Ben grinned. "Then again, maybe you aren't the only man who listens to ghosts.''

Chapter Eleven

It was a quarter till noon when Ben McQueen came tramping up through the cottonwoods after bathing in San Pedro Creek in the arroyo behind the governor's palace. He stopped in his tracks. What the devil? he thought. His uniform was missing. Despite its ragged, mud-stained appearance, Ben had hoped that Toby's mother might be prevailed upon to make his coat presentable again. He'd left his shirt, trousers, and long johns to dry on a mesquite bush. Now all that remained were his long johns, which he quickly donned. He searched beneath the bush and found his socks and boots, much to his relief. But the rest of his clothes were nowhere to be seen. He began to suspect the hand of Snake Eye Gandy in this and decided the hell with diplomacy, he was going to shoot the bastard and be done with it.

A twig cracked behind him and shattered a pleasant reverie in which Ben rehearsed dispatching Snake Eye Gandy straight to perdition. No doubt the devil had a berth marked for the Ranger. Ben suspected that Snake Eye could probably teach Ol' Scratch a trick or two in the process.

Ben glanced behind him and spied Toby on the path leading down to the creek. The boy's arms were filled with clothing: a fringed buckskin shirt, faded nankeen breeches, a worn leather gun belt and holster, a bear-claw shot pouch, a couple of broad-brimmed hats, and a Patterson Colt revolver.

"Got you some clothes, Lieutenant. Yessir, Mr. Gandy told me to take your coat and all to my ma to fix up. Told me to see you was dressed proper."

"Proper for what? A war dance?" Ben eyed the garments with skepticism. They were hardly regulation attire, but then this was hardly a regular situation. It was Texas. "Thanks," he said, and lifted the load out of Toby's embrace.

"Mister—General Abbot said for you to hurry. He got someone for you to meet," Toby added.

The shirt and trousers were a little loose on Ben but would shrink some when wet. One of the hats was too small, but the other settled properly on his head. Ben buckled the gun belt so that the holster rode high on his left thigh, the Patterson Colt butt forward and in easy reach of his right hand. The bear-claw pouch held a spare cylinder already loaded with powder and shot, the chambers dabbed over with bear grease to prevent sparks from igniting the other loads when one was fired. The pouch also contained a small canister of black powder and a couple of dozen lead balls wrapped in oilskin. Ben handled the Patterson Colt. It was identical to the weapon Virge Washburn had loaned him. The walnut grip rested easy in the palm of his hand. The gunmetal was cool to the touch. He slid the eight-inch barrel into the holster. Gandy was a difficult man to figure.

Maybe this was Snake Eye's way of making peace.

Toby whistled softly through his teeth. He was impressed by the transformation. This towering, red-haired hulk of a man seemed even more imposing than before. He looked as leather-tough as any Ranger Captain A. T. Pepper could put in the field.

"Well, I guess I'm ready," Ben said. "Now who am I supposed to meet?"

Sam Houston stood and looked Ben square in the eyes. The former president of the Texas Republic was accustomed to towering over most men, so the experience was a novelty. Ben noted that Houston immediately invited the lieutenant to take a seat while the hero of San Jacinto remained standing.

"So you're the young man Matt here speaks so highly of. McQueen, eh? I've heard that name." Houston wore a black frock coat, a frilly French shirt and brocaded vest, and tight gray woolen breeches tucked into knee-high black boots. In his early fifties, his silvery hair was the only part of his appearance showing age. His complexion was ruddy, his strong hands steady, his back straight as an arrow. Ben sensed that here was a man convinced of his own importance. But it was hard to fault one whose exploits and leadership had played such a major role in the birth of the Republic.

"I met your father. We fought together at Horse Shoe Bend. He didn't know me. We barely had time to make much of an acquaintance, as fast as Old Hickory was hounding the Creeks. But I heard the stories, how Kit McQueen single-handedly killed him a Red Stick chief. I, too, made something of a name for myself during that campaign." Houston grinned and glanced around the dining room. Seated at the table were Captain Pepper, Matt Abbot, and Ben McQueen. Another place had been set. Ben guessed it might be for Peter. He wondered if the general's son had managed to keep out of trouble. Surely with Clay Poole patrolling Main Plaza, Peter had weathered the evening.

Matt Abbot frowned with displeasure at Ben's choice of uniform. He leaned over and admonished the lieutenant.

"I daresay, Ben. The arrival of the former president calls for something a little more formal."

"Come, come, Matthew," Houston said, intervening on Ben's behalf. "From what Snake Eye told us of their earlier altercation, we're lucky the lieutenant has any clothes on at all." Houston chuckled. "Hell, Ben McQueen here looks to be in dress uniform, compared with my adjutants at San Jacinto."

Abbot shrugged and relinquished his point. The former general was in his own way as proud a man as Houston, but he was willing to humor the saviour of the Texas Republic. Houston could sway much of the public's sentiment and turn the populace in favor of annexation. Abbot knew that men with such high regard for themselves were often susceptible to flattery. "As you say."

"It's an honor to meet you, sir," Ben said. "Your victory at San Jacinto is legendary."

"And damn near accidental," Houston added. "My men didn't give me much choice. I simply held them back until Pepper here and Gandy and the others were mad enough to whip the devil himself once they cut loose." Houston emptied his glass of wine and helped himself to another.

"I believe you are too modest, Mister President," Ben said. Houston's exploits in the field of war, his Indian battles, the women he'd courted and duels he'd fought had become a part of folklore.

"Anson Jones is president now," Houston corrected. "I'm just an ordinary Texican."

"Begging your pardon, Sam," Captain Pepper spoke up, amused by the man's false humility. He wiped the back of his hand across his bushy mustache. "But I don't think you got an ordinary bone in your body."

"My sentiments exactly," Abbot said. "I daresay, if the presidency of the Texas Republic is behind you, perhaps first senator from the sovereign state of Texas lies ahead." Abbot waited, holding his breath. Sam Houston was uncharacteristically silent.

"I suppose we'll have to wait and see," he finally replied. Then he raised a glass of wine in salute. Ben, Matt, and Captain Pepper stood and raised their own glasses.

"Gentlemen. I give you the Republic of Texas, today. As for tomorrow . . ." Houston paused, enjoying the drama of the moment. "Tomorrow shall creep in its petty pace. And I shall give a speech at the fiesta. Perhaps all things will become clear." He gulped the contents of his glass. Stacia appeared in the doorway, an empty kettle in her hands. Steam curled from the pour spout. "I have had a long and tedious ride over from Austin. So if you'll excuse me, my good friends, the spirit is strong but my ass is tender, and I'd like to soak it in a hot bath." Houston bowed to the men at the table. Then he followed the woman out of the dining room and down the hall to his bedchamber and the copper tub she had filled with steaming water.

After he had left, Matt Abbot turned to Captain Pepper and sighed. "A most remarkable individual,"

Abbot said. "If he refuses a career in Congress, there's always the theatre."

"Looks like Captain Pepper's gone and signed us up another Ranger," Virge Washburn called out as Ben emerged from the governor's palace and stood in the shade of the long, wide thatch roof that ran the length of the building. Virge Washburn was leaning against a support post, whittling. Clay Poole sat in a straight-backed chair tilted back against the palace wall near an unshuttered window that looked in on the captain's office. He was sipping at a tin cup of coffee. Some of the brown droplets had collected in his beard. He held a flour tortilla he'd folded around strips of *cabrito*. The goat meat was lightly seasoned, not too spicy, for Poole had a tender stomach.

Snake Eye Gandy was perched on top of a pork barrel, cleaning the mud from his Patterson Colts. He had turned a wooden crate on end and was using the flat side for a table, on which were arranged the pieces of disassembled guns. He looked up, good-natured devilment gleaming in his eye.

"By heaven, he's fresh as bluebonnets in the spring," Gandy said.

"I hope he can sit a horse," Poole added, and took a bite out of his afternoon meal.

"He gentled Red Lady. She came over to him sure as if that roan had fed at his hand since birth," Virge said. "While she's give you nothin' but sore ribs and ·lumps on that hard head of yours."

Gandy and Virge both laughed at Poole's expense. The grizzled Ranger grumbled an unintelligible insult and concentrated on his meal. Meat juices dribbled onto the front of his buckskin shirt, but he seemed not to mind. A number of other stains had collected there over the past week. Once every month without fail, Clay Poole would amble over to the nearest creek, water hole, or spring-fed pond and submerge himself, clothes and all.

From the smell of him, it was plain to his associates that Clay Poole was about due for a dunking.

"You meet General Sam?" Gandy asked. "He's the best there is."

"How come you didn't join us?" Ben asked.

"Too damn many officers and the like," Gandy said. "And my guns needed cleaning after the fracas this morning. After the Comanche sign I seen, we'd do well to keep our guns loaded and primed."

"War parties?" Ben asked.

"Whole villages. On the move, but coming too far east. They ought to be following the mountains in from the Big Bend. I can't figure but it's like they were scared out."

"The warriors of the night," Ben softly intoned. "The blood-eating god." He glanced up. The Rangers were staring at him. Clay Poole was slack-jawed, his coffee cup clutched in his powerful grasp. A bulge in his cheek showed he had forgotten to chew. Virge audibly gulped.

"Damn," he muttered.

"You been jawing with that damn Comanche again," Gandy scoffed. "Brass Buttons, you been loading your pipe with loco weed."

Ben look sharply at the Ranger. Had the man been spying on him the other night at the ruins? Then he blushed, realizing Gandy had merely used an expression. His reaction intrigued Gandy, whose one good eye rarely missed a suspicious action.

"I've talked to him. And what he speaks is the truth," Ben said.

"Brass Buttons, you're a good man in a fight, but you've a lot to learn. Comanches ain't got no use for the truth. The only bucks you can turn your back on is dead ones. It's that way with most Injuns."

Ben glanced at Virge. Evidently Snake Eye knew nothing of McQueen's Choctaw heritage.

"Then it would seem, Mr. Gandy, we both have a lot to learn." Now it was Gandy's turn to look perplexed, which suited Ben just fine. Clay Poole finished the last of his lunch, licked his fingers, and studied his empty hand, regretting he hadn't brought more food.

"Fill your belly any more and you won't be able to sit a saddle," Virge said.

Poole looked wounded. He swallowed and belched. "Nursemaiding Peter Abbot is hungry work. I spent the whole night following him and that pretty little whore Cecilia around Main Plaza with nary a coin in my pocket to rustle me up some grub."

"Just as well. You might have wound up drunk in an alley instead of seeing Abbot safely to the German's hotel," Virge replied. He glanced at Snake Eye and winked. "I heard tell that Clay fluffed their pillows and tucked Abbot and his *puta* into bed."

"Liar. Black liar," Clay replied. His bushy brows furrowed and his eyes narrowed, crinkling his features. The meddlesome Virge knew how far he could push Poole without his grim-faced friend coming after him with a tomahawk.

"If you men will excuse me, I'll leave before the blood flows," Ben said.

"Ain't gonna be a fight," Poole said. "Virge, chicken-shit that he is, always runs off before I can lay a hand on him. But one of these days he's liable to trip. . . ." Clay Poole twisted his fists, one atop the other, as if wringing a chicken neck. He smiled in satisfaction and folded his hands across his belly.

Virge resumed whittling. The Comanche war chief was really taking shape in his hands. As for Poole's threat, he'd heard a hundred of them. Despite what an outsider might take for mutual animosity, the two men were *compadres*. They had saved each other's hide more than once. And would do so again without question.

Ben could sense this loyalty in every one of these rough-and-tumble soldiers of Texas. No wonder such men had prevailed during the revolution and driven the Mexican armies back across the Rio Grande. But the watchword of Texas liberty was vigilance and would remain so until the Republic agreed to annexation. With the armed might of the United States backing Texas, the threat of Mexican aggression might well be extinguished, leaving the state to develop and prosper. Ben could envision a rosy future for these Texicans. He wondered what the cost in lives would be to attain it.

"You look troubled, Brass Buttons," Snake Eye Gandy remarked, tapping the gun barrel into place on one of his Colts. He checked the action and the loads. "Things'll work out. They always do. Maybe you ought to pay a call on Señorita Obregon before I ask to escort her to the fiesta myself." He nudged Virge.

"I intend to," Ben said, refusing to be drawn into any further exchange. Gandy's humor was at best raw, and should Anabel become the object of an unflattering remark, he might have to take the Ranger to task, which would be an unpleasant and painful experience at best.

He left the porch and headed across Military Plaza, threading his way through stalls and vendors, makeshift stages, two-wheeled carts, and a colorful populace, young and old—men, women, and children who had come to barter and exchange gossip and to learn who had been born, died, or married in a dozen settlements north and south. For all intents and purposes, the fiesta had begun a day early.

Ben was midway across the plaza when the courtyard gate opened and three *campesinos* dressed in homespun, coarsely woven shirts, baggy trousers, and faded serapes stepped out into the plaza. The poor were always coming to visit Father Esteban, so none of the passersby paid the three men any mind.

However, yesterday's incident in the alley had left more of a mark on Ben than just the burn on the back of his neck from his assailant's quirt. His suspicions regarding Carmelita came flooding back. He tilted the brim of his hat to hide his features as the three peons hurried away from the priest's house, rounded the corner, and made their way down an alley between two imposing adobe houses whose inhabitants no doubt played an important role in San Antonio's social hierarchy.

For a moment, Ben hesitated and stood in the gray gloom of an overcast afternoon, undecided whether or not to follow the three men who had just left or to continue on to the padre's. The chance of seeing Anabel was the more appealing choice. But caution and curiosity got the better of him. He changed course and hurried to keep the *campesinos* in view as they made their way down the alley.

The lieutenant fought his way through the crowd,

past Germans and Mexicans, Anglos, mestizos, mixed breeds of all kinds. There were more merchants than customers, and more than once several towns-people with something to sell blocked Ben's path. He brushed aside a woman selling tortillas, an old man with a herd of milk goats, and a young woman who showed him some ankle and smiled provoca-tively as he sped past. Ben reached the mouth of the alley in time to see the three peons mount sleek, well cared for horses and walk their mounts over to the Calle Dolorosa.

Ben glanced about him and spied a brown geld-ing tethered behind a raised platform, from which, the lieutenant figured, Sam Houston no doubt in-tended to deliver his speech. The platform was still under construction. Workers hastily hammered away, nailing support beams and stringing the front of the platform with banners. The carpenters had tethered their mounts to a barber's pole in front of a shop near the alley. None of the workers paid the lieuten-ant any mind as he ambled over to the horses. Ben wasn't particular. He chose the first one he came to, a pecan-brown gelding with a black-freckled rump and white stockings. He untied the reins from the barber's pole and noticed a round-cheeked girl watching him. She had dark eyes, brown skin, and a smile that would one day break many a young man's heart. She wore a dusty yellow dress and mud-spattered, buckled slippers, and had skinned knees.

"My name is Emilia, what's yours?" she asked.

"Ben," the lieutenant replied, putting a finger to his lips.

"I'm ten years old," she said.

"You are a very pretty little girl," Ben said.

"I can be quiet as a mouse."

"Good."

"Or I can be very loud and tell those men you are stealing one of their horses," Emilia sweetly added.

"Why don't you be quiet as a mouse," Ben suggested.

"For a dollar I will," the girl replied.

Ben reached beneath his shirt and produced a small drawstring bag in which he kept a few coins that he saved for emergencies. He paid the girl, who seized the money in her stubby grip and scampered back down the wooden walk to a bench on which she had arranged her rag dolls. Ben suspected the diminutive, curly-topped blackmailer would own half of San Antonio one day. He untied the brown gelding and led the animal down the alley. Once out of sight of the plaza, he climbed into the saddle and, keeping his distance, began to shadow the three men he had seen leaving Father Esteban's. So far, curiosity had cost him a dollar. Ben didn't know it, but the price was about to skyrocket.

Chapter Twelve

The rain returned. It came in a slow, gray drizzle that made the very air heavy to breathe. The clouds themselves seemed to settle on the town, muting the voices of everyday life. The inhabitants of La Villita, the Old Town, retired to the humble adobe and thatched-roof homes that lined the narrow maze of alleys and muddy streets, some scarcely a block long.

Ben McQueen kept his hat lowered to conceal his features. He wrapped his upper torso in the threadbare serape he had found draped behind the saddle. He imagined faces behind the shuttered windows and the blank stare of open doorways. At any moment he'd be discovered and the denizens of these *jacales* would emerge to drive away the Anglo intruder. He dismounted by a one-room shack long abandoned to stray dogs, rodents, and wolf spiders. He tore a buckskin string from the fringes of his coat and hobbled the gelding to keep the horse from wandering off, then he entered the shack. The roof had been burned away and the window frames were charred black from a fire. The only articles of furniture in the forlorn dwelling were the blackened remains of a table, a bed frame, two stools, and, in one corner, the broken pieces of a cradle and a jagged shard of broken mirror.

Ben chose his steps with care. He was close enough to hear the voices of the three *compesinos* he had followed. A window at the rear of the shack looked out onto a makeshift corral whose fencing was a mixture of salvaged wood and thorny underbrush brought from the hillsides and piled up to form a natural barrier. He recognized the men in the corral and the wagon they guarded. Cal Ashworth had evidently abandoned his camp in the remains of the Alamo for a rather precarious place here in La Villita. He did not seem too intimidated by his surroundings, but then Ashworth had a Patterson Colt tucked in his belt and there was a telltale bulge beneath his frock coat. No doubt he wore a second gun on his right hip. Lester Harlan stood in the center of the wagon, whose canvas top had been rolled up on the side facing the entrance to the corral. Harlan cradled a double-barreled shotgun as if it were a newborn babe. It appeared he had reconsidered his association with Ashworth. The promise of easy money must have been a lure the hide hunter couldn't resist.

"I wish the others were here," Harlan called down to his employer.

The hook-nosed, bruised and battered Ashworth stiffly turned and faced his hireling.

"You'd be splitting your pay with them," he said.

"Then the hell with it," Harlan grinned. "I'll see things go nice and orderly-like." He patted the shotgun, then pointed to the gate. He didn't need to speak. Ashworth could see for himself. He had business to transact. And his customers were at hand.

The corral was an irregular circle about sixty feet in diameter. The two Anglos, their wagon, and their horses were the only occupants. The makeshift gate hung ajar.

Anabel Cordero, disguised as a young peon, glanced at her two companions. Miguel Ybarbo, his head bandaged, shifted nervously in the saddle, then dismounted. Hector, his older brother, caught Miguel as he stepped around his horse to assist the señorita.

"We are all strong young men. No need to help our friend here, eh?" Miguel nodded, deferring to his brother. There was wisdom in his words. Miguel's actions might reveal that their companion was a woman.

Hector maneuvered himself alongside the daughter of Don Luis Cordero. His loyalty to her was unremitting and steadfast, like that of Jorge Tenorio. Hector surveyed the motley collection of *jacales* surrounding the corral. They had entered Old Town unnoticed. But where was Jorge? The old throat-slitter had promised to keep watch as the three men approached the corral. But the damn *pulquerias* were enticing to a man with a thirst as great as Jorge Tenorio's.

"You should not have come with us, señorita," Hector muttered, unable to shake his gloomy thoughts.

"My place is here."

"But if there is trouble...?"

"My place is here," she firmly repeated. Hector was a good man, but he had to be silenced. This was no time to doubt herself.

Anabel led the way across the corral. Beads of rain rolled along the brim of her sombrero, only to be shaken loose with every step.

Cal Ashworth mistook Anabel for a young vaquero and discounted her at a glance. He turned to Hector, obviously the eldest of the three.

"El Tigre?" Cal Ashworth asked.

"I am El Tigre," Anabel said.

"I may have been born at night but it wasn't *last* night," Ashworth retorted. "I told the chili-eater with the gnawed ear I'd deal with El Tigre and no one else."

"We have brought the money you asked," Anabel said. She glanced around at Miguel, who reached beneath his serape. Cal Ashworth's hand snapped up, and he centered the business end of his Patterson Colt on Miguel's belly.

"We came unarmed," Hector said. "See, no guns." He lifted his serape to show he had no percussion pistols tucked away in his belt.

Miguel chuckled and untied a pouch of gold doubloons from his belt.

"Please, señor. Do not shoot us. *Por favor*," he taunted, and held out the pouch.

"Don't worry, Cal. I've got them covered," Lester Harlan said from the wagon. "First man so much as sneezes wrong, I'll cut him in half with a load of buckshot." Harlan scowled at the Mexican who mocked him.

Ashworth visibly relaxed at the absence of guns

among his customers. He grew more confident. Greed and pride were an integral part of his character. He sensed a chance to make a profit and jumped at it.

"We've brought the gold, two hundred and fifty dollars. Where are the revolvers?"

"Show them the case of Patterson Colts," Ashworth said.

"Right here under my left foot," Lester Harlan called out, tapping his boot against the case lid. "Twelve pretty revolvers. And tins of powder and shot."

"Then hand them over and we'll be off," Anabel said. The sooner this transaction ended the better. She nodded to Miguel, who stepped forward and dropped the bag of Spanish gold, the last of her father's plunder, in Ashworth's outstretched hand. The gun merchant hefted the bag. A slow frown crawled across his face, like fog creeping up from a riverbank, obscuring the true features of a landscape and placing the unwary traveler in danger.

"Funny thing about gold. Often when there's one bag, there's another."

Yes, danger.

Anabel tensed. She glanced aside at Hector and nodded. Then she returned her attention to Ashworth, who hadn't noticed the subtle signal that had passed from one "peon" to the other.

"We have brought the payment you asked. Now give us our guns," Anabel said.

"Well, young pup," Ashworth replied, stroking his two-day-old growth of chin whiskers. "Hard times breed hard bargains. Two hundred and fifty dollars was yesterday's price. The way I see it, my guns have doubled in value today. Bring me another two hundred and fifty in gold before sundown and we have a deal. Tomorrow it may just double again, so I wouldn't beat around the bush. Best you lads dig into your strongbox."

"We will pay the original price and not a coin more," Anabel stated flatly. She checked the wagon. Lester Harlan was still standing guard. But beneath the wagon she could make out two pairs of knee-high boots that belonged to Chico Raza and Tomas Zavala. They had entered the corral from the wagon's blind side. Harlan's attempt to stay dry in the drizzling rain would be his downfall.

"You'll pay my price," Ashworth replied. His lip curled as he spoke. "I imagine Captain Pepper over at the Ranger headquarters would be mighty interested to know some of El Tigre's bandits were hiding under his very nose."

"Then you leave us no choice," Anabel told him, a note of resignation in her voice. Ashworth sensed a threat and turned his gun on her. "Adios," Anabel said, and touched the brim of her sombrero. Suddenly she whipped it from her head and slapped the gun from Ashworth's hand, then slapped him across the face, momentarily blinding him. Ashworth staggered back and tried to ward off blow after stinging blow. Unable to see and caught completely off balance, he stumbled back against the wagon.

Harlan, shotgun in hand, hesitated only a second, shocked that one of the bandits was a pretty señorita. The delay cost him his life. Zavala slit the canvas siding and Chico Raza dove through the rent in the fabric and caught Harlan as he turned to face him. Raza's left arm encircled Harlan's throat while his right plunged a knife into the hide hunter's back. Harlan pitched backward as Raza manhandled him to the wagon bed. Zavala clambered into the wagon to help Raza subdue the dying man.

Miguel and Hector drew knives from their boot tops and rushed to the aid of Anabel Cordero as she continued to assail the gun merchant. Ashworth shouted for the hide hunter to help him and then, with one hand raised to protect his face from the woman's vigorous onslaught, fumbled for the gun tucked in his waistband. He freed the revolver, but too late. Miguel Ybarbo rushed past his older brother, dove beneath Anabel's attack, and plunged his dagger into Ashworth's heart.

The entire action lasted less than a minute. Anabel retreated a few paces, her breathing rapid as the adrenaline coursed through her veins. Miguel stepped aside and stole the revolver from his victim's dying grasp. Ashworth sagged against the side of the wagon; a stain darkened the front of his frock coat and spread out from the knife hilt which protruded like some grisly badge upon his chest. His legs buckled. Ashworth sank to his knees. He died, held upright by an arm that had caught in one of the wagon's front wheels.

Chico Raza climbed down from the wagon as Tomas Zavala lowered a heavy wooden crate of Colt revolvers over the side. Both men were grinning as they worked.

Anabel remained where she was, unmoving. The sudden violence had left her drained. It could have been avoided, but Ashworth had given them no choice. She looked down at his crumpled form, then to the black ring on her hand. Her father had lived a life of violence, fighting against what he took to be injustice, determined to restore the honor and prosperity of his family.

On this rainy afternoon, she had begun to realize what it meant to be the daughter of Don Luis Cordero.

She wasn't the only one dumbstruck. Hidden in the *jacal* a few yards from the corral, Ben McQueen could scarcely believe his eyes. He turned and put his back to the wall, muttering "son of a bitch" beneath his breath. Anabel had played him for a fool, using her wiles to blind him while she plotted treachery. And he had fallen for every flirtatious glance. He'd traded his innate caution for the promise in a pretty girl's smile.

He drew his Colt, checked the loads, then returned to the gaping ruins of the *jacal*'s rear window. He watched as the bandits loaded their weapons in the gray mist, and recognized Zavala and Raza as the two men who had attempted to ride him down. He saw one of the bandits, a dark-featured man with a thick mustache and black hair, step away from the wagon and carry a gun belt and holstered revolver to Anabel. She strapped the weapon on her waist and adjusted her serape to hide the gun. She tucked her hair beneath the sombrero while nervously searching the surrounding buildings. Nothing but silence and the humble facades of mud-brick buildings—gray mist, gray walls, stained, rotting wood. Even if there were witnesses, who would speak against Anabel and her men? She was among friends in La Villita. She had nothing to fear. Old Town was the one place in San Antonio her secret was safe.

Anabel's gaze swept over the man in the window and darted back in alarm. Her mouth dropped open and icy fingers clutched at her spine.

"Ben," she whispered.

Ben McQueen lifted his gun. He didn't know if he could bring them all down, but he'd do his best to see that these men joined Spotted Calf in the calaboose.

But before he could issue a command for the bandits to throw their weapons in the mud, a piece of pottery cracked behind him. Ben whirled around, his gun held waist high. He saw a shadow, glimpsed a man with silver-streaked hair. Jorge Tenorio swung his rifle with all the rough, solid strength in his arms. The walnut rifle butt caught Ben flush against the side of his head.

Ben stumbled and fell against a side wall. The world reeled crazily. He tried to retain his hold on consciousness, tried to bring his Colt to bear on his attacker, but his hands refused to obey his commands. The gun dropped from his fingertips. He sank to his knees. Was that Anabel framed in blinding light?

The brightness became unbearable. But he had no mouth to scream. Ben was grateful when the darkness came. He ceased resistance and plummeted into the abyss.

Chapter Thirteen

Light and darkness. Pain like a steep grade a man must climb. It was the path home, out of a nightmare. He saw a jaguar drinking from a pool of blood. The jaguar opened its jaws wider, then wider still to reveal the face of a man who stared back and grinned and licked the blood from his lips. Evil was aroused. Something darker than sin lurked on the edge of unconsciousness, waiting, leering. Ben sensed its presence and crawled upward. Pain was the way back, leading him like a beacon while unbridled horror nipped at his heels.

He opened his eyes to the night-shrouded *jacal* where he'd been left bound and gagged. His wrists were tied behind his back. The side of his head hurt like hell, but he was alive. As Ben's eyes adjusted to the night, the moon momentarily emerged from behind a rain cloud and illuminated the interior of the roofless shell of the *jacal*. Ben was alive, all right, which was more than he could say for the two men propped against the wall. Ashworth and Harlan had been carried from the corral and left with Ben.

The lieutenant turned his eyes away from his grisly companions and managed to sit upright. His head throbbed and his lips felt bruised and puffy beneath the gag. The world momentarily reeled, then steadied itself. Ben had no idea how long he had been unconscious. Perhaps he had come to and drifted off more than once. No matter. It was night. The hour was impossible to tell. Those disturbing images he had seen in his mind's eye left him confused and shaken and were slow to fade. But he didn't have time to worry about them. Maybe later, when he was free and had rounded up a certain señorita and her desperados.

He struggled against the rawhide cords securing his wrists. His hands were numb and it took effort to move his fingers. In another half hour, he wouldn't be able to feel a thing. If he was going to free himself it better be soon. He took his bearings and settled on a plan. A rawhide rope attaching his bound wrists to another set of bonds firmly imprisoning his ankles left him little choice but to awkwardly roll to the corner of the *jacal*. Once over, then twice, and then again before the fire-damaged remains of a crib dug into his ribs. A little extra discomfort didn't matter now. He felt around on the dirt floor and sifted through straw and the pieces of a crib frame and a shattered stoneware cup half buried in mud and ashes. He cut himself, cursed, then with satisfaction realized he had found the shard of mirror.

Concentrating on his swollen fingers, he managed to grasp the jagged glass and, with his back to the wall, began to saw at the rawhide. It was slow going. Twice he dropped the shard, and only with maximum effort was he able to retrieve it.

Perspiration blinded him and dripped from his swollen features. His red hair was matted to his skull. Sweat streamed from every pore as he struggled to free himself. First one strand parted, then another, then a knot parted and a third strand. Seconds crawled past like hours. He lost his hold on the piece of mirror for the fourth time and, shifting his weight, accidently managed to break the shard into even smaller pieces.

Ben lowered his head. "Damn it," he sighed, the gag muzzling his words. Anger welled in him, starting in the pit of his stomach and spreading like wildfire until he trembled with fury. Then a muffled growl sounded deep in his throat and increased in volume until it became an animalistic cry of rage. His muscles swelled and the remaining rawhide bindings cut into his flesh as he pulled and twisted. Then, with an audible snap, the rawhide parted and his hands were free. He tugged the gag from his mouth and bit away the last strands of rawhide cutting off the blood supply to his hands. Feeling slowly returned, as did the use of his fingers. He fumbled with the rawhide rope that was looped around his ankles. They hadn't been as securely bound, and in a minute he had freed his legs and was standing. He wasn't surprised to find his gun belt missing. No matter, he thought, I know where I can get another. Ben leaned against the wall and allowed the circulation to bring life to his limbs. Moonlight faded, obscuring the two corpses near the doorway. Cal Ashworth and Lester Harlan were no great loss. Ben doubted any tears would be shed over their fate, for indeed it was one both men had tempted. They had called the tune and now had paid the piper.

But Anabel and her armed escort were something else again. Ben McQueen resolved there'd be a reckoning. He intended to come calling on the señorita this very night, and to bring along a trio of Texas Rangers to act as chaperons.

He had waited long enough. Ben stumbled across the room and, with unsteady steps, entered the narrow, night-wrapped streets of La Villita. A dangerous place at night? Ben pitied any man who got in his way.

Peter Abbot watched an evening shower chase the townspeople from the plaza. Lanterns swung to and fro, as if casting lazy signals in the gentle wind. Sodden banners hung heavy above the wooden walkways. The Alameda Hotel and its main competitor, the Ridenour House, appeared to be doing a thriving business. An amber glow flooded the hotel porches as it steamed through unshuttered windows. A variety of well-dressed townsfolk, Anglo, German, or Mexican, mingled in the Alameda's bar and the Ridenour House restaurant. The haciendas of the wealthy whose courtyards fronted the plaza also showed signs of celebration, despite the inclement weather.

Peter Abbot's hand flew across the paper, leaving clean, quick, subtle streaks of charcoal that captured the plaza, now abandoned by the very townspeople who had decorated it and who only an hour ago had been dancing under the starless sky.

"She looks kind of like a lady, all decked out for the ball only to find her escort's run off and there ain't no dance," Snake Eye said, peering over the artist's shoulder. A restless man by nature, he had followed Peter Abbot onto the veranda that stretched across the front of the governor's palace.

"You have the soul of a poet, Mr. Gandy," Peter remarked. He had heard the man approach, but had never lost concentration as he hurried to capture the moment. His keen observation noted the smallest detail: the play of lamplight in the puddles; the stark darkness of the church and priest's house, a sharp contrast to other homes; the cantina and the hotels, all of which bore the brunt of the festive crowds. The rowdy elements were contained in Main Plaza, and pity the drunken lout who lost his bearings and attempted to celebrate with the town's leading citizens.

"'Soul of a poet.' Hell, don't tell that to Virge. I never would hear the end."

"The secret shall die with me," Peter replied. The south walk needed a wash, and the subtlety of the background was too forced and needed to blend more with the shadows where the lamplight ended. Glancing up to study the angle of the hotel balcony overlooking the street, Pete caught a glimpse of movement in the plaza. Snake Eye noticed it as well. Gandy's keen eyesight, however, had been honed not by a pursuit of art, but by years spent on the frontier dodging Comanche arrows and Mexican lancers.

"By jingo. It's Ben McQueen," he said. "I'd know that broad-beamed younker anywhere."

Moments later, a rain-bedraggled Ben McQueen came lurching out of the night. He stumbled toward the porch, braced himself on a beam, and then stepped into the glare of the lantern Snake Eye held up before him. Ben was drenched to the skin, his lip was puffed, and the side of his head was swollen and caked with dried blood.

"Son, you look like you been kicked by a Missouri mule," Snake Eye said.

"For chrissake, Ben, what the devil happened?" Peter asked. "And where's Father? Is he all right?"

A cold chill creeped along Ben's spine and he became more alert.

"Your father?" he gasped. "Why would I know anything about your father?"

"I saw it for myself," Gandy interjected. "Carmelita showed up with a message that the general was supposed to hurry over to the padre's. She told us you and the brown robe had gathered some of the town's important Mexican leaders over at the priest's house to discuss these here plans for Texas becoming a state."

"And you let him go, just like that?" Ben groaned.

Snake Eye shrugged. "Seemed like the thing to do, after she showed us what you sent along to prove what she was about."

Peter was obviously worried. He set his sketch paper and box of charcoal sticks aside. Behind his glasses, his expression betrayed his concern. His features were suddenly tightly drawn and bloodless.

Ben looked from one to the other. Then he turned and stared at the funereal and somber silhouette of the church spires and the adobe hacienda alongside.

"What do you mean?" he said in a hoarse whisper.

"She showed us the medal. The old woman said you gave it to her as proof of her story," Peter told him.

Ben's hand shot to his neck and ripped open his shirt to below his rib cage. He stared down at his rain-soaked chest. His heart plummeted. The pain from the rifle blow had been nothing compared to what he felt now. Peter had spoken the truth. The medal was gone!

Chapter Fourteen

Father Esteban had an attentive audience at his kitchen table as he told his story. Sam Houston's hardened expression reflected the gravity of the situation. The kidnapping of Matthew Abbot might well precipitate a war. Ben McQueen, his jaw swollen, stood behind Houston. Ben's gaze smouldered as he shifted it from the priest to Carmelita. He had learned one of the bandits was her son. Ben was in a dark mood. He'd been played for a royal fool and lost not only the man he was supposed to protect, but the symbol of his family heritage. He reached to his chest as if unable to believe the medal was gone.

Captain Pepper sat at the end of the table, while Peter Abbot listened from a corner of the room near the back door. He sat on a stool and from time to time rubbed the bridge of his nose where his spectacles had rubbed a raw spot in his flesh. Virge Washburn had searched the priest's house and checked on the church itself, to no avail. He'd dispatched Clay Poole and Snake Eye Gandy to La

Villita several hours ago. Pepper wasn't expecting much, but he went through the motions. It was a case of shutting the barn door after the horse had escaped, and he knew it.

"Dawn soon," the padre observed aloud to no one in particular. The rain had stopped. Defying the spring rain's legacy of soggy streamers and mud, the fiesta would begin early and no doubt continue well on into the night. Already a ragtag band consisting of a couple of guitarists, three fiddlers, and a man playing a brass trumpet had gathered on the balcony of the Alameda Hotel and were beginning to wake the residents in the surrounding neighborhoods with a cheerful tune.

Such a gay beginning was wasted on the people in the kitchen. Any reason for celebration had ended with the kidnapping of Matthew Abbot. Father Esteban glanced over his shoulder at Carmelita, who sat by the stove, her round features defiant in the face of her captors. The priest shook his head and faced Houston again.

"My sister brought the general over into La Villita. There he was taken prisoner, bound, and placed on a horse. They rode out late yesterday afternoon." Esteban sighed and took a sip of coffee. "I learned this from Carmelita. My sister left without speaking to me. She knew I was against any such plan." He glanced at Ben. "One of my sister's vaqueros had your medal, Señor McQueen."

"Why should she do such a thing? Who were the men with her?" Captain Pepper firmly asked.

Esteban nodded and folded his hands upon the table. It was obvious the entire affair deeply troubled him.

"Once as a child," he began, "I went exploring

a cave on my father's ranch. Being a reckless youth, I managed to get myself stuck in a narrow passage several feet below ground. It was like being buried alive. I have never forgotten the experience of being trapped with no way out. Fortunately, my father's segundo, Jorge, heard my cries. He found and freed me." The priest gulped his coffee, set the stoneware on the table, and stared at the muddy silt at the bottom of the cup. His future looked about as bleak. "I am trapped again, señores, and truth is the only way back for me." He searched the faces of the men in the kitchen, but found no compassion, only suspicion and anger. The priest did not blame them. "My name is not Obregon. It is Cordero. Anabel and I are the children of Don Luis Cordero."

"My God," Captain Pepper said.

"So El Tigre has cubs, eh?" said Sam Houston. "Well, well, well. Now that is something."

"My father was a man of violence. A man of deep passions. And a long memory. He hated norteamericanos when first you came to this land. He chose to fight. He died trying to drive you out."

"And you?" Houston's deep voice demanded. The former president of the Texas Republic did not enjoy being roused from sleep. He had come to the priest's house wearing a nightshirt tucked into nankeen trousers and a Colt revolver tucked in a wide leather belt that circled his waist. There were pouches beneath his eyes, but his gaze was rock steady.

"So the tiger of the mountains really is dead," Captain Pepper muttered aloud.

"I am a priest. I take my vows most seriously. And I have tried to lead my flock, whatever the color of their skin, in the ways of peace," Father Esteban said directly to Sam Houston. Then he lifted his gaze and looked at Ben. "Anabel was always his favorite. Daughters and fathers, this is a special bond. She is so much like him. The land is in her blood. Like his. And the pride... like his."

"What does she hope to gain by kidnapping an official of the government of the United States?" Ben asked, keeping the emotion out of his voice. He wanted to sound as businesslike as possible. Anabel wasn't the only one with pride.

"War," Esteban replied. "The tension between Mexico and the United States is like kindling. This incident might well set the relationship ablaze." The padre stood and crossed to the stove. He refilled his stoneware cup, taking care to ignore Carmelita's accusing stare. "My father's full name was Don Luis Cordero de Tosta. We are related by marriage to Santa Anna."

"He's in exile in Cuba," Sam Houston pointed out. He had kept himself informed as to the whereabouts of his old enemy, the former president of Mexico.

"Should war break out, there are many factions who would see him restored to the presidency. That would revive our family's fortune as well." Esteban turned and held out his hands in a classic gesture of helplessness. "It was my father's dying wish." He glanced down at his brown robes. "My fortune is stored for me in heaven, not in Mexico City." He returned to the table and sat opposite Houston, looking from the former president to the Ranger captain and then to Peter Abbot, who appeared distraught over his father's kidnapping.

"She won't harm General Abbot. Once war breaks out, she'll probably try to ransom him," the padre said.

"Over my dead body," Ben said. "Where is she heading?"

"My father's hacienda, across the border, in the

mountains. Who can say? I have never been there,"
the padre replied.

"And I will not tell you the way," Carmelita
interjected. She blessed herself with the sign of the
cross. "This I swear."

Ben, despite his anger and sense of betrayal,
had to admit a grudging respect for the rotund old
woman. They could stake her out on an anthill
Comanche style, he figured, and she still wouldn't talk.

Comanche...

He had an idea, one that might just work if it
didn't get him killed. He excused himself from the
gathering, hurried from the kitchen, and ran into
Snake Eye Gandy near the front door. The Ranger
had spent half the night searching the *jacales* in La
Villita, just in case the priest was lying and Anabel
and her prisoner hadn't left town after all. However,
his search had proved fruitless.

"You learn anything?"

Gandy shook his head. "You look like a burr's
been put under your saddle."

"I'm not waiting any longer," Ben said.

"They've had several hours' head start. And
rain's washed out the tracks. Now, unless you know
something I don't know..."

"Not me," Ben said. He was playing a hunch,
based on the hasty exchange between Anabel and
the Comanche at his capture. "Spotted Calf."

The only action at the jail consisted of a pair of
mud daubers trying to figure out the best corner in
which to build a nest. The insects hovered in front of
the door and refused to give ground until Ben swept
them aside with the back of his hand. He peered

through the barred window. The sky had cleared and the sunlight warmed his shoulder and soothed his battered cheek. Spotted Calf lay on the dirt floor of the adobe jail, motionless. Indeed, he seemed dead. But then, without looking toward the door, he spoke.

"Bitter Creek has returned to watch his red brother die."

Ben unbolted the door to the jail. Snake Eye's shadow fell across him as Gandy grabbed McQueen's arm. Snake Eye had been at Ben's side, hovering like a one-eyed guardian angel, hoping to talk sense into the rawboned young man, or to back his play.

"Have you gone plumb loco?" Gandy asked.

Ben pulled free and entered the darkened interior. The Comanche on the floor sat upright, surprised by the soldier's actions.

"I have come to watch you die or live. The choice is yours."

Spotted Calf cast a wary glance toward the open door. He spied Gandy's shadow on the ground, gun in hand. The Comanche returned his attention to the man towering over him. He waited, his silence an unspoken question.

"The woman is gone. Anabel Cordero and the bandits of El Tigre have stolen guns and escaped toward the mountains." Ben knew he was grasping at straws, but one look at the Comanche's expression told him he had struck pay dirt.

"You lie," Spotted Calf said.

"She has stolen something that belongs to me. I will not rest until I get it back."

Spotted Calf heard the anger in the white man's voice. He felt the anger in the white man's heart and realized Ben must be speaking the truth. The Comanche scowled. The woman had promised to free him if the brave kept her secret. The Comanche had fulfilled his part of the bargain. But the woman had left him to die the white man's slow death, shut off from the mountains and the good wind.

"I think you know where she has gone," Ben said. Spotted Calf stood, and his dark, flat-nosed features grew impassive and guarded. "Take me there," the soldier added.

"You do not know what you ask. The dark ones have come to the mountains. We would ride to our deaths." Spotted Calf lowered his head.

"Better to ride to your death like a warrior than wait for it here," Ben said, and turned his back on the Comanche with obvious disregard for the brave's former prowess. He might as well have been standing before an old woman.

"Wait," Spotted Calf said as the soldier's big frame filled the doorway. "I hear the wisdom in your words. I will lead you."

Ben swung around and stared at the chief. From outside the jail, Gandy whispered, "You can't be serious. You can't trust him; you're his enemy. He'd as soon slit your gullet as spit."

"Give me your knife," Ben said.

Gandy hesitated, then drew a broad-bladed bowie knife from the sheath beneath his left arm. Ben took the knife and with its gleaming point carved a hole in his own thumb. Blood trickled down into his fist. Spotted Calf understood, and moved forward and held out his right hand. In a matter of seconds, two wounded thumbs were pressed together, mingling the blood of red man and white.

"Now I am not his enemy, but his brother in blood," Ben said, handing the knife back to Gandy.

"All this big medicine doesn't mean a hill of

beans, younker. We don't need a goddamn Injun to lead us into a trap. We'll find Cordero on our own." Gandy could see that his words were falling on deaf ears. He stepped aside in disgust as Ben brought Spotted Calf into the light. The Comanche shielded his eyes and studied the rapidly clearing sky. It promised to be a warm, clear day. Spotted Calf sucked in a lungful of fresh air. The brave grinned, obviously enjoying the effect his release was having on his old adversary. Spotted Calf held up his shackled wrists for Ben to unlock the chains.

"When we're clear of town," Ben told him.

"Sombitch!" Snake Eye cursed. His face was mottled red, ugly mean. "I ain't about to trust my life on the trail in the company of this red devil." He spoke with absolute finality.

"No one's asking you to," Ben replied. Then, with the Comanche at his side, he started toward the barn. With luck they'd be on their way before noon. Ben glanced down at his self-inflicted wound. Ben could only hope the Comanches held such rituals in as high regard as the Choctaws he'd been raised with. A hell of a lot was riding on a bloody thumb.

Chapter Fifteen

Toby stood in the sunlight, sweat beading his dark brow. He held a cloth sack stuffed with bread and half a smoked ham for the men to eat when they made camp come nightfall. Provisions for the journey—jerked meat, coffee, beans, tortillas, and a couple of slabs of salt pork—had already been packed. Ben had reoutfitted himself with a borrowed Patterson Colt and the muzzle-loading rifle the army issued to all its soldiers. Whoever had clubbed him had forgotten to take the bear-claw pouch. Ben looked across the rumps of the horses, hoping in vain to catch a glimpse of Snake Eye Gandy. There was nothing to see but mesquite trees, bunchgrass, and sparrows flitting among the spiny arms of an ocotillo. Ben checked the extra loads in the pouch. If he was riding to his death, as Spotted Calf said, at least he wouldn't go unarmed. For his part, the Comanche had selected a horse for himself and had worked diligently to ready the animals for the journey. Chains rattling with every movement of his arms, the brave inspected the hooves of the horses they would ride into the mountains of Mexico.

Toby hooked his thumbs in the rope belt circling his waist. "Things is sure gonna be quiet around here with you gone, Mr. McQueen." He wanted to go with the Rangers more than anything in the world. Still, a day of fireworks, music, and food would salve his wounded feelings. He patted the roan and then, with the exuberance of youth, trotted off toward Military Plaza, where the fiesta was fully under way.

Clay Poole and Virge Washburn looked none too happy about traveling in the company of the Comanche, but they kept their doubts to themselves.

Captain Pepper had asked for volunteers to join Ben, but, as Virge Washburn had wryly observed, he and Clay Poole were the only Rangers in town at the moment. Neither man would have hesitated had it not been for the nature of the guide. The two hard cases had spent the past ten years fighting Comanches. Now they were being told to ride with one of the very same braves they had been chasing. It just didn't make sense. But they seemed resigned to the situation.

Standing in the stable yard, Ben and the others were surprised to see Peter Abbot emerge from the barn. He led a brown gelding saddled and ready to ride. The general's errant son carried a revolver holstered high on his right hip and a rifle slung over his shoulder. He wore nankeen pants tucked into high-topped black boots and a coarse linen shirt, a serape, and a flat-brimmed black hat. He had draped his satchel of sketch paper and charcoal across the back of his saddle. Sunlight glinted off the lenses of his spectacles as he joined the men in front of the barn. He looked nervous and unsure of himself. Ben felt the same way but refused to show it.

Sam Houston and Captain Pepper stood aside as Peter approached. He nodded to Ben. By rights, the young man figured, he should have been enjoying the fiesta, finding a variety of libertine young señoritas to flirt with and reveling in the abundance of food and wine.

Flies circled mounds of fresh horse droppings. The shadow of a hawk drifted over the gathering of men. Peter Abbot stared defiantly at the Rangers until they looked away. Their opinion of him was obvious.

"You don't have to come along. No one will think the worse of you," Ben said.

"You're going after him," Peter said.

"He's my responsibility," the lieutenant replied.

"He's my father." Peter dabbed at his pale features. It wouldn't be long before his forehead was sunburned and peeling. "Look. He and I have never seen eye to eye. But despite everything, I still love the man. It's my right to go after him, Ben. And I will, even if it means trailing you from a distance."

Ben nodded. He couldn't argue with the sense of responsibility Peter felt. Ben himself would follow the man who had taken his medal, to the ends of the earth if need be. He'd retrieve it or die. Yes, Ben McQueen understood the demands of blood and family.

Sam Houston sauntered past the horses as Ben climbed into saddle. The creak of leather, the smell of oiled guns and horseflesh made the hero of San Jacinto wistful for earlier days.

"My place is in Austin, son, trying to make the best of this terrible situation, else I'd be going with you. I must also notify President Polk of these tragic events."

"You'd be welcome," Ben said.

Houston produced an Arkansas toothpick, a bone-handled knife with a twelve-inch blade of double-edged hammered steel. The knife was encased in a simple buckskin sheath. There was nothing fancy about the knife. It was a simple, ugly, efficient weapon that had seen plenty of use. And would again. The lieutenant tucked the sheath in the left side of his belt.

"I thank you, sir," Ben said.

"Keep your powder dry, Lieutenant McQueen," Houston said. "Good speed, all of you." He stepped back. Spotted Calf, in his stolen brocaded vest and blue frocked coat, winced as he leaped into the saddle. His wounded shoulder didn't seem to hamper his movements. He rode up alongside Ben and looked straight ahead, as if seeing beyond the horizon. The joy of his newly won freedom had worn off, to be replaced by a journey that would take him back to the mountains where a dark god waited.

Peter Abbot and the Rangers lost no time in mounting. Clay Poole's hammerhead stallion bucked and fought the weight of the man on his back.

"Be still, you goddamn nag," Poole roared, "or I'll bust your head with my tomahawk!" His threat took effect and the stallion settled down.

Virge chuckled aloud. "You been ridin' a stool too damn long, Clay."

"Shut up, you . . ." Poole's insult trailed off as he spied the horseman coming toward them out of the arroyo.

"Lieutenant," Poole called out to the man in the lead.

"Well, I'll be damned," Virge muttered.

Ben turned as Snake Eye Gandy walked his bad-tempered stallion up out of the mesquite-choked arroyo. The grizzled Ranger offered no explanation as he rode up abreast of Ben McQueen. He sat silent for a moment, then shrugged.

"Maybe I'll tag along for a while."

"Suit yourself," Ben replied.

"Yeah," Gandy said, glaring at the Comanche. The Ranger tucked his topknot beneath his sombrero and fixed Ben in a rattler stare. "You're a crazy sombitch, McQueen."

Ben refused to be cowed. "Go to hell."

Snake Eye Gandy chuckled and glanced aside at the Comanche. "Sure thing. Hell it is. Reckon you know the way, Spotted Calf?"

He did.

Chapter Sixteen

Fire Giver looked out across the ancient landscape and listened to the voice in the wind. He heard secrets that reassured him. There had passed as many nights as the fingers on his hands. In that time, Tezcatlipoca had fed well. Fire Giver stood and walked the edge of the ridge overlooking the box canyon his god had led him to. Down below, at the far end of the canyon, the whitewashed walls of a hacienda gleamed in the moonlight. In the center of the canyon, a settlement had sprung up where poor peasant farmers, Chisos Indians, and the families of the vaqueros had made their homes. Consisting of maybe two dozen families, the settlement had provided crops for themselves and Cordero's men. Goats and cattle had grazed on the chino grass here and in other canyons hidden among the serrated ridges and upthrust peaks of northern Coahuila. In return, the farmers received the protection of Cordero's vaqueros. Comanches came to this canyon to trade, not plunder. Don Luis Cordero provided a measure of safety the poor were unaccustomed to.

Three days ago, Fire Giver had put a grisly end to that illusion.

Behind where he stood on this rampart of volcanic stone and upthrust limestone debris, a fossil-encrusted boulder about twenty feet in length and ten feet wide had been sculpted by the elements into a distinctly ominous resemblance of a crouching panther, poised, waiting to spring atop the unwary traveler. The panther's front paws, smooth-weathered stone encrusted with tiny shells, were black with dried blood and ashes. They had served as a divine altar, a sacred receptacle for the hearts of the sacrificed. The women and children and few men in the settlement never knew they were under attack until the battle was all but lost. The warriors of the night had descended in darkness and carried off the inhabitants to die beneath the sacrificial knife that Fire Giver wielded with such expertise.

But the grim god had yet to be glutted. Fire Giver knew this. He had heard it in the moaning wind. As evening deepened he turned away from the edge of the cliff and with war axe in hand made his way along the ridge and down to the encampment Striker had found. The shaman picked his way among sumac bushes, prickly pear, and ocotillo cactus. Limestone gravel gave way to bunchgrass and oak shrubs and mesquite trees. There was water here, a silty, shallow creek that was barely adequate to meet the needs of his band. Young Serpent had led a group of young warriors into the edge of camp, where they were waiting for Fire Giver to return to the arroyo so they could make their complaints known. Young Serpent had discarded his eagle headdress and his atlatl and throwing spears. He did not want to show disrespect for the shaman.

Fire Giver descended from the ridge in a cloud of luminescent insects that swirled around the high priest with every step. Fire Giver saw the gathering of warriors awaiting him. Between the jaws of his jaquar-head helmet, the shaman's eyes seemed to burn with an unearthly intensity. His multicolored robe made a solid, smooth-lined silhouette of his wiry frame and, along with the helmet, provided an imposing stature to the man.

"Why are my children come to me?" he asked. The remainder of the braves were resting in the comforting glow of half a dozen campfires.

"Sacred One," Young Serpent began. He had been elected to speak by virtue of the fact that his mother had been Fire Giver's sister and the other warriors figured the shaman might not take offense if it was a relative who questioned his choice of campsites. "There is too little water here. We are forced to build shelters for ourselves, while in the canyon on the other side of the mountain of the Sleeping Panther, there is good water and shelter made of stone just waiting for us."

Fire Giver nodded and stepped around the braves, then motioned for them to follow him back to the camp. The shaman stopped at the first campfire he came to, reached down, and plucked a length of branch from the outer ring of coals. He held the branch so that all the men with Young Serpent could see it.

"This is the *home* of the mountain people," Fire Giver said, indicating the glowing red tip of the branch. He stepped out of the firelight, and in a matter of seconds the pulsing red tip had attracted a pair of moths that fluttered and swirled around it. "See, these winged ones are the people of the canyons who will return to their home." He blew on the branch until the glowing red tip burst into flame. Tongues of fire flared up to engulf the moths. "And we are the flames. We will wait and watch, and when more of the mountain people come within our reach..." He held the branch beneath Young Serpent's nose. The moths had been reduced to gobs of molten wings and shapeless gray-black bodies.

But Young Serpent longed for his village.

"When shall we return to the Valley of Eagles?"

"You will know the time," said Fire Giver. "All of you will see the sign and know it is time to return to home. I speak for the Smoking Glass and tell you this."

Chapter Seventeen

Sparks billowed up into the evening air as Clay Poole dug up the sotol roots he'd roasted in a bed of ashes. Each root was about the size of a potato, emerging crinkly black from its bed of coals. However unappealing the sotol looked at first glance, sliced in half it revealed a delectable orange-colored, fibrous meat with a taste similar to sweet potato. As harsh as these desert mountains seemed, a man need not starve to death if he knew what to look for. Moisture could be squeezed from the pods of a prickly pear and, once peeled, the pod itself provided nourishment. Tinajas where the rainwater collected in hollows of eroded stone could be discovered by following animal tracks or noticing the flight of bees.

Ben was a conscientious student. Ten days on the trail and he could identify many of the plants that might supplement an otherwise drab diet of salt pork, tortillas, and beans. He'd even acquired a taste for sotol. He consumed his share without hesitation and topped it off with frijoles wrapped in a tortilla and washed down with black coffee.

The Rio Grande lay behind them. They had chosen a camp near a spring in the foothills of the Sierra Madre Oriental. The three Rangers were breaking the law by being in Coahuila, but none of them seemed concerned. Snake Eye wasn't the kind of man to let a little thing like a border keep him from pursuing the kidnappers of Matthew Abbot.

Ben McQueen sipped black coffee and took the measure of his makeshift invasion force. An artist, a Comanche war chief, three Rangers, and an army lieutenant did not make for the most cohesive group. Gandy and the other Rangers were simply grateful that Spotted Calf hadn't murdered them in their sleep. They couldn't understand why Ben trusted the brave. As far as Ben was concerned, Spotted Calf had given his word, and his word had been bound with the mingling of his blood with the lieutenant's. Ben glanced at Peter Abbot's huddled form. Peter had slumped wearily onto his bedding, propped his head against his saddle, and closed his eyes. Was he asleep or thinking of his father? Peter had held his own through the long days on the trail. Ben wasn't surprised. Abbot was no dandy. He could ride and shoot as well as anyone. Peter simply marched to a different drummer, to a cadence his father had never been able to understand.

Spotted Calf sat apart from the men around the campfire and finished his meal. A different hunger glinted in his eyes, directed toward Clay Poole, who was busy checking the percussion caps on the spare cylinders he carried in a buckskin pouch slung over his shoulder. Ben could imagine what was going on in the Comanche's mind. Up until now, against single-shot weapons, the "lords of the plains" had held their own against the white man. With the advent of these "many-times-firing guns," the tide had turned and the red man's days of mastery were at an end.

Unless, of course, such weapons came into the hands of Spotted Calf and his tribe. The war chief rose from his blanket. Immediately two pairs of eyes turned his way. Virge Washburn and Clay Poole watched as the brave walked across the camp to stand alongside Ben. The wind stirred the branches of the mesquite and drew the campfire smoke into the night sky. They had camped near a spring with a ridge to north and west. Hoping to conceal their presence, they'd built their campfire in a mesquite thicket in the center of a patch of lechugilla cactus whose tall, thorny stalks were bound to deter any nighttime aggressor. The dark shadows of the mountains rose against the night sky. As Spotted Calf studied them, a sense of foreboding filled his spirit. He seemed oblivious to Ben's presence, though the lieutenant stood close at hand.

"Tell me of the blood-eating god," Ben said. It was a particularly fiercesome term and one he had not encountered until recently.

"It is best not to talk of such things, especially when we are so close."

"To Cordero's hacienda?"

"That too. Maybe two moons from here," Spotted Calf said. "We will find it. If we have not been killed."

"I will not die," Ben replied. The brave's gloomy demeanor was beginning to affect him. "I thought the Quahadi Comanche were not afraid to die."

"To die in battle is one thing," the brave

explained. "But it is said the dark ones steal your spirit as they kill you. It is a bad thing." He stared at the mountains. They had been home and haven for his people during the long winter months. He had always felt safe here . . . until now. Spotted Calf glanced at the soldier.

"I should have a gun," he said.

"Take me to Cordero's canyon."

"Then I will have a gun?"

"Then you will have your freedom."

Something rattled in the underbrush and both men turned to face the threat. Ben drew his revolver. The Comanche snatched up a fist-sized stone. About twenty yards in front of them a sumac bush shook and trembled. Ben's eyes searched the night. His heart leaped to his throat as he scanned the darkness. The dark ones, the blood-eating god, the Warriors of the Night—all these ominous legends crowded his thoughts and left him poised and alert. His hand trembled. He exhaled slowly. The shaking stopped. What is it? What the devil is out there? He frowned and wished he hadn't thought of the devil.

Spotted Calf hurled the stone at a patch of shadow darker than the shapes around it. The missile struck flesh, and a garish squeal erupted from the intruder. Ben almost fired off a shot but caught himself just in time as a javelina, a breed of wild pig around whose water hole the men had camped, broke from behind the underbrush and scampered off through the lechugilla. Ben sighed in relief and looked askance at his companion's flat, battered, dark-skinned features, but the brave remained taciturn. Spotted Calf sauntered off toward the campfire. He walked with heavy, plodding steps, as if his squat, round-shouldered frame bore the weight of some tragedy he alone could foretell.

Ben leaned against a limestone outcropping after clearing out the prickly pear sprouting at its base. He tilted back and stared up at the sky, and imagined Anabel Cordero watching the same starry night. His anger toward her had cooled. She certainly wasn't at a loss for courage, the way she went after Ashworth with only a sombrero against his Colt. He was remembering the night on the balcony of the hacienda and the ease with which she had won his trust. He'd been only too happy to give it. Had it all been a ruse on her part? If so, she was a damn fine actress, or maybe he had just been the perfect audience, a man looking to be healed.

"You spook the javelina?" Snake Eye asked from off to Ben's left. Ben jumped and, after he'd regained his composure, scowled at the Ranger. "Best you keep alert," Snake Eye warned. "One of them ghost warriors the Comanche talks about is liable to sneak up and put a knife in you." Gandy chuckled and walked over to the rock. "Been circling the camp. Ain't seen hide nor hair of trouble. Just that ol' scared desert pig. She damn near trampled me trying to get to safety."

"You don't believe Spotted Calf."

"Not as far as I can toss him." Gandy looked at the silhouettes of the mountains against the night sky. "There's enough to ride shy of in this country without looking for trouble. Injuns is always talking about spirits and curses and such." The Ranger shifted his stance and added, "But I reckon you know all about that, being part Injun and all." Gandy jabbed a thumb back toward camp. "Peter and I been talking some since leaving San Antone."

"I'm quarter Choctaw," Ben said. "It's not something I'm ashamed of." His tone of voice was as hard as the rock at his back. "If you've got a problem with that, we can settle it now."

Gandy's glass eye reflected the moonlight and became a coldly sinister orb. He ran a hand through his silver-streaked hair, scratched at his stubbled jaw, then let his long arm fall to his side.

"You're a regular Texas twister when you're on the prod, younker, " he said. "Abbot told me about your wife. I had me a wife once. Comanches killed her, took her breasts for medicine bags. I been killing 'em back ever since. We be who we be, I reckon, and that's the size of it." He yawned. "Anyway, I just wanted you to know I wasn't a bastard for no reason at all. My slate's been writ on, too."

Ben hesitated a moment, uncertain how to reply to the Ranger's casual revelation. At last he realized there were no adequate words. So he said the first thing that came to mind.

"Think Clay left us any coffee?"

Snake Eye shrugged. "Reckon we could go find out."

The two men started back to camp. They kept to a deer trail that threaded its way through the barrier of lechugilla cactus. Coyotes howled in the night, their chorus a lost and mournful sound interrupted by the echoing roar of a panther. Death prowled the dark hills. It stalked on four legs. And on two.

In Blanco Pass, between McQueen's campsite and Cordero Canyon, Tomas Zavala ignored the deepening shadows of night and went about his usual routine. He'd watered and grazed his horse and prepared himself a meal. Zavala was not a man easily spooked, even when camping alone in these ancient mountains. Someone had needed to stay behind and keep watch for any sign of pursuit. Blanco Pass was ideally situated, about a day and a half from Cordero Canyon. With a spring-fed creek for fresh water, a lean-to nestled back in a grove of scrub oaks for shelter and concealment, and enough food for a week, what more could a man ask for? Zavala sighed. He had volunteered to stay behind because he had no wife or family to greet him in the lair of El Tigre, not like Chico or Hector. They were fortunate; both had taken wives, and Hector even had two children.

Zavala wrapped another helping of frijoles in a tortilla and filled a cup with the coffee he had brewed. The campfire popped and crackled and cast a cheery glow. He took a bite of the tortilla and chased it down with the black, bitter coffee. Food to warm his belly, and afterward . . . he glanced at the bottle of tequila in his saddlebag and grinned. Now all he needed was a wiling señorita to crawl beneath his blanket and keep him warm throughout these cool, high-country nights. Well, a man couldn't have everything. He scratched at his scarred left ear, the legacy of a brawl in a cantina up on the Rio Seco in Chihuahua. A pretty señorita too free with her kisses had cost Zavala a piece of his ear and, after the gunsmoke cleared to reveal a jealous lover laying dead, had left him an outlaw with a price on his head and wanted by the Federales. Don Luis Cordero had given him food, tequila, a fine horse, and a place to live. Tomas Zavala was a man of simple wants and simple loyalty. With the death of El

Tigre, he had simply shifted his devotion to Anabel Cordero. It was easier to follow than to lead. In San Antonio, Zavala had been fearful of capture. But here in the Sierra Madre, he was master of his fate. Despite Anabel's sense of caution, Tomas was certain the Rangers wouldn't cross the border. And even if they did, no damn gringo was going to find Cordero Canyon.

Tomas finished his meal and brought his plate and coffeepot to the source of the creek, where the water bubbled up out of the earth beneath a ledge of volcanic stone at the base of a cliff. The creek never reached more than a couple of feet deep before playing out about a quarter of a mile down the canyon.

Zavala rinsed out his coffeepot, cleaned his plate, and sauntered back to camp. He set aside the coffeepot and plate and added a couple of stout branches to the flames. Kneeling by the fire, Zavala uncorked his bottle of tequila and emptied a quarter of its contents down his gullet. Then he drew one of his Colt revolvers and set the bottle aside.

Now here was a weapon. Five shots as fast as he could cock the hammer and pull the trigger. He pitied the Comanche raiding party that ever came to steal the horses of Cordero. As for the Rangers, well, one day the riders of Cordero would head north and settle with those Texans who had ambushed and destroyed El Tigre and his followers.

"The daughter of Don Luis shall lead us," Zavala said aloud. The creek bubbled merrily behind him. The new logs sizzled and snapped in the fire. The vaquero's voice was the only other noise.

The revolver clicked, being cocked; then Zavala eased the hammer down, between cylinders. He stared into the flames of the campfire and imagined himself riding at the head of a heavily armed column of men who looked to him for guidance and followed his lead. He saw himself charging into battle, his Colts blazing, his enemies fleeing before his wrath.

A shadow detached itself from the underbrush. Then another. And another. They made no sound. One shadow took shape, became a man whose fierce eyes peered from his eagle helmet. It was Striker. He raised his obsidian-encrusted war club and came on at a run.

Zavala, in his reverie, could almost hear the jingle-jangle of gold coins pouring into his saddlebags. He softly laughed. The tequila warming his gut merely fueled his fantasies.

Images of a rosy future layered one atop the other, each sequence better than the one before, until they all came crashing down and splintered apart like fragments of shattered glass, in jolting pain. Zavala never heard the rush of the blow that filled him and left him sprawled alongside the campfire. What dream was this? Hands quickly turned him over on his back. Through veils of his own blood he saw three demons with eagle heads and knives of serrated black stone. Zavala screamed. It didn't do him any good. Then the demons with the knives went to work on him.

And his dreams became nightmares.

Chapter Eighteen

"Where the hell is everybody?" Jorge Tenorio said as he sat astride his weary mount in the middle of Cordero Canyon. A solitary afternoon breeze stirred the woven-reed flaps covering the windows of the houses. Anabel, at his side, ordered Chico Raza and Hector Ybarbo to fan out through the settlement. They were only too happy to comply. Both of them had taken wives, and Ybarbo had two children who should have been running out to greet their father as the men of Cordero returned home.

"Ramona," Hector called out. "Children, why do you hide from your father?" The question reverberated through the canyon and returned unanswered.

"Natividad?" cried Chico, with the same results as his friend.

"No parade to greet you?" Matt Abbot asked, taking a moment to rub his aching back. The grueling pace had left him drawn and pale. He moved stiffly. His thick neck was sunburned and peeling.

But his posterior and spine were the major sources of his discomfort.

Miguel reached out and jabbed his rifle into the retired general's shoulder. "Keep quiet, you!" Abbot groaned, and Anabel, seeing what had happened, turned and rode back to Miguel and grabbed the rifle from his hand. She was tired and her patience with his bullying ways had worn thin.

"Leave the *norteamericano* alone! He will not be harmed. You understand me?"

Miguel did not like being taken to task in front of the prisoner. He muttered an unintelligible reply and stared at the ground. Anabel did not have the time to prolong the reprimand. She was more concerned with the whereabouts of the families. The settlement appeared totally deserted.

"Do not try to antagonize my men, Señor Abbot. You can only suffer for it. Sí?" She rode back to Jorge and followed him to the edge of the settlement. About a hundred and fifty yards up the canyon, at the west end, Don Luis had built his hacienda to face the sunrise. However, what looked to be a solid cliff behind the house was actually an illusion, for the ridge took a dogleg turn to the north just beyond the hacienda. This cul de sac, flanked by volcanic ridges, concealed a bubbling pool of spring water, oak trees, and a carpet of nourishing chino grass.

"What was that?" Hector Ybarbo shouted. "I saw something." He pointed to a jumbled pile of rocks on the south side of the canyon near the settlement. The boulders were the result of an earlier rock slide. One section in particular, a broad, flat chunk of table rock about ten feet in diameter, had come to rest atop the rubble, which itself was almost thirty feet in height. The table rock provided a perfect vantage point for a sentry to keep watch over the entrance to the canyon. One of the three men Don Luis had left behind to protect the families should have been on guard. Hector rode over to the slide area and studied the precipitous mound of jagged limestone debris. At last he turned to the others and shrugged. He had found nothing out of the ordinary. Jorge suggested to Anabel that perhaps the hacienda itself might hold a clue to the disappearance of the canyon's former inhabitants. She called out for the others to follow her and raced off toward the hacienda. Her tired gelding covered the distance with a determination born of its mountain breeding. The horses of Don Luis Cordero would run till they dropped.

Tenorio managed to catch and pass the woman and was the first to ride beneath the arched gateway in the east wall of the hacienda. Adobe walls, ten feet tall, formed three sides of a rectangle—north, east and south. The house itself completed the rectangle and sealed off a center courtyard a hundred and thirty feet across and ninety deep. A corral was attached to the outside of the south wall. And on the far side of the corral, an open-sided shed sheltered a blacksmith's forge.

Anabel was perturbed that Tenorio had been the first to enter the courtyard. No doubt he was still trying to protect her, but he would have to learn that she could take care of herself. Behind Jorge and Anabel, the other vaqueros and their prisoner crowded through the arched entrance in the stone wall. Only Hector had remained in the settlement. He had dismounted and was searching each adobe cabin.

Anabel dismounted and slid her father's sawed-off shotgun from its saddle scabbard and started toward the front door. From the courtyard, the place seemed deserted. The only residents were a pair of Mexican jays that had perched on a hitching rail in front of a low-roofed barrack built against the north wall.

"It's a curse. We should have freed Spotted Calf from the Rangers," Chico bemoaned, and blessed himself.

"Idiot," Jorge replied. Despite being the oldest of the lot, the long journey back to El Tigre's lair seemed to have affected him the least. He tilted his sombrero back on his forehead and wiped a hand across his mouth. "Some promises cannot be kept. The Comanche was no friend. And the Rangers would not have handed him over for the asking. Was he worth your life? Or mine?"

"Silence," Anabel replied. This time she led the way to the heavy door of paneled oak. She grabbed the iron latch and pulled. The door creaked open and a flurry of crows burst through the open doorway right in her face. She gasped and raised a hand to ward off the attack. The shotgun roared and the last of the crows vanished in a blizzard of black feathers. Buckshot blew a chunk out of the doorsill and peppered the back wall of the living room. Miguel and Matt Abbot had to fight to keep from being dislodged from their mounts as the startled horses bucked and tossed their manes and pawed at the air.

Anabel turned red with embarrassment. Furious at herself, she drew her Colt revolver and stalked through the door. Sunlight streaming through unshuttered windows illuminated the interior. The hacienda was much the same as she remembered. Save for some Indian blankets hung from the walls, there was little in the way of decoration. The house reflected the builder, her father. It was sparsely furnished with thick, solid, hand-hewn furniture, protected by laboriously constructed adobe walls. The hacienda bespoke strength and permanence. And like the settlement in the lower end of the canyon, it was chillingly devoid of life.

Ben McQueen took stock of Blanco Pass and the lengthening shadows of late afternoon and suggested his party make camp. A shallow cave carved out of the walls of the pass offered protection from the elements. Snake Eye gave the suggestion his blessing after scrutinizing the surrounding walls of the pass. He preferred the open range and didn't like feeling hemmed in. Here in the Sierra Madre, darkness came early as the sun dipped past the broken-backed ridges of the western skyline.

Clay Poole trotted his skittish bay up to the mouth of the cave and peered into the depression that time and flash floods had scooped out of the base of the cliff. He took his time and proceeded with caution. Such natural shelters were generally already occupied by a variety of creatures, spiked and fanged or with flashing claws.

"Careful now," Virge called out as Clay gingerly entered the cave. "Watch out for rattlers."

"She ain't deep," Clay said. "I can already see the back wall. Appears to be purty clear."

Virge walked his mount up to the cave and fished a six-inch-long dried rattler's tail from his saddlebag. He gave the rattles a violent shake. The telltale warning had an instantaneous effect on Poole's horse as it stood just inside the cave.

"Whoa—whoa—shiiit!" Clay landed flat on his back in the sand and his horse, a broom-tail bay, scampered out of the cave and into the fading light. Virge roared with laughter and slapped his thigh and held up the rattlesnake tail as Clay Poole emerged from under the limestone ledge. It didn't take Clay long to realize he had been tricked. He saw Ben McQueen cut off his escaping horse and waved his thanks. Clay grabbed his battered hat and threw it on the ground. The fringe of brown hair around the sides of his head stuck straight out from his skull. He brushed sand from the beard that hung down his chest.

"Virge Washburn! You've gone too far. Climb off that nag o' yours and I'll part your hair proper." He hauled the tomahawk from his belt. "God, you know I hate them rattlers." He advanced on Washburn, who good-naturedly held up his hands in a mock surrender.

"By heaven, take you on the Mescan side of the Rio Grande and you get plumb touchy," Virge replied.

"I'll touch you right enough!" Clay retorted, waving the tomahawk under his compadre's nose. Snake Eye Gandy rode between them and defused the quarrel before it turned serious.

"Virge. Since you're so full of piss and vinegar, ride on up the valley aways and make sure we aren't in anybody's backyard." Gandy glanced over his shoulder at Ben. Even though the Rangers were ostensibly under the lieutenant's command, Snake Eye Gandy had a habit of issuing orders and checking with McQueen as an afterthought.

Virge shrugged and rode off without waiting for Ben to give his approval.

"Dumb bastard," Clay muttered. "He couldn't even count to eleven with his pants open." He started back to the cave as Ben and the others dismounted. Peter volunteered to take the horses down to the creek and the others quickly handed over the reins to him. The creek was a stone's throw from the cave, and Peter had no trouble in leading the horses to water and making them drink.

The rest of the men set about gathering firewood, which was plentiful enough among the scrub oaks that formed a greenbelt through the pass. But they'd barely begun their labors when Virgil came riding back at a dead gallop.

"What the hell?" Snake Eye muttered.

Ben shifted his stance to check behind the oncoming Ranger. No one was chasing him. But that didn't make Ben relax any, not the way Virge was riding.

"That bastard is trying it again," Clay scowled. He was determined not to fall for another of his friend's ruses.

Virge halted his mount with a savage tug on the reins. The animal skidded in the soft earth near the creek. The Ranger looked ghastly white as he waved his hat and motioned for the others to follow him.

"Saddle up, lads. By God, what I've found yonder no man should have rode up to on his lonesome."

"Virge, we've had a bellyful of your shenanigans," Snake Eye warned.

"If this is another trick . . ." Clay added.

"I wish to God it was," Virge said in a shaken tone of voice. "God knows I do." And with that he wheeled his horse about and rode up the pass toward a grove of scrub oaks that grew dense at the base of the north cliff. Behind him, his companions remounted in silence. Clay was the last to swing a leg over his saddle.

"If this is a trick..." he repeated.

It wasn't.

Ben had to look away, though he recognized Zavala as one of Anabel's men. Peter doubled over, sank to his knees, and retched. Clay Poole dismounted and walked over to the butchered remains of the vaquero. Zavala's hands and feet had been severed to keep him from pursuing his attackers when they one day joined him in the world of the dead. His chest cavity had been ripped open and his heart torn out and tossed into the fire for a sacrifice, although it appeared some of the organ had been gnawed on. His features were frozen in a look of abject horror. The blow that caved in the back of his head evidently hadn't killed him outright. How long the poor victim had suffered was anyone's guess. Clay drew his Colt revolver and aimed it at Spotted Calf, who was keeping his distance from the grisly remains.

"You sonuvabitch. Murdering heathens! It ain't enough you kill a man, but you got to butcher him like a fattened hog." He thumbed the hammer back and fired as Ben lashed out and kicked the man's arm upward. The gunshot reverberated the length and breadth of the pass.

"That's enough," Ben said, dismounting in front of the enraged man.

"The hell with you," Clay roared, and tried for another shot. This time Ben batted the gun aside and leveled the burly Ranger with a solid right to the jaw. Clay slammed back against a tree, shook his head to clear his vision, and tried to resume his attack. This time he faced Snake Eye Gandy along with Ben.

"Hold it there, Clay," said Gandy.

"You seen what his kind done? A bullet's too damn quick. But it'll do. You been wanting to douse his lights yourself!" Clay blinked tears and tried for a clear shot at the Comanche, but Ben and Snake Eye refused to budge.

"Truer words were never spoke, Clay," Snake Eye replied. "And I'd be standing at your side if this were the work of the Quahadi or any other stripe Comanche." Gandy looked down at the mutilated corpse. "None of his kind had a hand in this. They don't eat on their kill. Or open a man up like so." Gandy rubbed a hand across his mouth and shook his head. "The poor sod's had his heart yanked clean out, maybe while he was still alive, judging by the look on his face." He pointed toward the carcass of Zavala's horse. "They even slit the throat of his horse yonder. No Comanche I ever heard of would kill a fine animal like that."

"Even the buzzards ain't touched him," Virge muttered, looking up at the deepening hue of the sky. Pastel yellow, vermilion, and lavender, the westering sun spilled its bouquet of color across heaven.

"Because the dark ones have been here," Spotted Calf spoke up. His voice was thick with dread.

"Even the scavengers will wait until the sun has passed across the body many times." Spotted Calf glanced around, and there was fear in his eyes, something few men had glimpsed in a Comanche. "The spirit-takers have come as in the stories the Dream Walker used to tell us. And they have brought the blood-eating god with them."

"I've heard enough, you crazy buck," Snake Eye said.

Ben wasn't sure what to believe. But suddenly the ancient mountains had taken on an air of menace, and he knew he would be glad when they had reached the hacienda and rescued Matt Abbot. Only after Clay holstered his gun did Ben relax his guard. He returned to his horse and tethered the animal to a tree upwind of the corpse. He returned to Zavala's camp and began piling rocks around the dead man. Peter Abbot scrambled to his feet. He wiped a hand across his mouth and stumbled over to help Ben bury the man. Spotted Calf dismounted but continued to keep his distance. Clay kept a watchful eye on the brave, but Gandy and Virge helped gather stones. Though Zavala had been an enemy in life, his pursuers felt pity for him in the terrible manner of his dying. No man, they all believed, should have to meet his maker in such a way.

From a limestone rim overlooking the pass, Striker watched as the men below built the mound of stones over the body of the man he had killed. His two companions, Cut Lip and Gray Snake, wanted to wait until night and then attack these intruders. But there were too many. Striker was older by ten winters, and time had taught him the value of patience. Better to allow these white-skinned men to continue into the trap Fire Giver had prepared for them. It wouldn't do to alarm them and cause them to scatter. No. Let the men come on. Come on to their deaths.

Chapter Nineteen

Darkness greedily consumed Cordero Canyon. Stygian shadows engulfed the settlement and obscured the nearby canyon walls. The vaqueros hurried about their chores. The horses were led to the corral outside the wall and a guard was posted to watch over the mounts. Hector pulled first duty. He didn't mind. He was too worried about his wife and children to even think of resting. Lamps were lit and soon the front windows of the hacienda were filled with amber light. The smell of boiling coffee and frying meat helped to ease the gloom that had settled over the fortresslike hacienda.

Although the broad, spacious dining room was the center of activity where the men waited for Chico Raza to serve up his specialty, chili and tortillas, lamplight also filtered from a rear bedroom in the single-storied house. And while the men in the front cleaned their weapons and speculated as to the strange disappearance of the settlement's inhabitants, the woman who had brought them here confronted her own private ghosts.

After issuing orders to her men, Anabel made her way down a brief, narrow hallway to her father's bedroom. Summoning courage, she opened the door and stepped inside. Memories came rushing up to engulf her on wings of night, though there was little to remind her of the man who had lived in this room or slept in the ponderous bed. A nightstand and washbasin filled one corner. A coiled lariat hung from the wall. The room's one article of luxury dominated the center of the room. Flanked by two ladder-backed chairs stood a small, square table topped by a parqueted chess board. Pawns and knights, bishops, queens, and all the rest were arranged just as she and her father had left them.

"*What about the game, Papa?*"

"*Leave it. One day we will finish. Until then—*" He had hugged her. Anabel could still feel the pressure of his arms, the warmth of his embrace. It was the last time she saw him alive.

Anabel opened her eyes and looked down at the chess set. As an act of finality, she reached out and toppled the black king and lay the piece on its side.

"Checkmate," Anabel whispered as the memory unraveled and returned her to the present. Jorge Tenorio stood in the doorway, hesitant. He did not wish to intrude. She sensed his presence and faced him. He held the shotgun out to her.

"I reloaded it for you, Señorita Cordero."

"*Gracias,*" she replied, taking the weapon from him and closing the bedroom door behind her as she joined him in the hall. "You think I am a foolish girl."

"A woman with a shotgun always has my utmost respect," Jorge told her and, with a gleam in his eye, added, "No matter how bad her aim."

Anabel resisted the urge to smile. She led the way down the hall and into the dining room. Miguel was pacing the room. Chico Raza was in the kitchen stirring the contents of a cast-iron cook pot. Matt Abbot, unbound thanks to Jorge, sat slumped across the table. He looked up as Anabel and her *segundo* entered the room.

"The horses are in the corral?" she asked.

"We will take them to pasture tomorrow morning," Jorge said.

"My dear young woman, you have no idea the enormity of your actions," Matt said. "Is there no way that I can reach you, to make you understand what you have done?"

"I have kidnapped a general of the United States. Now there will be no peaceful settlement between my country and yours," Anabel said, beaming. "I will ransom you for much money." She sat across from him. "Then I will buy guns and raise an army for Santa Anna when he is restored to power."

Matt shook his head, astounded at her naivete. "My dear misguided young lady. Money for my return, indeed. You'll not see much for me. Why, I daresay there are some in President Polk's circle that would pay you to keep me here." Abbot laughed ruefully. He folded his hands beneath his chin to prop his head up.

"We don't believe you," Miguel sneered, pacing like a caged mountain cat.

"Then you are all damned by your own foolishness," Matt replied.

"I'll show you who is the fool, old man," Miguel said, kicking a stool aside. He slipped a pearl-inlaid dagger from his boot top and advanced on the prisoner.

"No," Anabel said. "Go outside, Miguel. Wait for me there."

Miguel glanced from Matt to the woman and then to the dagger, whose double-edged blade glittered in the lamplight. At last he returned the blade to his boot sheath and stalked from the room.

"A proud young man, Señor Abbot," Jorge said. "It would not do to provoke him."

"He provokes himself," Matt replied.

Chico entered and set a black pot and a stack of tortillas in the center of the table. He left the room and returned with bowls and spoons from the kitchen.

"You think Tomas will stay the entire week in Blanco Pass?" Chico asked.

Jorge shrugged and softly chuckled. "That one follows orders worse than any of you. No, he'll stay until the tequila runs out. Then I wouldn't be surprised to see him come trailing in."

"And he will be shocked by what he finds," Anabel added. She looked at her *segundo*. Jorge had survived all these years living by his wits, a fast horse, and a gun. She trusted his instincts and, like her father, was unafraid to ask for his help. She gazed down and saw her reflection on the surface of the black ring.

"Tell me, Jorge. What do you think has happened here? Where are our people?" she asked in Spanish, not wanting to include her prisoner in the discussion.

"Who can tell? I have found no blood. No sign of a struggle in the *jacales* down in the canyon. If the Comanches had come, there would be bodies. The settlement and this hacienda would have been burned." Jorge scratched his head, then rubbed his grizzled chin. His eyes were red and tired-looking. "Something bad has happened. But I don't know what."

"You talk like a frightened old woman," Chico interjected. "Maybe our people are hiding back in the hills, waiting for us to return. And when they see smoke coming from the chimney and the lanterns in the windows of the hacienda, they will come down from their hiding places." He dug into his chili, spooning the thick red chunks of meat and beans into his mouth.

Anabel shoved clear of the table. She had no appetite for dinner. Matt Abbot wrinkled his nose as he sniffed the spicy stew Chico placed before him. The prisoner chanced a mouthful. His features reddened from his forehead to his throat.

"More pepper, señor?" Chico grinned.

"No. I think you've just about got the right mixture," Matt said. He refused to let his captors see him squirm. He watched Anabel leave the room, then turned toward Jorge.

"All right, you old cutthroat, what the hell is going on?" Matt's gaze narrowed. "I've been a soldier long enough to know when there's a fly in the buttermilk."

Jorge leaned forward over his meal and began to eat. "You will know when I do, Señor Abbot," he muttered.

Matt stared at his meal. Somehow he wasn't reassured.

Anabel paused on the porch to allow her eyes to adjust to the night. Miguel was standing by the barracks near a wall that Don Luis's vaqueros had dug into the hard floor of the canyon.

She waved to Hector on the wall. When he returned the greeting, she started over to join Miguel. The darkly handsome young man straightened as she approached. He turned and climbed the stone steps to the roof of the bunkhouse. Anabel considered following him, then changed her mind. Sometimes Miguel Ybarbo could be as petulant as a young girl. Anabel walked up to the front gate. The metal bolt grudgingly, slowly slid back. She pulled the heavy door open and stood beneath the arched entranceway. She no longer could make out the settlement, for the moon was hidden behind a cloud. She stepped a couple of yards outside the wall. The enormity of night threatened to overpower her slender form. Youthful fears assailed her. She was grateful for the shotgun cradled in her arms.

Was that a noise? No. Only her imagination. Her father had never shown fear, and neither would she. Anabel refused to retreat, not until she had proven to herself and to the night that she was master of her own fate.

But the night had no heart and she had only her courage. Everything was reduced to simplicity. Anabel had to prove something; to her father's ghost, to herself, and to what lurked on the borderline between the shadow and the light.

She waited.

She watched.

Then a patch of darkness took on substance. And another. And another. The blood in her veins turned to ice. Like beasts, like men, they charged her at a dead run. Anabel thought at first she was hallucinating, for the beast-men made no sound.

Seconds passed, and now she could identify shields and clubs and obsidian axes and heard the pad of bare feet upon the dirt. She broke free of the spell that night had cast upon her and turned to run inside the gate. She stopped in her tracks as a warrior in eagle headdress materialized out of thin air to block her escape. The warrior raised a war club in his right hand.

Anabel reacted purely on instinct. She brought the shotgun to bear and loosed both barrels. The shotgun muzzle spewed flame that lapped at the warrior's feathered coat. The brave flew backward, cut nearly in half by buckshot, and landed on his shoulders in the courtyard. The gate was clear. Anabel rushed through and pulled the door shut behind her and rammed the bolt home. She heard the horses in the corral neigh and shriek in terror. Hector and Miguel opened fire from the wall as Anabel hurried to join them. Jorge ran out of the hacienda and met the woman at the stairway. Chico appeared on the roof of the hacienda, ready to fight.

By the time Anabel and Jorge reached the wall overlooking the corral, the fight had ended. The soldiers of Tezcatlipoca had withdrawn into darkness, leaving Miguel and Hector to feverishly reload.

Anabel sagged against the wall and looked down at the carnage below. "Oh, mother of God," she whispered. Her breath came in ragged gasps as she struggled to comprehend what had happened. Not one horse in the corral had been left standing. Some were dead; the others lay bleeding to death from half a dozen wounds.

"No!" she screamed. And the word reverberated and returned to taunt her—"No! No! No!"—while the poor creatures in the corral shuddered and died. One, by one, by one.

Ben McQueen, his rifle at his side, knelt alongside Spotted Calf as the Comanche drew on the dirt floor of Blanco Pass. Snake Eye Gandy wandered over at Ben's request and looked on as Spotted Calf completed a crude drawing of Cordero Canyon. He indicated the placement of the settlement and the hacienda at the west end of the canyon and gave an indication of the terrain to either side of the hacienda.

"There is a creek south of Cordero Canyon, on the other side of the ridge," Ben said.

"If he ain't lying," Gandy muttered.

"I speak straight," the Comanche replied, turning to look over his shoulder at the Ranger. "Do not be afraid."

"The only thing I'm afeared of is that you'll skedaddle before I can put a bullet in your worthless hide," Gandy retorted.

"You are a worthy enemy, Snake Eye," said Spotted Calf. "It will be an honor to kill you."

"That's enough out of both of you," Ben growled. "We've got trouble aplenty without you two trying to lift each other's scalps." Ben glared at them both until they quieted and grudgingly set aside their differences. Ben took a twig and pointed to the south ridge. "Snake Eye, if you follow south creek here, reckon you could work your way across the ridge after nightfall and enter the canyon from the blind side?"

"The hills are steep, but there is a trail down," Spotted Calf pointed out.

"What do you think?" Ben asked the Ranger. "I'll come at them right through the front door. Think you and Virge could sneak in the back?"

"Hell, Brass Buttons. This here's your party. You call the tune and me and the boys will dance to it as best we can." Gandy clapped Ben on the shoulder, then looked around at the dark mountains surrounding them.

"I won't be sorry to leave this damn pass behind," he said. He walked back to his bedroll near the campfire and stretched out. They had made camp in the oak grove, not far from the mound of stones that marked Zavala's final resting place. Virge Washburn had volunteered the first watch. The grisly discovery he'd made had left him unable to sleep. He was out among the shadows, watching, listening, lest Zavala's murderer return to kill them all.

Ben nodded to the Comanche. "You'll ride at my side into the canyon."

"It is good," Spotted Calf replied. "But hear these words, my brother. When we reach the canyon, our bond is broken and I will be a tame Comanche no longer."

"You have said it," Ben replied. He patted his rifle stock. "And I will be ready." There was nothing else to be said. The darkness hung gloomy as a shroud. Too restless to sleep, Ben left the brave's side and wandered off toward the spring. He squatted down and cupped water to his mouth and over his shaggy red mane. He stared down at his reflection as the moon emerged from behind the scudding clouds. He studied his features and marveled at how serious he seemed. His brow was creased with worry lines that aged him beyond his twenty-four years. His eyes looked hard as flint. He opened his shirt and stared at his naked chest where the medal should have been gleaming in the glare of a silvery moon.

Gone. Stolen. The blood heritage of the Mc-Queens. And his fault. His fault. Ben knotted his fist and drove it into his reflection until the image was lost in a blur of black and silver ripples spreading out across the dark pool. He stood and turned away, and his gaze settled on the burial mound. The stones were the color of bleached bones. What the hell was loose in these mountains? Ben McQueen had the uneasy feeling he was about to find out.

Chapter Twenty

Fire Giver stood upon the table rock atop the rock slide, in full view of the hacienda. He had arrived before dawn so that the men on the wall would see him at first light, the sun rising behind him. He wore his richly colored robes and his jaguar helmet. He brandished the sacrificial knife in his right hand and raised his left hand to the rising sun as if drawing strength from the golden light, or perhaps summoning it into being. And seven men of the eagle clan sat at the base of the rocks and played upon the drum and the shell trumpet and reed flute. From the hills the warriors began to chant, and their voices rolled down from the ridges like distant thunder. A storm was coming, with no way to avoid it, a tempest of wanton killing and destruction. And all to please the Smoking Glass, the god of darkness. With the sun at his back, Fire Giver stood tall and stretched out his arms, pointing the sacrificial knife toward the hacienda. The shaman's shadow stretched along the canyon floor as if threatening to storm the walls of the hacienda.

Fire Giver saw power in this phenomenon. He imagined fear in the faces of those he had lured into the canyon. Several days ago, he had scattered his warriors across the hills to find other sacrificial victims. The drums were calling them back. While his force swelled in size, the shaman had prevented his enemies from escaping by killing their horses. But he had lost three of his men in the process. The many-times-firing guns puzzled him. The few rifles his people had encountered had all been single-shot, muzzle-loading pistols and rifles. The ferocity of the gunfire from the walls had sent his men scurrying to the safety of the boulder-strewn slope.

Now Fire Giver must be content to wait, to bide his time while his men returned in groups of two and three. In a day or two, he would have a large enough force to storm the walls and destroy his enemies.

Tezcatlipoca was hungry for hearts.

Fire Giver looked down from his place of authority and spied Young Serpent with his men, keeping faithful vigil. *Young Serpent is too impatient,* the shaman thought. *I long to return to our village as much as he. But I know what must be done. Only after the blood flows like red rain, after hearts like red flowers are offered on altars of stone, will the sacred sign be given.*

Far to the south, hidden among mountains as old as time, the People waited. And died. For them, Fire Giver and the eagle clan had begun their quest. They must not fail.

*   *   *

Noon.

A bee landed on the top of the east wall. It crawled along the sun-washed surface until it came to Anabel's hand, then crawled across her slender brown fingers and took to the air, circling her twice. The bee came and went unnoticed. Her attention was focused on the shaman in the jaguar mask and feathered robes.

The eerie blasts from shell trumpets and the droning drums was wearing on everyone's nerves. Now and then Anabel and her vaqueros glimpsed masked warriors darting among the rocks on the slope. Like living shadows, there one moment, gone the next.

"Just look at him," Jorge muttered. "Standing atop that rubble for all of us to see. Sí, this hombre has the *cajones* of a bull."

"Well, if he or his kind come within the range of our Colts..." Miguel said from the corner where the east wall joined the south.

"Now we know what has happened to our families," Hector muttered. "They must have taken them prisoner."

"It isn't a sure thing," Anabel replied.

"I think it is," Hector said. "Your father was at peace with the Quahadi and many other tribes." He reached inside his buckskin shirt and produced a broad beaded belt, a symbol of peace among most tribes of the desert mountains.

"I took it from the mantel," Hector explained. "Your father used it to make peace whenever a new chief brought his men to the canyon to hold council and trade for guns and horses."

"These are not Comanche," Jorge said.

"No matter, they're all alike. Any Indian will

trade," Hector said. "If you've got something he wants." He held up a brace of single-shot pistols. With the Colt revolvers at his side Hector was confident he could handle any situation that might arise and, as he no longer needed the pistols, they would make an excellent trade gift. He might even be able to buy back his wife and sons. That was worth a little risk, and he said as much to Anabel.

"No," she replied. "You would go to your death."

"I do not think so, Señorita Cordero," Hector replied, glancing toward the lone brave atop the rock slide a little over a hundred yards away. "I will bring them the medicine belt and show that we come as friends." He turned and started down from the wall. Anabel was torn between permitting him to go and calling him back. Perhaps there was still a possibility that some kind of peace could be made with these mysterious warriors. It might be worth the effort after all.

"Wait. I should go. It is my place," Anabel said.

"No. Señorita. It is my wife and children who are missing. It is for me to meet with these chiefs."

Anabel glanced at Jorge, who shrugged and said nothing, though it was obvious he disapproved. Miguel seemed anxious for his brother to go. If there was a chance for an end to the hostilities, he felt it was certainly worth the risk—as long as it wasn't his risk.

"Go then, but be careful."

"*Adiós*," Hector said. He glanced at his younger brother.

"*Vaya con Dios*," Miguel said. "I will close the gate after you, eh?"

The two brothers hurried down into the courtyard. Hector quickly gathered up a few trade goods, draped a couple of blankets across his shoulder, and then, with the Comanche medicine belt held before him like a shield, nodded to Miguel, who opened the oak door. Hector looked around at the hacienda and spied Chico Raza and the *norteamericano* watching him from the roof. He waved to Chico, who returned the salute. Clapping Miguel on the shoulder, Hector stepped through the gate.

"He's about there," Jorge announced, despite the fact that Anabel and Miguel could see just as well as the *segundo*. Even Chico and the captive Matthew Abbot were standing on the wooden walk behind the east wall, attention centered on the distant figure who had just reached the rock slide after making his way unharmed down the canyon.

The stench from the corral was enough to turn the strongest stomach. The carcasses of the dead animals had begun to bloat in the heat. Their flesh was black with flies. Anabel knew something would have to be done but she didn't want to take any action that might endanger Hector. She watched as Hector raised a hand in greeting and then spread the blankets upon the ground. The bargaining had begun.

"I don't like this," Jorge muttered. Half a dozen warriors materialized out of the rocks and slowly advanced on the solitary peacemaker who had bravely left the safety of the hacienda.

"My brother knows what he is doing," Miguel nervously countered. Hector was indestructible, he thought. Nothing could harm him. Anabel raised a spyglass that had belonged to her father and peered through the eyepiece. She could make out the man in the jaguar mask, who seemed to be the chief. She moved the spyglass and Hector slipped into focus. He was speaking with a good deal of animation, indicating the blanket and the trade guns he had brought. He turned as the other warriors left the protection of the boulders and advanced on him. She had never seen the likes of such men as these, with their eagle masks and feathered armor and their obsidian-studded axes and clubs. One of the braves held a spear set in the notch of a throwing stick, poised to hurl it at Hector if he tried to reach the Colt revolver tucked in his belt. Hector continued to talk, but the warriors surrounding him offered no indication that they understood. Then one of the warriors to Hector's right suddenly and without warning raised his club and swung it in a short savage arc against the back of Hector's skull.

"No!" Miguel blurted out from the wall. "No!" He opened fire with his revolver in a hopeless gesture, for the rock slide was well out of range. Hector stumbled forward as the warriors swarmed over the struggling man and pinned his arms and then proceeded to carry him up the mound of boulders until they reached the table rock that served the shaman as a makeshift dais. In a matter of seconds they had stripped away Hector's shirt and stretched him out across the stone. The warrior in the jaguar mask drew an obsidian knife from his belt and raised it toward the sun, then thrust down.

Hector's scream reverberated the length of the canyon as the shaman cut his heart from his chest and held it aloft. Anabel dropped the spyglass and sagged against Jorge, who helped her stand aright. No one on the wall made a sound. Miguel had emptied his revolver. Smoke curled from the barrel.

He continued to stare with disbelief. Anabel regained her senses and turned away. The screaming had mercifully stopped. She stumbled along the walkway until she came to the corner of the wall overlooking the corral, where the dead horses continued to fill the air with their stench.

"Jorge," she said. "See that the carcasses are burnt."

"Señorita?" He had lived a long life and had seen many terrible things, but nothing so awful as what he had just witnessed.

"Burn the damn horses!" Anabel shouted. She swung around, her features flush with anger, her limbs trembling. Tears welled in her eyes. She noticed Matt Abbot standing close at hand. She drew the revolver from her belt. Abbot tensed, uncertain of her intentions. Then, to his surprise, she handed him the gun, butt first. "There is powder and shot in the hacienda," she said.

"What are you doing?" Miguel blurted out. "You give guns to our prisoner?"

Anabel looked out across the canyon at the boulders and clumps of mesquite and scrub oak, the tall brittle grasses dancing in the wind, all of it foreboding now. How many blood-hungry killers waited for their next victim to venture outside the walls? She stared at Miguel and her eyes were as cold as naked steel.

"Niño—por Dios! We are all prisoners now."

Chapter Twenty-One

It was three hours shy of sunup when a column of six tired men rode their weary horses out of an arroyo that snaked through the cordillera and brought Ben McQueen's colorful column to within a half mile of Cordero Canyon. Ben called a halt and Snake Eye Gandy trotted up alongside the lieutenant and took a moment to allow his Appaloosa to crop a mouthful of chino grass.

"Bright as a Comanche moon tonight," the Ranger said, looking up at the stark white hills bristling with cactus and clumps of mesquite clinging tenaciously to the rocky soil. "I've told Virge to stay with you. I'm thinking one can ride quieter than two along that ridge."

"Suit yourself," Ben replied. He respected the older Ranger's judgment. McQueen held out his hand. "We'll give you about a half-hour head start. Good luck."

Snake Eye shook his hand. "Seems to always

boil down to that. Good luck or bad—and a man must take his chances."

"And keep his powder dry," Ben added. The Ranger glanced ahead at Spotted Calf and considered warning young McQueen to keep on the lookout for treachery, but he knew his words of wisdom would fall on deaf ears.

"Be seeing you, Brass Buttons," Snake Eye said as he started his horse up slope. The noise of the hooves striking loose rocks and rubble seemed deafening to the men below. Ben could only hope that the trail that ran along the crest of the ridge made for quieter going.

He signaled to Spotted Calf to continue on, and the Comanche obediently complied. Then the lieutenant trotted up alongside Peter.

"You all right?"

"I may not sit for a week," Peter grinned. He removed his wire-rimmed spectacles and cleaned the round lenses on the hem of his linen shirt. "Won't be long now," he mentioned. "I don't feel exactly happy about it. More like a toreador standing in the middle of a bullring. I mean, the crowd's cheering and his heart's swollen with pride, but then there's the matter of that damn bull...."

"I feel the same way," Ben replied.

"Yes? But you're different, my friend." Peter eased back and studied the red-haired young man riding tall in the saddle alongside him. "I've watched you these past several days. You're not the same Ben McQueen who squired me around Philadelphia and showed me all the pretty girls. You've taken to the trail like a thirsty man to water. I'm enduring this ordeal. But you seem born to it."

"Maybe I am," Ben said. He studied the looming hills and the jagged silhouette of the mountains rising up beyond the ridges. Peter had called it correctly. Ben McQueen felt he had been riding toward this moment all his life. He had never felt more alive.

Virge Washburn nodded in the saddle. He had started to slide from horseback when Clay Poole tossed a pebble that struck him in the back of the neck. He straightened up, startled, and slapped at his skin, then craned his head around and scowled at his tormentor.

"You cut that out," he warned.

"Suits me. The next time I'll just let you slide out of the saddle and break your fool neck."

"I ain't never fallen off a horse yet."

"Cause I'm around to look after you," Poole said.

"You don't need to play nursemaid to me," Virge complained.

"Somebody's got to," Poole chuckled.

Virge didn't like his weaknesses showing. Beneath his breath he muttered something Poole couldn't quite hear, although he heard the words "fat" and "meddlesome" and "old." Then Virge touched his heels to his horse and the gelding trotted forward and put a little extra distance between its rider and the Ranger at the rear of the column.

"I have kept my word," Spotted Calf said, leaning forward on his horse. Along with Ben, the Comanche studied the moonlit passage and the cluster of mud-walled adobe houses and *jacales* in the center of the box canyon and the stark fortresslike walls of the hacienda farther back. The only way in or out, save for the treacherous deer trail up on the crest of the ridge, was straight up the wheel-rutted path they sat astride of. A half hour after leaving Gandy, the column had halted twenty yards into the canyon. There they stalled an extra fifteen minutes to give Snake Eye time to work his way along the south rim and get himself in position.

The men waited in silence, all except the Comanche, who seemed more nervous than any of the white men.

"Cordero Canyon," Spotted Calf said with a wave of his hand. Thoughts of revenge faded the closer he came to El Tigre's lair. Now, with his quarry in plain sight, his first instinct was to get as far away from these black ridges as possible.

"Yes, you have kept your word," Ben said. He unslung his rifle and removed a powder flask and shot pouch from his saddlebag. He handed the rifle to the Comanche. With Zavala's corpse still fresh in his mind, Ben could not bring himself to release Spotted Calf unarmed to face the danger of these rugged mountains. Still, he was glad Gandy wasn't here to see the gesture. The Comanche stared at Ben in amazement. Slowly he extended his hands and took the rifle from the white officer.

"Our paths must not cross again, Bitter Creek," Spotted Calf said. "For if that day comes you will see only a red man you must kill."

"And you will see only a white enemy," Ben said.

"It is the way of things," Spotted Calf replied. Then he raised the rifle in salute. "But this night I say farewell, my brother."

Spotted Calf rode back up the draw, the darkness swallowing him and muffling the hooves of his departing horse.

"We could be ridin' into trouble," Virge Washburn cautioned as Ben trotted his horse to the head of the column.

"I'll lead the way," Ben said. He glanced around at the three men behind him. "Come along if you've a mind to." The lieutenant didn't wait for a reply but started down the path toward the settlement.

Hoofbeats reverberate off the canyon walls: clatter-clatter-clop-clop, like drums keeping time to the beating heart. Pulse throbs, veins feel about to burst with each passing yard. And the starkly silent adobe huts and thatch-walled jacales, ominous and ill-lit by moonlight, draw nigh. Atop a mound of boulders, the remnants of a rock slide, fireflies spiral and swarm, drawn by what power unseen, spinning and aglow?

"Where the hell is everybody?" Ben muttered, echoing the sentiments of the day before.

They were among the houses now, squat, humble-looking structures whose blank windows and doors watched the intruders thread their way through the settlement. Virge was to the right and Clay and Peter fanned out to the left.

Ben could feel the sweat bead his lower lip and trickle down the back of his neck. His chest tightened with every breath and tension, like a branch in a gale, bowed to the breaking point, nearly snapped.

Movement in the dark. The fireflies swirled

with furious intensity. Time hung in the balance. Then explosions rocked the night.

Ben reined up as gunfire rippled along the walls of the hacienda nestled against the western slope. For a moment he thought they were under fire from Anabel's bandits. Gun in hand, he almost squeezed off a shot despite the distance, before realizing that the people on the walls were fighting a battle of their own.

Gunshots erupted on the south ridge. Snake Eye in trouble? Ben didn't have long to worry. In a matter of seconds he had problems of his own. A warrior detached himself from the roof and in a blur of motion hurtled through the air and slammed into the lieutenant, knocking him from the saddle. Ben landed hard and lost his grip on the Patterson Colt. His attacker crashed onto his chest. Ben could make out the warrior's yellow and black streaked features, framed by an eagle headdress. The warrior was about to cleave his victim's skull with an obsidian hand axe.

Ben's hand shot out and batted the axe aside. The obsidian blade bit into the earth inches from his skull. Ben caught his attacker by the throat, dragged him forward, and shoved free of the man astride his chest. Both combatants scrambled to their feet. The warrior charged like a maddened bull, his squat, muscular body leaning forward as he swung his war axe. Ben threw a handful of dirt in the warrior's face, momentarily blinding him, then stepped aside and caught his attacker by the back of his feathered body armor. Ben added his own strength to the warrior's momentum and drove the axe-wielding killer headfirst into the nearest adobe wall. After a sickening crunch, the body sagged lifeless in

Ben's grasp. He dropped the man and turned to look for his gun. A spear thudded into the wall.

Striker, eldest of his clan, fitted another spear to his atlatl and hurled it at the white man. The crafty warrior wasn't prepared for the big man's speed. Ben spied his revolver on the ground and dove for it. Striker's second spear tore the back of Ben's buckskin shirt, glanced off the ground, and buried itself in the doorway of a *jacal*. Ben landed in the dirt, one arm outstretched, and reached the Patterson Colt. He rolled to one knee, brought up his Colt, and aimed. Striker was gone, leaving only a patch of empty moonlight in the space between the two *jacales* where he had been standing.

The noise of battle seemed to come from every direction. Ben heard a gunshot, followed by a scream, off to his right and headed toward it. He rounded a *jacal* as three eagle clan soldiers dragged Virge Washburn from the saddle. The Ranger crumpled to earth as obsidian long knives and war axes rose and fell in the moonlight. Virge tried to stand, tried to lash out with the barrel of his Colt. Then he collapsed, bleeding from a dozen wounds.

"Bastards!" Ben shouted, then charged. The warriors turned away from the dying man to face the new threat. Ben shot one through the heart. An axe flew toward him, fanning his cheek. Ben shifted his aim and fired. A dark figure doubled over. Ben fired again and again, the gun kicking in his iron grasp. Explosions and shrieks of pain and fury and Ben's own wild war cry filled the air. The third warrior staggered backward as bullets dusted his quilted coat. Then there was no one left to shoot at and Ben was standing over Virge. The Ranger looked up at

Ben and clutched at his trouser leg. Ben knelt at his side.

"Tell Clay . . . watch for . . . watch . . . hell, I'll tell him myself." Virge coughed and died. The hairs rose on the back of Ben's neck. He turned and spotted Striker standing on the roof of an adobe house not ten feet away. At this range the warrior wasn't about to miss with his lethal-looking spear. Ben snapped up his Colt and squeezed the trigger. The hammer struck an empty cylinder. All five chambers were spent. Ben had a loaded cylinder in his pouch, but no time to reload. He spotted one of Virge's guns tucked in the dead man's belt. He didn't hesitate. He only had one chance, and took it, but the revolver snagged on the Ranger's shirt and Ben knew he had lost his gamble. A shot rang out as Ben tore the revolver free and swung around in time to see the warrior on the roof drop his spear and throwing stick and topple to the ground. Striker bounced once against the hard earth, raised up, then collapsed and breathed his last.

Ben McQueen's benefactor rode his horse between the buildings and waved his smoking rifle toward the lieutenant. Ben was stunned to see Spotted Calf. Then the sound of battle galvanized him into action. He ran toward the war chief and vaulted up behind the brave on horseback.

"Ha-hey, my brother. The bond remains," Spotted Calf said.

"I never thought a Comanche could be such a pretty sight," Ben yelled in the man's ear. "What brought you back?"

"A man must walk his path," Spotted Calf said. "He cannot change what will be." The brave nudged his mount's rib cage and issued a harsh command,

and the horse galloped off toward the hacienda. Gunfire still flared along its walls. It looked like more trouble, but there was no other choice. Ben spied two riders several lengths in the lead, no doubt Peter Abbot and Clay Poole. The two riderless horses belonging to Ben and Virge had already reached the hacienda. A third horseman blasted away at his unseen attackers, reached the floor of the canyon, and galloped toward the front gate. Ben figured it had to be Snake Eye Gandy. Evidently Gandy had abandoned any thoughts of stealth or subterfuge for the comparative safety of those ten-foot-tall walls.

The gate swung open and the riderless horses were brought inside. Then Peter Abbot and Clay Poole darted through the opening, followed by Gandy, who wheeled his Appaloosa beneath the arched gateway and fired his guns back at his pursuers.

Ben clung to horseback and loosed a couple of shots at a pair of suspicious-looking shadow figures as they retreated into the night. Short, obsidian-tipped spears came whirring out of the dark in reply and narrowly missed the two men on horseback. Ben gritted his teeth and waited for one of the shafts to plunge between his shoulder blades. Then the walls of the hacienda loomed overhead and Ben could hear Gandy holler a welcome as he retreated out of harm's way.

The arched entrance sped past, and after what seemed an eternity Spotted Calf jerked his mount to a savage halt. His horse reared and skidded in the dirt and collided with Ben's riderless mount.

Ben slid off the horse's rump and took his bearings in the courtyard. Chico Raza stood by the gate door. The bandit promptly bolted the door and drew his revolver. Gandy, Clay, and Peter Abbot stood in the yard. Above them on the walls, Jorge Tenorio, Miguel Ybarbo, and Anabel Cordero were astonished at the identity of these new arrivals. Anabel had seen riders coming from the settlement and assumed they were some of the lost people returning to the hacienda. Seeing Peter and the Rangers, Anabel and her men trained their guns on the intruders in the courtyard. Snake Eye Gandy and Clay Poole lost no time in selecting targets on the wall. Peter's left arm hung limp at his side; his shirt was bloody near the shoulder.

"Peter!" Matthew Abbot recognized his son and, with no thought for the situation, hurried down from the wall.

Spotted Calf reloaded his rifle. He searched the wall, spied Anabel, and raised his muzzle loader. Ben noticed the Comanche's actions and stepped forward to place his hand on the rifle barrel.

"No," he said. One shot could trigger a melee that few would survive. He forced the rifle down. "Take to the walls, men," Ben called out. He lifted his gaze to Anabel. "Or we can shoot each other down and the survivor gets to wait for those butchers outside to finish him. Or *her.*"

The guns were aimed but no one fired, as the wisdom in Ben's admonition began to sink in.

"Peter, My God, it is you," Matt Abbot blurted out. He hurried down from the wall and crossed the courtyard at a run. Ben was surprised to find the former general not only armed but apparently fighting alongside his captors. As Matt hurried to embrace his son, Snake Eye Gandy holstered his guns.

"Ben's right. We got bigger trouble than each other. I don't know who these bloodthirsty devils are, but I came upon their handiwork back of the ridge younder." The Ranger shook his head; his wiry shoulders sagged. "I seen the remains of a whole passel of folks, and every one of 'em carved like that Zavala fella."

Chico, shaken, staggered forward. "The children? Did you find the children and the señoritas?"

"I found 'em. And wish to God I hadn't," Gandy replied. "It's a sight to plague a man all his days."

"No—Natividad—oh, no." Chico moaned.

"What of Zavala?" Anabel called down.

"Buried him yesterday," Clay spoke up.

Chico blessed himself at the mention of his friend's demise. Then his expression turned hard and mean.

"How did our *compadre* die?" Anabel pressed the matter as she descended the steps. Miguel swaggered at her side, showing his contempt for these gringos.

"Not quick enough," Gandy exclaimed.

"He had been mutilated. Like some kind of sacrificial lamb," Ben added. "We buried him where he lay."

Anabel closed her eyes a moment. She regretted all that had happened, and even blamed herself. Drums began to softly toll an implacable warning that soon all of the people in the hacienda would suffer a fate similar to that of Tomas Zavala.

"Say—where's Virge?" Clay spoke up. He glanced around until his gaze settled on Ben McQueen.

"He's gone under," Ben said.

Clay scowled and turned away. "The sorry son of a bitch." The Ranger walked back to his horse and began to unsaddle the skittish animal. He tossed the saddle into the bed of a wagon that had been left in the shadow of the north wall, near the summer kitchen. A blue enamel tin coffeepot rested on the top of the stove, and the good smell of strong coffee filled the air. Clay didn't wait for an invitation, but sauntered over to the cast-iron stove and helped himself. Chico followed him and held out a cup for the Ranger to fill. Since it appeared they weren't going to shoot one another, he saw no harm in drinking together.

Jorge Tenorio, on the wall, was torn over whether to watch the courtyard or the canyon. Dawn was a couple of hours off and there was still the threat of another attack.

Down below, Ben looked at Anabel and had started to speak to her when he noticed the gleam of moonlight reflected on the shiny surface of an English silver crown dangling from around Miguel's neck. Even the scrawled "GW" was visible. Ben turned toward the handsome young vaquero.

"That belongs to me," Ben said firmly.

An arrogant smile lit Miguel's features. He had no use for this particular *norteamericano*. The big man's size did not impress Miguel. The vaquero had few equals with gun or knife. As far as Miguel was concerned, Ben was just an oversized target.

"It is mine now, señor. Unless you wish to try and take it."

"Miguel . . . enough. No more children's games," Anabel said.

"*Por favor*, señorita, but this does not concern you." Miguel stepped aside and lowered his hand to the revolver holstered on his hip. Tension immediately returned to the courtyard. "You want something from me, Señor McQueen, you must take it."

"Have it your way," Ben casually replied. His right fist shot out and caught Miguel off guard. The vaquero had been waiting for Ben to reach for his gun. McQueen's fist struck his target with an upper-cut that lifted Miguel off his feet and laid him on his back in the dirt. Ben leaned down, took the medal, slipped the chain over his head, and sighed as he tucked the keepsake in his shirt.

From his vantage point on the wall, Jorge made the wry summation, "That boy never will learn," and returned his attention to the canyon.

Ben looked at Anabel. "I want to talk with you."

She shrugged, indicated the house against the west wall, and started toward the front door. Gandy motioned for Spotted Calf to give him a hand, and the two men picked up Miguel's unconscious form and carried him into the summer kitchen, where they stretched him out on one of the tables. Matt brought Peter over to the lamp hanging from one of the posts.

"I'll tend your arm, son. There's hot water next to the coffee and we can clean that wound."

"It's just a scratch," Peter remarked, but he followed his father. He felt strangely happy and couldn't understand it. Here they were, more than a hundred miles from the border, surrounded by murderous savages and without hope of rescue, and he was almost elated. He couldn't make sense of it, and didn't try very hard.

Ben followed Anabel into the house and closed the door behind him. She spun about to face him, her lustrous black hair whipping the air. Her dark gaze smouldered as she waited for him to speak.

For the past two weeks Ben had rehearsed this moment. He'd played it over and over again in his mind. Now, alone with Anabel, the phrases he'd so painstakingly construed failed him. Nothing seemed adequate or even remotely represented the emotions warring upon the battlefield of his heart.

Reacting on instinct, he reached out, pulled her to him, and kissed her. She made no attempt to resist as his mouth bruised hers. Then, when it was over, she stepped back and slapped him. They stared at one another like wounded animals. Ben slapped her in return with about the same force as she had used. Her cheek grew red as his. Her eyes flared and she struck again. This time he caught her wrist. She hesitated, and then, instead of pulling free, rushed forward and kissed him, taking the offensive and stealing his breath away. This time when they parted the soldier and the señorita warily retreated to opposite sides of the entranceway.

"Well, now that we understand each other..." Ben said. He touched the brim of his hat and made a hasty exit.

"Sí," Anabel weakly replied, and sagged against a ladder-backed chair. "We understand." With the taste of her enemy lover fresh on her lips, Anabel Cordero proceeded to reload her gun.

Chapter Twenty-Two

As a presage to sunrise, the eastern sky shed its purple cloak of night and flushed, pale pink, then donned vestments of gilded gold clouds. Amber light washed the hacienda and its backdrop of hills, then swept down the canyon like a flash flood.

Fire Giver climbed to the table rock and stood with arms upraised to greet the morning light. His loud, clear chant rang out for all his people to hear and take courage from. The prayer song carried across the killing ground to the walls of the hacienda.

"Smoking Glass,
The darkness ends.
Your spirit will dwell in us
until the darkness returns.
The light brings warmth.
But the dark brings power.
I am the hands of the blood-eating god
The Destroyer of Enemies.

> *I am the heart of the blood-eating god.*
> *Through me my people live."*

The warriors appeared along the canyon walls. Many of them looked to Young Serpent, for he had braved the thunder weapons and led the raid on the horses in the canyon. Standing on the hillside, Young Serpent's heart was heavy with sorrow. Striker had been slain. Corpses had been carried from the canyon floor under cover of night and hidden among the mesquite trees and boulders on the steep hills to the north and south. Seven of Young Serpent's clansmen had already been lost. And still, Fire Giver demanded more blood. Young Serpent could only wonder when their hungry god would be appeased.

Now the warriors were gathered. A great battle was coming; of this Young Serpent had no doubt. And maybe after tonight Tezcatlipoca would reveal his wishes and show them the way home.

"It is a bad thing, these deaths. The thunder sticks strike us down like petals in the wind," Cut Lip spoke up. He was only a year older than Young Serpent. Stocky, with a deep chest, Cut Lip, it was said, could run night and day without tiring. Scars marked his limbs and torso, the legacy of other battles. But today there was fear in his voice. Perhaps it came with the dawn. He wasn't alone in his dread of the white eyes and their weapons. Many of the warriors held a deep-seated dread of facing the thunder sticks. But they feared the wrath of their god in the person of Fire Giver even more.

"A bad thing. The Smoking Glass must have needed warrior's blood," said Young Serpent.

"It may need more before we leave this place," Cut Lip muttered.

"If it be my blood, I am ready to die for my people." Young Serpent fixed his steely-eyed stare on the walls of the hacienda barely fifty yards away. "But I shall not die alone."

Another time and place and Jorge Tenorio would have been exchanging gunshots instead of pleasantries with Snake Eye Gandy atop the walls of El Tigre's lair. The two men had lived all their lives at war, either with the Comanches, the harsh elements, or with each other during the struggle for Texas's independence.

Jorge wiped a hand across his mouth and yawned. It was about time to summon Miguel to stand guard.

Snake Eye scratched at his half-scalped skull. The scar tissue always seemed to itch when his life was in danger. He had counted fifty-three strangely clad warriors dotting the canyon walls to either side of the hacienda. There were probably more.

"I kinda wish they was Comanche. At least I understand them," the Ranger remarked. "And that fella on the rock gives me the willies." Snake Eye patted the blued-metal gun barrel of his Patterson Colt. "Wish he'd step on down from them rocks and mosey on over so I could fill his hide with lead."

"If he comes, it will be at night," Tenorio said. "And with his warriors, and we will not hear them until they are upon us, too many for our guns to stop." The segundo had heard the legends of these warriors in their feathered armor and beast-masks. But he had always thought such stories were tales told and retold around Comanche and Yaqui campfires to frighten the young into silence. It seemed he couldn't have been more wrong.

Jorge shifted his attention to the courtyard. Miguel and Chico had retired to the barracks. Across the courtyard, Clay Poole and the Comanche were stretched out on long tables underneath the roof of the summer kitchen. With a half bottle of tequila beneath his belt, Clay had relaxed enough to be able to sleep, although not without complaining that it was a sad day when he'd have to bed down with Comanches and Mexican bandits.

Snake Eye glanced at the Mexican standing alongside him. He coughed, reached in his pocket a moment, and found a couple of *cigarillos*, one of which he offered to Jorge.

"*Gracias*," said the older man, who produced a battered brass tinderbox from a pouch on his belt. Soon both men were enjoying their smokes.

"I had you in my sights, back in April when we ambushed you boys west of the San Antone River."

"Why did you let me live?" Jorge asked.

"My horse spooked and threw my aim off," Snake Eye said. Smoke curled from his nostrils. The aroma of coffee and the smell of tobacco helped a man feel alive.

"Maybe it's just as well, gringo."

"Oh?"

"*Sí*. You may need me to save your ugly hide tonight," said Jorge.

Snake Eye started to return with a caustic reply, but he looked up at the warriors lining the canyon. "Hell," he muttered. "You may be right."

There was a firing port in the front gate, and it was here Spotted Calf came to watch the Fire Giver make strong medicine to weaken his foes and impart strength and courage to his people. The sight of the warriors kindled memories deep within him of creation legends and stories of the time when the Ones Who Came Before walked the earth and the Elder Gods warred with one another until the Great Spirit banished them from the realms of men.

He did not understand the words of the Shaman, nor did he wish to, for these were things better left unheard. Better to be deaf than to understand the meaning of such songs and go mad. He felt a presence behind him and turned, keeping a tight grip on his rifle. His look of alarm became a scowl of anger as he saw Anabel standing a few paces from him.

"Why have you come here?" he scowled. "I have no ears to hear you."

"Still I shall speak," Anabel said. She kept her hands folded before her and felt relatively safe. If he made a move toward her, Chico, on the wall above, would intervene.

Spotted Calf's flat, burned-copper features lost none of their hostility. But she planted herself right in front of him, allowing the Comanche no room to walk around her.

"I did not keep my word with you," she said. "It was a bad thing." Anabel fingered the dark stone on her ring. Sunlight glinted off its shiny surface as if it were ablaze with black fire. "I did what was best for my people. You would do the same for yours. But I wanted to tell you."

"Now you speak straight. But it will not save you," Spotted Calf said. He cradled his rifle in his arms and patted the stock.

"I will not plead for peace between us," Anabel

said. "I wanted you to know there was sorrow in my heart for breaking my word. But it had to be done."

"One of us will not leave these hills alive."

"Let it be as you have said," Anabel replied, uncowed by his threat. Defiant to the last, she stepped aside. The daughter of Don Luis Cordero thought she caught a glimmer of renewed respect in the Comanche's sideward glance as he walked past.

Miguel watched Anabel Cordero make her way across the sun-drenched courtyard and decided he could not live another moment without confronting the señorita about the decisions she had made within the past few hours. He waited beneath the north wall near the house while Anabel drew closer. Behind her, Spotted Calf found a patch of shade near the summer kitchen and caught a few moments' rest, while close at hand, Jorge and Snake Eye were wolfing down a meal of bacon and beans.

Miguel left the wall and headed for the front door to cut the woman off. Anabel spied the jealous young vaquero and slowed her pace. She could see at an instant that he was upset. For the sake of his brother, poor Hector, she subjected herself to his caustic attitude.

"Señorita Obregon, a word with you. If you have the time," Miguel said.

"Always time for my friends," she answered.

"Yes. I see. Like the norteamericano officer, the one called McQueen. You invite him into the house of your father, to sleep in one of the very beds your father built with his own two hands. And mine. Yes, I helped El Tigre. I was always at his side. A place of honor, señorita." Anabel caught the aroma of tequila on his breath. She started to admonish him, then changed her mind. After what he had seen the day before, witnessing his brother's terrible fate, he deserved to drink himself into a stupor. But the rest of them couldn't afford the luxury. They had to remain alert. Death awaited the unwary.

"My father was grateful for your loyalty, as am I, mi amigo."

"Friend? No. No, señorita, no friend. That title is reserved for the gringos who once were our enemies. Yankees like McQueen who you invite into your bed!"

"Lower your voice," Anabel snapped. "You are drunk."

"Sí. But not blind, eh?" Miguel wiped a forearm across his mouth. "They have brought us horses. We could take them and ride out of here."

"And what of McQueen and the Rangers?"

"Let them rot within these walls. It is what Don Luis would have done."

Anabel started to make an angry retort in defense of her father. In all honesty, she could not. Deep down, she knew El Tigre would have greeted the arrival of the Rangers like a godsend and not thought twice about stealing their mounts and abandoning McQueen and the others to the devil warriors who had murdered Hector, Tomas, and the inhabitants of the settlement.

"I am not my father," she said.

"No," Miguel concurred.

"But now I am El Tigre. And I will not run away from your brother's killers. Hector's spirit cries out and I answer, 'Vengeance.' How do you answer, Miguel, or do you even hear his voice?"

She turned from him and continued on into the

cool interior of the thick-walled adobe house. The sitting room was empty except for Matt Abbot, who slept in a cushioned, leather-backed chair. In the dining room, last night's chili had been left in the middle of the table, a cast-iron centerpiece of congealed sauce and fatty chunks of meat alongside a platter of cold tortillas.

Peter was nowhere to be seen. She left the former general to his rest and studied the hallway and the door to her room at the end of the abbreviated corridor. Thinking to catch up on her own sleep, she headed toward her bedroom, then stopped by the door to the spare bedroom and placed her hand on the oaken panel. The door swung open. And against every propriety, she stepped into the room.

Ben McQueen woke a few minutes after noon. It took him a moment to get his bearings. He'd dreamt of ravens and jaguars and red knives. The room itself had little in the way of amenities, but the solid oak four-poster bed had a mattress of straw ticking overlaid with a soft woolen cover, and Ben had slept well. The moment his eyes opened, his senses keyed and he reached for the revolver he kept beside him under the covers. He bolted upright and drew a bead on Anabel, seated in an armchair at the foot of the bed. Ben recognized the young woman in her short-waisted brown jacket, tight-fitting chocolate-colored breeches, and black boots. Her long black hair was tied back from her face with a leather string.

"I reckon this is the second time I ought to be thanking you," Ben said. "This makes twice you've had me unconscious and haven't put a bullet in me."

"In San Antonio, Miguel wanted very much to slit your throat, even though Jorge had knocked you out and you were no threat." Anabel rose and walked to the door, then back to the bed. Her revolver was plainly visible, holstered at her side. "You see, Ben, we share the same problem." She drew her gun and aimed it at the man stretched out on the bed. "I cannot decide whether to kill you...or kiss you."

Ben lowered his gun and leaned back against the headboard. He'd slept in his clothes, a buckskin shirt and nankeen trousers. His calf-high boots were streaked and scarred from riding through the thorny brush country of Texas and Mexico.

"There's folks outside these walls that just might make the decision for us," he said.

Anabel's eyes lowered. She saw her features in the black ring and turned the stone aside so as not to meet its accusing stare, then said, "Perhaps we ought not to wait, then." When she looked up, her warm eyes held promises and her moist, parted lips were an open invitation that Ben was only too willing to accept. He leaned forward and reached out. His pulse quickened and his cheeks turned hot, as if in fever. Closer now, and he could feel the same heat radiating from the señorita. Then Peter Abbot burst into the room and the moment shattered like dropped crystal.

"I hope I'm interrupting something," he said, grinning broadly. He pointedly ignored the disapproving stares and open hostility emanating from the man and woman on the bed. "I know who these savages are," he blurted out, waving his bandaged arm excitedly in Ben's direction. "And I know how we can beat them." He turned and started back down the hall. Ben and Anabel looked at one another and reached the same conclusion. Ben climbed out of bed and buckled on his gun belt. Then he and the señorita followed Abbot down the hall and into the dining room.

Peter was seated at the table, his hands clasped beneath his chin. He welcomed them in a low voice, a mischievous smile on his face. Matt Abbot wandered into the dining room and took a seat alongside his son. The former general yawned and looked from Ben to Anabel to his son and, sensing he had intruded on a meeting of some importance, started to leave. Peter reached over and placed a hand on his father's arm.

"Stick around, General," Ben spoke up. "I want you to see me pound your son's head into the table if he doesn't wipe that grin off his face."

Peter looked indignant. He removed his spectacles and rubbed the same spot on the bridge of his nose. He put the spectacles back on and cleared his throat. Ben recognized his friend's flair for the dramatic and indulged him.

"Aztecs," Peter triumphantly replied. "They're Aztecs, or at least some kind of precedent race. I've read about them. I've been to Mexico City and seen the temples." Peter glanced over at Anabel. "You've seen them too."

She nodded. "But their culture was destroyed by the conquistadors long ago."

"Not all. Look outside your walls. Don't ask me how or why or what pit they've crawled out of," Peter said. "But I tell you, we are surrounded by those same blood worshipers who used to rip the hearts from their sacrificial victims to satiate their dark god."

Ben shrugged. "I've read of Cortez and Montezuma, but how does that help us now?"

Peter's eyes widened with excitement. "I've been studying them from the roof. The man atop the rock slide must be the shaman, the very personification of a deity. If anything were to happen to him—"

Ben understood what his friend was getting at. The Spaniards had killed the high priests and so demoralized the Aztecs that Cortez and a handful of men had conquered an empire. The shaman was the key.

"You see my point?" Peter asked.

"Yes," Ben replied. "Tonight, one way or another, a god must die."

Fire Giver felt a sense of triumph at dusk as he stood upon the table rock that had become the ceremonial dais from which he intended to oversee the destruction of his enemies. His personal guard had ringed his position with gathered underbrush. At the given time the brush would be set ablaze. The circle of fire would light up the rock slide and outline the shaman. Fire Giver wanted his enemies to see their destroyer.

As the sky turned velvet black and shadows crept the length of the canyon, the drums and flutes fell silent and Young Serpent approached the shaman, as he had been ordered. It was always with a feeling of trepidation that one approached the manifested god of darkness, and the warrior wondered if he would be taken to task for his openly expressed desire to return home.

Young Serpent climbed to within about six feet of the dais and announced himself. "You sent for me?" Fire Giver's eyes seemed to glow within his jaguar mask. He nodded and, drawing the sacrificial knife from his belt, knelt and scratched a circle almost four feet in diameter in the stone. Then he straightened and stood in the circle.

"This night the blood-eating god shall glut himself on the hearts of our enemies," said Fire Giver. "Let my words pass from ear to ear. Before the night passes, I shall make our path clear."

"May it lead home," Young Serpent replied in all earnestness.

"I am the power; my strength shall be in the arms of my people. Tell them," the shaman chanted.

"It will be as you have said." Young Serpent breathed a sigh of relief. He turned and from this vantage point took a moment to study the walled hacienda the Warriors of the Night would soon assault. What were the strangers within the walls thinking? Did they feel safe? Did they know how close they were to death? Their weapons were noisy and wreaked terrible havoc. Many of Young Serpent's clansmen might well perish during the attack. Tezcatlipoca was a demanding god. Still, it was worth whatever price to rid his people of the spotted sickness that had claimed so many lives in their village to the south. He stared at the walls of the hacienda, his mind full of questions whose answers were only hours away.

Ben adjusted the focus on the spyglass by lengthening and then shortening its length. Young Serpent's image shimmered into focus. Daylight was fading fast. Ben shifted his stance and the shaman filled the eyepiece.

"Now there's a fierce-looking son of a bitch," Ben muttered. He swept the slopes with the spyglass, but the other warriors had vanished, as if the earth had swallowed them up. It was unnerving to think that so many of the bloodthirsty bastards were probably watching him right this instant, and that he could not see them.

Anabel made her way along the south wall and joined Ben at the corner where he had been standing his watch for the past couple of hours. He smiled at her approach. She was as great a puzzle to him as when first they had met. Had it been but a little more than two weeks ago? He had taken time to shave and wash the dust from his face, and brush his thick red hair back from his face. He tilted his sombrero high on his forehead and tucked the spyglass in his belt.

At first glance she looked like a vaquero in her short-waisted jacket, cotton shirt, and breeches. A black sash circled her waist. A holstered Patterson Colt rode high on her hip. She leaned her elbows on the wall and folded her hands while she toyed with her father's ring, its obsidian stone like the heart of night.

In the courtyard below, the men worked together, enduring an uneasy truce for the common good. Clay Poole, Chico Raza, and Jorge Tenorio rolled the straw-littered wagon out from the north wall as Miguel and Snake Eye led Gandy's Appaloosa and a chestnut gelding over to the singletree and harnessed the animals to the wagon.

Gandy made a quick inspection of the axles, all of which had needed repacking. It had taken most of the afternoon, but now the wagon seemed sound enough. He glanced up at Ben, shrugged, then nodded, a noncommital acceptance of the freight wagon's condition. In the summer kitchen, Peter Abbot, with his bandaged shoulder, and Matt had escaped the more strenuous labors. Father and son had taken it upon themselves to clean and oil the weapons. Several Colts lay before them on the tabletop, broken down into barrel, cylinder, and grip.

"Are you having doubts?" Anabel said.

"No," Ben answered.

"It is a good plan," she said by way of encouragement, just in case he needed it. A couple of hours ago she had stood aside and allowed Ben to issue orders to her own men, as well as to the Rangers under his command. Her vaqueros had grudgingly accepted his leadership. They did not pretend loyalty, as such a pretense could have fooled no one. There were two factions within these adobe walls that were sworn enemies. No—three by her count: Spotted Calf would no doubt turn against them all once they were clear of the canyon.

Ben had put together a simple plan, but one that for all its simplicity might just work. They had six horses and ten riders. Four men—Ben, Spotted Calf, Jorge, and Clay Poole—would lead the way on horseback, followed by the remaining six in the wagon, which would be pulled by a two-horse team. The concentrated gunfire from the wagon ought to mow down any attackers who got in their way. With the warriors afoot, they could easily be outdistanced. Getting clear of the canyon was the hard part. While the wagon made its dash to safety, the men on horseback would try for the shaman. Snake Eye had bristled at being assigned to the wagon, but Ben had stood his ground. If anyone could see Matt Abbot safely out of these mountains, Ben had insisted, Snake Eye Gandy was the man.

Stars began twinkling into existence as the sky grew dark. Ben surveyed his surroundings. A man could do worse than make his home here—or his grave. He looked at Anabel, who seemed amused by his appearance.

"You look like a *bandito*, not a soldier," she said. "Maybe you should ride for me, eh?"

Ben shook his head. "My place is north, across the Rio Grande. It could be your place too."

"Never!" she replied. He had touched on a nerve, and it showed.

"Your father is dead, Anabel," Ben said.

"His struggle lives. I am Cordero. As long as I wear the ring of my father, there shall be no peace."

"If we live through the night, I'll be bringing Matt Abbot home," Ben said. "But what shall I do with you?"

"Maybe I surprise you, Señor McQueen," the woman countered in a velvety-smooth tone of voice. "But for now, let us be friends, *sí*?"

Ben agreed, though the irony wasn't lost on him. Friends, yes, but they might have been more, much more, save for time and the Rio Grande.

Chapter Twenty-Three

And so it began at a quarter past midnight.

First came the fire as the dry brush surrounding the table rock was set ablaze. In the center of the lurid light, Fire Giver stood with his great axe raised above his head.

After this, the Warriors of the Night rose from the ground like spirits of the dead rising on Judgment Day, only these came not to dance with angels, but as harvesters of death, red rescuers whose eyes burned with battle lust. They were berserkers come to appease the blood-eating god, their only thought to kill and kill again until the walls of the hacienda ran crimson with blood.

Up went ladders of mesquite limbs tied together with vines. They attacked from north and east and south. Wood clattered against the adobe walls, but the warriors themselves made no sound, shouted no war cries. That was the eeriest part of all, a host of slayers moving in silent unison, storming the walls, racing forward toward the gate. One of their own who had scaled the wall was to unbolt the heavy oaken door and swing it open.

But the warriors hadn't expected the gate to open so soon. And they were wholly unprepared for the deafening volley from the revolvers of the men on horseback who charged into their midst, blasting away to left and right, trampling helmeted braves under the flashing hooves of their horses. Behind the horsemen came a freight wagon barreling through the entrance. Snake Eye Gandy cracked his whip and howled at the team of horses as he urged them to greater speed. Patterson Colts spat flame and leaden death as the wagon lurched from side to side. Iron-rimmed wheels skidded in the dirt. Hurled spears cracked and clattered off the sides of the wagon and shattered against the spokes.

Ben McQueen rode low in the saddle and blasted away at the throng of attackers. It was plain to see they'd been caught off guard. Guns blazed as Ben, Clay Poole, Jorge Tenorio, and Spotted Calf charged the ranks of armed slayers. Spears hurled out of the night as Ben fired at shapes and shadows that moved toward him.

Ben's horse slammed into a club-wielding warrior and the man went down with a muffled scream of agony as the horse caved in his ribs. The animal lost its footing and stumbled forward. Ben brought the animal's head up and saved himself not only a fall, but certain death.

The attackers had fallen back in disarray from the onslaught of mounted riders and the deep-sided freight wagon, which was afire with the rattle of guns. Anabel tried to pick her targets and carefully squeezed off round after round, but the wagon had too uneven a ride and it was all she could do to stay erect, grip the sides of the wagon, and space her shots as best she could.

Peter Abbot managed to prop himself up and blasted away at the enemy. Matt Abbot knelt by his son, fired a shot, fell, hauled himself upright, and fired again. "Damn it, Gandy," he shouted as the wagon jolted and bounded.

"Look out!" Gandy shouted back, sliding off the seat and scrunching down into the wagon box. Another flurry of obsidian-tipped spears battered the wagon. Guns blazed. Anabel saw a warrior spin and fall. Another attempted to leap into the wagon. Peter rose up and shot the man. The brave screamed and fell backward and disappeared beneath the wheels. Miguel, alongside Anabel, emptied one revolver and grabbed another from his coat. Chico crouched at the end of the wagon and struggled to unjam the cylinder on his Patterson Colt. A cap had fallen off the nipple and lodged in the hammer mechanism. A spear caught him between the shoulder blades. He straightened, dropped his gun, and tried to claw at the shaft jutting from his back, then sank forward onto the wagon bed. Miguel turned and tugged on the spear. Chico screamed as the obsidian blade broke off in his back. Miguel tossed the spear shaft over the side of the wagon. Chico looked up and Anabel scrambled to his side to cradle his head.

He was trying to speak. His lips moved, formed words, but the thunder of guns and clatter of the wagon drowned out his voice.

"What?" Anabel said. "I can't hear you. I can't hear!" He sagged in her arms and his head rested against her breast. She shook him. His eyes continued to stare blankly into space. Matt Abbot clapped a hand on her shoulder, turned her around, and shoved a loaded revolver in her hands.

"He's dead. You can't do any more for him. Here, help yourself." Anabel took the gun and crawled back to her place near the wagon seat.

Gandy clambered up onto the bench seat. "We're clear," he shouted. The ground sped past. The warriors surrounding the hacienda gave chase, but afoot could not hope to catch the horses. "Nothing but open road," the one-eyed Ranger shouted. "By jingo, we're free!"

Almost. Then the gelding collapsed, a broken spear shaft protruding from the animal's side. When the animal died, the singletree and hitching post twisted, the wagon lurched violently to the left, and the harness buckled and broke. The wagon's momentum carried it over the gelding's carcass.

"Jump for it!" Gandy shouted, releasing the reins.

The others didn't have a choice. With a resounding crash, the freight wagon flipped over. One moment, Anabel was clinging to the side, the next she was briefly airborne, and then she was tumbling into the dirt.

Ben heard the crash and swung around as the freight wagon flipped and rolled completely over. When it came to rest its spinning wheels were like the appendages of some sort of insect lying on its back, dying, and clawing at the air. The Warriors of the Night abandoned the hacienda and swarmed toward the overturned wagon. In a manner of minutes they'd reach Anabel and the others.

Jorge galloped past Ben and raced off to rescue

the señorita he devotedly served. But the only thing that would really help any of them was to end the fighting. And Ben knew the only way to accomplish that. "Jorge, no!" Too late. Ben turned his mount. Forty yards away, Fire Giver watched them from his fiery vantage point. The shaman's voice ebbed and swelled in a frightening chant.

"Well, Lieutenant, what'll she be?" Clay Poole hollered. Blood seeped from a gash on his cheek.

"Ha-yah-hey. Let it be said we walked the path," Spotted Calf called out. "Bitter Creek—is it not time to fight or die?"

Action spoke louder than words. Ben's horse reared and pawed the air and charged past the Comanche and Clay Poole. But both men quickly followed Ben's lead. They rode straight for the shaman. Whatever else happened, the god must die, or all was lost.

Miguel staggered out of the night and hurried toward the Appaloosa where it stood trapped in its leather traces, unable to break free of the harness post and the dead gelding. Both of the animal's forelegs were battered and bruised, but the stallion seemed sound enough. Miguel Ybarbo wasn't about to be picky. The Appaloosa was his escape from the canyon, and nothing else mattered. He pulled a knife from his boot and proceeded to feverishly slice the tangled leather harness. Sweat and blood mingled on his forehead where he had raked himself across ocotillo cacti when the wagon flipped. It hurt like hell, but not as much as having your heart torn out. Miguel was not about to share the fate of his brother.

"Leave the horse. Come back to the wagon. We need every gun."

Miguel froze at the sound of Anabel's voice and the click of a gun hammer being thumbed back. "I no longer follow you," he replied without turning around. "I ride for myself."

"Get back to the wagon," Anabel repeated. "We will need the horse for the wounded."

"You mean the damn gringos," Miguel snapped. He cut through the last couple of harness straps.

"I mean the wounded," Anabel repeated.

Miguel stared past the Appaloosa to the nightmarish figure of the shaman wreathed in flames atop the mound of boulders. No, Miguel wasn't staying just so he could be another sacrificial victim for the shaman's dark god. He gathered up the reins with his left hand and with his right returned the knife to his boot sheath, then straightened and reached inside his torn jacket. His hand closed round the wooden grip of a short-barreled, single-shot percussion pistol. As he made no move toward the holstered Colt revolver on his hip, Anabel suspected no treachery from the desperate young vaquero.

Suddenly he spun around, his right hand snaked out, and the short-barreled belly gun spat flame. Anabel fired at the same instant. Then there was silence.

Snake Eye reached down and dragged Peter to the safety of the overturned wagon. Matt scrambled up alongside his son. All three men hurriedly reloaded. Peter had a clumsy time of it. His fall had opened his shoulder wound, and it needed rebandaging. Gandy peered over the edge of the wagon, his ugly features framed by the spokes of a wagon wheel.

"They're coming. Reckon they smell the blood," he said.

"Look there." Peter Abbot had his back to the wagon and pointed toward the shaman in his circle of fire and the three horsemen bearing down on the boulder-strewn rubble.

"There you go, Brass Buttons," the Ranger muttered. "Aim steady and watch your backside." Snake Eye hunkered down and finished reloading his guns. Like his two companions, he was preparing to sell his life for as high a price as possible.

Ben leaped down from his horse and ran toward the rocks, with Clay Poole and Spotted Calf at his side. The mound of boulders loomed dark and forbidding, and from his fire-lit dais the shaman taunted them in a language the three men could not understand. But his gestures and tone were unmistakable. From out of the darkness, warriors dislodged from beneath ledges and behind boulders. In a matter of seconds Ben McQueen was fighting for his life. A man leaped out and swung a war club that opened a gash across Ben's chest. The warrior darted closer and slashed at the big man. Ben parried the blow with his strong left arm and shot the man in the chest. The warrior flopped against a boulder and slid down with his legs outsplayed. A second warrior landed on Ben's shoulders and knocked him to the ground. The warrior tried to knife his fallen foe, but Ben twisted away, forced an arm free, fired up into the man's masked features, and tossed the lifeless corpse aside.

Clay Poole emptied his revolver into the throng. He dropped a man with a bullet to the shoulder, gut-shot a second. He split a skull, eagle headdress and all, with his iron-bladed tomahawk. He drove forward, firing and slashing and leaving a trail of dead and dying, until a spear caught him high in the chest and a second one low in the abdomen. He staggered backward, toppled over a boulder, and dropped to the floor of the canyon.

Ben emptied one revolver, then drew his second and charged up the same trail Poole had tried. Warriors rose up to kill him, but he shot them as they came. Spotted Calf appeared at his side as the warriors, determined to protect their high priest, attacked like a pack of wild beasts. But the warriors were not the only men driven to blood fury this night. Ben and Spotted Calf stood back to back among the rocks just a few feet below the burning underbrush illuminating Fire Giver in his circle of power. Revolvers thundered, each shot seeming to claim a victim, and when the guns were empty, Ben drew the double-edged Arkansas toothpick. The Comanche swung his rifle like a club. He crushed the skull of one man, broke the neck of another. Ben parried and slashed. The heavy, razor-sharp blade sliced flesh, shattered bone, and became crimson to the hilt.

Fire Giver looked down in dismay as his warriors died. Taking his great axe, he swung it overhead and hurled it at the men below. The chiseled obsidian blade struck Spotted Calf between his neck and collarbone. The Comanche stumbled, sank to his knees, and fell face forward, dead before he struck dirt. Ben buried his knife up to the hilt in a short, powerfully built warrior with a split lip and breath that smelled of dried blood. He lost his hold on the knife as the warrior fell away. Then turning Ben saw the Comanche lying dead.

"No!" he roared out, and battering free of the last of the shaman's defenders, he scrambled up the remaining few yards and leaped the fiery barrier to stand upon the table rock opposite Fire Giver.

The shaman had blackened himself with a paste of ashes and blood. His eyes burned with divine rage as he drew the *tecpatl*, the sacred knife, from beneath his cloak. His waist-length hair was matted with dried blood. He was strong and lithe, like his totem animal, the jaguar. He prepared to strike, to fight viciously to the death.

Ben stripped away the remnants of his shirt. His powerful physique was crisscrossed with gashes. The pain only fueled his fury. The savage in his blood had come to the fore. And it had come to kill.

Fire Giver lunged. Ben tried to leap out of harm's way but lost a strip of flesh in the process. The ceremonial knife had tasted blood. Fire Giver danced back and circled the larger man. He touched the knife to his lips and smeared his mouth with Ben's blood. The two men continued to stalk one another, to feint and dart back, looking for an opening, a weakness.

"Come on," Ben said, waving the shaman forward. "Come on, you bastard. Here I am. You have the knife. But it won't save you. Not this day!"

Fire Giver halted. He raised the sacrificial knife overhead and began to softly chant. It was an unnerving display. The man was drawing the power of his dark god down upon him. He touched the knife to his heart and then pointed it directly at Ben.

The moment of truth, Ben cautioned himself.

Live or die, here and now. The medal on his naked chest caught the firelight and seemed to glow with a life all its own. Ben closed his hand around the talisman, the legacy of the McQueens. The pain from his wounds lessened as renewed strength flowed into his limbs. Though some might call it madness, Ben knew the medal itself and the legacy of courage it represented were the source of his rejuvenation.

Fire Giver attacked, seeking a quick thrust to disembowel his enemy. The shaman was a panther. He was a blur of quickness and skill. But for all the shaman's savage swiftness, Ben was faster. He caught the shaman's outstretched arm, turned and twisted and snapped Fire Giver's wrist. The knife clattered to the stone. The shaman howled in pain. Ben caught him by the throat, first gripping him with one hand and then with both, and raised the man aloft. Fire Giver managed a feeble shriek as Ben's fingers dug into his flesh and closed off his windpipe. The shaman kicked Ben until his sides were purple with bruises. Ben would not let go. The shaman rained blow after blow upon Ben's shoulders and head. Ben would not let go. The shaman's fingernails, like talons, raked the arms that held him until the limbs ran red with blood. And still Ben would not loose his hold.

"Damn you," said Ben through clenched teeth. *Enough killing. Enough! The slaughter must stop.* "Die! Die! Die!" He lost all sense of time. He only knew that he must not ease up. Muscles corded the length of his biceps, back, forearms, and belly.

Wreathed in flames for all to see, the Fire Giver's struggles grew feeble. Patterns of light danced before his eyes. He saw the face of a leering human.

Impossible. His legs dangled loose now. His arms slowly sank to his sides and hung lifelessly.

Five minutes, or was it ten? Time had no meaning. On the canyon floor the gunfire ceased. Ben took no notice, but stood as one transfixed staring into the bulging eyes of a dead man. He could not look away. His fingers felt leaden, his back muscles ached horribly, and still he would not release his hold. He did not even notice how still the canyon had become. He paid no mind to the warriors who had abandoned their assault and who now filed past the mound of boulders and the two men in the firelight, the shaman and his destroyer.

Young Serpent led his remaining clansmen out of the canyon. The night of blood was ended. The shaman's own death had been the looked-for sign. The blood-eating god had claimed his own and was appeased. Young Serpent was certain. It was time to begin the journey home. The curse had been lifted by quest and sacrifice. In a matter of minutes the Warriors of the Night had left the canyon, slipping away like shadows, like the vestiges of some terrible dream.

"Son." It was Gandy's voice. He had climbed the rock slide and kicked a path through the burning underbrush. "Son. Put him down now. It's over."

Ben blinked. His body shuddered as if he were coming out of a trance. Fire Giver's corpse slumped to the table rock, a lifeless husk of a man, dead at McQueen's feet. Ben stumbled forward. His voice was hoarse and tinged with sadness. His movements were clumsy now, the result of his spent rage.

"She's dead, isn't she, Gandy?"

The Ranger gave a start. "How'd you..." Then he nodded. "Yes, son, Jorge came riding up with her. Seems she caught Miguel trying to run out on us and shot him. But he sent her under as well."

"I knew it. Standing there with my hands around his neck, looking into his face," Ben said. "It just came to me: Anabel was dead." He leaned on Snake Eye for support. "Help me down from here."

The Ranger nodded. The way was simple. One needed only to follow a trail of death.

Peter and Matt sat astride their horses and were waiting at the base of the rock slide when Ben and Snake Eye appeared. Jorge sat alongside them. The *segundo* had wrapped Anabel in a serape and draped her across the back of his horse.

"I will bury her in the mountains. Not here, but someplace where the wind carries the scent of cactus flowers, and not the stench of death." Jorge looked down at the red-haired young man. "She would have fought you to the death, señor. She liked you, Ben McQueen—too much, I think. But for her father, her duty... ah, who can say."

Ben stepped around the man's horse and touched the still, wrapped figure in the blanket. Something dropped from the folds and landed in the dirt. Her feather's ring. What had she said? Yes: *While I wear it there can be no peace.* With the toe of his boot he nudged dirt over the keepsake until he had buried the black stone ring in the dust of the canyon floor. *Be at peace, señorita.* At long last, peace.

Jorge started forward. Once free of the canyon he would head south to Vera Cruz. After all, it was his country. And it was hers.

An hour later, Ben had found a spare shirt and Clay Poole had been laid to rest, along with Virge

Washburn and Chico Raza. Miguel they left for the carrion birds. As for Spotted Calf, while Gandy and the Abbots scratched graves in the hard soil, for the Rangers and a bandit, Ben laid the Comanche to rest in the branches of a mesquite tree near the mouth of the canyon. He placed his rifle in Spotted Calf's stiffening grip and sprinkled a pinch of ashes from the Comanche's own medicine pouch upon the warrior's closed eyelids. Spotted Calf, whatever his crimes in the white man's world, had been true to the sacred path. Snake Eye, Peter, and Matt arrived on horseback and looked on in respectful silence as Ben McQueen sang a burial chant his mother had taught him. For Clay and Virge there had been a psalm, and the words were fitting. But a dead Comanche brave deserved more than a christian "Ave."

> *"Brother to the wolf*
> *And to the hawk*
> *Grandfather spirit has*
> *called you, to hunt*
> *with him in the land of*
> *your ancestors.*
> *May the buffalo be plenty.*
> *Plenty game of all kind."*

Ben thought of Anabel Cordero; he couldn't help it. And added, as much for her sake as the Comanche's.

> *"Swift horses are yours.*
> *Warm wind and all*
> *things that shine."*

Ben glanced back at the stygian corridor between the ridges. Here at the entrance, the bones of a Comanche would mark this canyon as a place of death. It seemed fitting.

The lieutenant rejoined his companions and climbed into the saddle. He turned his back on Old Mexico and started north toward home. And if the night hung somber and still, like his own brooding thoughts, no matter. Ben McQueen intended to ride clear to sunrise.

Author's Note

 In late June of 1845, Texas formally accepted annexation and became part of the United States. By January of 1846, a formal state of war existed between the United States and Mexico. And almost a year to the anniversary of the death of Anabel Cordero de Tosta, her dream was realized. Santa Anna returned from exile in Cuba. He landed at Vera Cruz on August 16, 1846. One month later the Napoleon of the West marched triumphantly into Mexico City and once again assumed the role of president. At about this same time, an American army began its assault on the impregnable stronghold of Monterrey. As usual, Ben McQueen and Snake Eye Gandy were in the thick of things . . . but that's another story.

If you have been captivated by THE MEDAL, Kerry Newcomb's saga of an American military dynasty, turn the page for an exciting preview of a best-selling historical novel by Kerry Newcomb, finally available again in paperback.

SACRED

IS

THE WIND

This moving novel of the American West will be on sale in May 1992. Look for it wherever Bantam Domain Books are sold.

March 1865—Montana Territory

No dreams. Only silence of the heart. No song, only waiting. Storms raging over Spirit Mountain, north winds whipped into a tempest, spinning down from the bitterroots where eagles roost in the crevices of the Great Divide, north wind, new wind, bringing rain to the forests below Spirit Mountain and the village of the Morning Star people who claimed the mountain as their own. The mountain, not the *maiyun* dwelling there, for who can claim the Spirits. Men can only do their best, can only lift their hearts in prayer and raise their voices to be carried off by the wind. It is for men and women to tread the paths of their days beneath the ghostly scrutiny of the *maiyun* and the love of the All-Father, the Great Spirit, the Beginning and the End.

In the last days of the buffalo, in the last days of the horse, Panther Burn had done his best. And it had not been enough. His features bunched in concentration as he tried to keep the faces of his friends from returning to his mind.

"*Ta-naestese!*" he muttered. "Go away. Go away." He turned on his side and dug his shoulder into the bulrush mattress, from which he had not moved for the past hour, ever since his father had sent him here to await the verdict of the council. He sighed, deeply, almost a moan. He glanced up, at the entrance to the tipi. Steps sounded. Panther Burn propped himself up on the backrest of willow shoots, waiting for the rawhide flap to be pushed back and the tall lean length of Yellow Eagle, his father, to scramble through. The coals crackled, popped, sent an ember arcing toward him. He caught the glowing morsel and, ignoring the pain, extinguished it in his palm. He listened as a shadow fell across the entrance, hesitated, then glided past; the footsteps faded. It might have been his mother. For Crescent Moon would never have shamed her son by entering and offering again the venison stew both her husband and Panther Burn had earlier refused. This was not a time for full bellies. Not when, elsewhere in the camp, another mother mourned her dead sons.

Panther Burn dropped the spent coal from his hand. There was an irregular crimson patch of burned flesh in the center of his palm, but the pain was nothing compared to the hurt within his heart. Blood trickled toward his fingers; he wiped his hands on his buckskin shirt, the one his mother had made him before he left on the hunt. A warrior's shirt, he had thought then, as now...only now he would have torn it from his body if it weren't for causing his mother grief. And one mother grieving in the camp was enough...all because of him...his pride...his honor.

It began with a hawk.

It was a sprawling land of emerald meadows in those days, a lovely cloud-swept land, a killing ground, a realm of beauty and death. Nothing stirred among the deep thick stands of pine, no glimpse of movement save over all the sudden swift shadow of a hawk. The cry of the hawk rang out over the rolling landscape to dash against the Absarokas in their snowcapped granite robes of silence, the shrill cry returned in a succession of ghostly echoes. It is said that among the craggy battlements where the pine forest gives way to hard barren ground, the spirits wait, walk, dwell, and now and then sit content, as if in audience to the deeds of men. It is said, and the Cheyenne believe, that the spirits argue in voices of thunder, they weep in the wind, they slumber in the gentle rains washing the earth in forgetful tears.

But on this second morning of the Muddy-Face-Moon, men not *maiyun* hunted in the foothills of the mighty peaks to the west. Panther Burn of the Spirit Mountain Cheyenne raised his coppery arms in unabashed prayer. He faced the east and thanked the All-Father for the gift of morning. A young man of twenty years, he stood just under six feet tall. His dark black hair hung past his shoulders; a single braid would have been lost in the thickness of his hair had the strand not been interwoven with two gray eagle feathers. His eyes were like flint chips, capable in anger of flashing sparks of light. He was naked to the waist, though a beaded medallion fashioned of porcupine quills and blue and white trading beads hung around his neck. He stood strong and lithe in buckskin leggings, breech-cloth, and beaded moccasins. His voice rang out, rich in tone, strong and commanding; his invocation cut through the stillness like an arrow in flight. In the deep band of purple-black above the golden glow of sunrise swelling upward from the horizon, a single star continued to flicker as if with a life of its own, joining in this warrior's song of the soul.

"All-Father...thank you for today," sang Panther Burn as warmth gradually eased into his chilled torso. "Thank you for this new beginning. Thank you for the mountains and the rivers." He lifted his gaze to the dying, dazzling sky jewel overhead. "Thank you for the morning star. Where it sings, I am with my people. I am never alone." His hand drifted to the medallion against his chest. Within the round patch of stitched buckskin the beads had been worked into a striking design, a square cantered on a corner and set off by four lines, one to a side, radiating outward like rays of light—the Morning Star. His hand touched the medallion, gently gripping it as he repeated the song-prayer. When he finished, darkness had been leached from the sky. The March sun offered but a false promise of summer's warmth here in the high country. Panther Burn glanced down at the camp nestled in a pine grove at the base of the hill. Three figures, his companions on the hunt, were up and about, each tending to his own business, each welcoming the morning in his own way. The wind sighed in the buffalo grass, whipping black strands of hair against Panther Burn's cheek. There was power here in the Lonesome. And magic. But Panther Burn was not ready yet to understand the ways of magic and the spirit. He only knew that his heart was filled with life. He felt ready for brave deeds, great heroics that he might join his father in the Dog Soldier Society, *hotame-taneo-o*, the bravest of the brave. But Yellow Eagle, his father, had ordered his son and these three others to continue the hunt while the Dog Soldiers carried war to the mighty Crow. What honor was to be gained in the death of *vaotseva*, the deer? Full bellies for the people of his village, yes, but what of the heart, what of the spirit? Heart and spirit know hunger as well. The shadow of the hawk swept up the hillside, passed across the brave, rushed down to lose itself amid the treetops.

An arrow thwacked into the earth at Panther Burn's feet, shattering the young man's moment of reflection. Panther Burn flinched, leaped back, much to the amusement of one of his companions below, who held his bow aloft and shouted up the slope.

"I have counted coup on the panther," laughed High Walker. He was a year younger than Panther Burn and one of the pranksters of the village from which they had all set out three days before. One packhorse was already loaded with rawhide packets of smoked venison. Another kill and the four young hunters could return home. High Walker continued to bait his friend. He trampled the dirt with a quick dancing step. "Now I may join the Clan of my father," he laughed, "I have counted coup and proved my worthiness." Little Coyote, High Walker's brother, the eldest of them and a man seldom given to smiles, ignored the antics of High Walker and busied himself with the Hawken rifle he had used to bring down their first kill. He sang his morning prayer in a soft voice, all the while readying his weapon. With his ramrod he tamped home a charge of powder and lead shot, placed a firing cap over the nipple, and gingerly lowered the hammer to hold the primer in place; he grew quiet, prayer completed, rifle loaded. Knows His Gun, the third brave by the campfire, was a slim, diminutive young man. Small-statured and conscious of it at a trace over five feet tall, Knows His Gun generally followed, seldom led. His character was flawed with an insolence that befitted a man, broader, taller, and better able to contend with the enemies his attitude might help to create. Contrary to his name, he was the only one of the four without a rifle, a fact of which he was bitterly aware.

"Perhaps I should count coup as well," Knows His Gun remarked as he reached for his elk-horn bow. Little Coyote nudged the weapon away with his foot. "The panther will laugh with High Walker because they are friends," Little Coyote said, his solemn expression misleading. On closer observation his brown eyes registered concealed amusement. "But he might return your arrow to someplace other than your quiver. And right up to its turkey feathers." Knows His Gun started to complain that he was not afraid of Panther Burn but he held his tongue, for everyone knew Little Coyote as a man wise in the ways of truth, capable of recognizing lies when he heard them.

"Better to give thanks for this morning," Little Coyote added, glancing upward as the hawk suddenly ceased its lethargic spirals above the treetops and shot from the sky like a bolt of lightning. A tanager, its red head and bright yellow plumage gleaming in the dawn's glow, glided from the top of a hundred-and-seventy-foot-tall ponderosa pine and headed toward its nest among the branches of a smaller pine halfway up the slope opposite the camp. The tanager's high-pitched cry was cut short by an onrush of lethal talons as the hawk knifed through the air. Dark and deadly, its rust-red tailfeathers streaming back like living flames, the hawk snatched its prey from the sky. The impact sounded like a pistol shot to the men below. Its cry of triumph ringing down the wind, the hawk soared upward over the hilltop and lost itself among the conifers. Little Coyote glanced around and noticed Panther Burn standing like a statue on the hillside enrapt by the sight, a look of eagerness shining from his coppery face and flint-chip eyes. At last Panther Burn appeared to sense Little Coyote's stare, for the statue came to life and broke into a hurried trot down the last few yards of hillside.

"I hope you remember your father's words," Little Coyote said, a premonition of impending disaster lurking on the fringes of his thought.

"Too well," Panther Burn replied, tossing the arrow back at High Walker, who danced out of harm's way. "Yet it was I who cut the sign of our enemies, the Crow. It was I who alerted our village."

"And you who watched your father and the other Dog Soldiers ride out to track these Crow dogs who have entered our hunting grounds," Knows His Gun remarked offhandedly, yet not without the knowledge of how his words stung the son of Yellow Eagle.

"And it is for us to bring food to our people," Little Coyote said. "Which we will not accomplish standing here." Little Coyote stooped over and took up Panther Burn's Hawken rifle, noting with satisfaction that it was already loaded and primed. Panther Burn might yearn to disobey his father, but at least he was setting a good example for the others.

"I think the others were afraid of how bravely we would count coup upon the Crow," High Walker said, siding with Panther Burn. "They are afraid we would cover ourselves with glory and shame them with our bravery." He slung his bow and quiver over his shoulder and took up his Hawken and gave a loud cry that echoed over the hills. Their horses nearby grazed unperturbed, already well accustomed to the antics of the young braves. Bees darted among splashes of pink and white bitterroot. The world ignored High Walker's challenge.

"Our horses are fast," Knows His Gun piped

up. "Our arrows fly swift and straight." He was as eager as any of them to make war against the Crow.

Little Coyote shook his head in resignation and started toward the horses while High Walker and Knows His Gun disguised the remains of the camp. Panther Burn fell into step, taking his rifle from Little Coyote but keeping to one side, as if unwilling to walk behind even a friend. He respected Little Coyote and preferred the company of this quiet young man. But despite his love for friend and father, Panther Burn's heart yearned to prove his worth to Yellow Eagle, to all the people of the Spirit Mountain Cheyenne. He longed to wear the buffalo hat of the Dog Soldier and be accorded the respect due the members of this society. Little Coyote read his friend's thoughts but said nothing. He tossed a blanket over his horse and tied his rawhide bridle around the mare's pink-flecked muzzle and proceeded with Panther Burn to gather the other ponies.

"I too would build my lodge among the Dog Soldiers," Little Coyote revealed at last. "It is just that I am one who can wait. This, my friend, is a good day." He led three horses now while Panther Burn had bridled the other three. "And I am not ashamed to be a hunter."

Panther Burn paused. His pinto, a sturdy brown-and-white-patched stallion, nudged him forward, eager along with the other two mares to continue abreast of the horses trailing Little Coyote. Panther Burn lifted his eyes to the treetops as a dark-plumed crescent shadow swept up from the ponderosas, climbing in long lazy spirals to the sky, casting its shadow over the unforgiving earth.

"Ah, my friend, there are hunters," said Panther Burn, "And there are . . . hawks."

Panther Burn balanced his Hawken rifle across the back of the pinto and pulled on the rawhide shirt his mother had stitched for him. Crescent Moon had labored many hours over the shirt, stitching the Morning Star symbol on the left, over the heart, and the stark red-beaded design of fire on the right. It was a shirt befitting a warrior, not a hunter, and Panther Burn had been loath to wear it even at the risk of disappointing Crescent Moon, but a brisk north wind changed his mind and he donned the soft rawhide shirt. The wind reminded him that this month was also called by some *punu-ma-es-sini*, the light snow moon. For three hours now he and Little Coyote had been riding together, leaving Knows His Gun and High Walker to hunt on the opposite slope of the ridge. Half an hour ago Panther Burn had cut buffalo sign and with Little Coyote followed the tracks in silence. The scattering of cloven hoofprints took them through a dry wash and up a long arduous climb along a gully that forced Panther Burn to take the lead and Little Coyote to follow. The surefooted pinto beneath Panther Burn chose his steps carefully. The animal had been bred to the rocky slopes, perhaps had climbed these same ridges, before Panther Burn had caught him and turned the animal from a wild mustang into a half-wild mustang. Good graze at the top of the draw, Panther Burn thought to himself as the pinto quickened its stride; good graze and water luring the animals into hurrying up such a winding, broken path as this. Savage-looking chunks of broken granite jutted out from beneath a veneer of topsoil. Brush against one of these and lose a chunk of flesh from your leg, strip it to the bone. Step wrong and a ledge could break away, sending horse and rider tumbling down the gully, leaving both broken, buried in gravel, carrion for wolves. The pinto angled to the left. Panther Burn almost lost his balance; his fingers tightened on the reins, his legs firmly clasped the stocky frame beneath him. The animal sidestepped again, leaped a break in the granite, and trotted up the remaining few feet to bring Panther Burn out on a broad plateau carpeted with tall yellow grasses dotted with tender emerald shoots. The land gradually sloped into a broad fertile valley. Spring storms had washed life into the valley. Though patches of snow still clung to the shadows lining the battlements better than ten miles across from where the two braves stood, the green shoots clinging to life here by the gully increased in gay abundance, spreading outward in an avalanche of newborn life. Despite the chill north wind stirring the dry yellow stalks of yesterday, spring had come to the land between the ridges. Tall stately pines masked the apron of land beneath the granite battlements. Bitterroot formed pools of pink and white flowers throughout the valley. And dotting the tableau, serenely oblivious to the hunters on the ridge, a herd of buffalo wandered over the rich feeding ground—one older male, a younger bull, half a dozen cows, and four calves.

Neither brave spoke, their glances to one another conveying all the information they needed. Panther Burn had first discovered the tracks that had brought them to the valley. It was for him to make the kill. Holding his rifle by the rawhide-wrapped stock, he gestured toward the older bull. Little Coyote nodded. They would approach the grazing animal from either side, Little Coyote to head the animal toward Panther Burn, whose responsibility it was to make the kill. Panther Burn was grateful that Little Coyote had suggested leaving the packhorses in the care of High Walker and Knows His Gun. It made two less horses to have to worry about. Buffalo are a peculiar lot. Oftentimes an entire heard will stand placidly feeding while all around them hunters fire their guns, dropping animal after animal. Another day the slightest commotion might set them off in a thunderous onslaught of hooves and slashing horns, trampling everything in their path. Those days were gone, Panther Burn ruefully reminded himself. *Ve-ho-e*, white men, had brought an end to the vast herds sweeping the plains, white men who killed for sport, who took the hides and left the prairies choking on the stench of rotted meat. *Ve-ho-e* had made the rifle Panther Burn carried. And though it shot farther than a bow and perhaps killed quicker, he wondered if the price might not be too high for such a weapon. For the rifle was not of the people. Such thoughts confused him. And now was not the time to think of right or wrong.

The herd below ignored them as the Cheyenne braves slowly descended the slope and reached the floor of the valley. Panther Burn tried to swallow, his mouth dry as granite shale. One of the calves had ceased its playing, stopped to stare at the approaching riders. To the calf's poor eyesight, the hunters appeared to be two more buffalo, albeit strangely shaped ones. The young bull was better than a hundred yards away, cropping the green shoots sprouting up through old growth around a pool of melted snow. As Little Coyote made his way around opposite his companion and began to double back, the wind shifted, carrying his scent to the old bull. It was six feet tall from hoof to humped shoulder blades, ten feet long from horn to tail, and to see its great shaggy head rise suddenly and a great and terrible bellow issue from its throat was enough to strike fear into the bravest heart.

The bull lunged forward, veered toward Panther Burn, recognized the blocked route, and lowered his head, charging forward, eyes blazing, slaver on its lips. The move was unexpected. So was the bison's speed. Panther Burn jerked on the reins and the pinto danced to one side as the bull lunged past, its curved horns narrowly missing the pinto. Little Coyote galloped past in pursuit. Gravel and dust spattered Panther Burn's face as he wheeled the pinto and took off after Little Coyote. Alerted by the bull, the rest of the herd fled the meadow, heading toward the shelter of the rocky battlements to the north. Panther Burn eased the hammer down on the percussion cap and whipped his pinto into a reckless gallop and gradually closed the distance on Little Coyote and the buffalo bull. He watched as Little Coyote raised his rifle. The bison veered to the left, its horns slicing toward Little Coyote's mare.

The Cheyenne was forced to fire his rifle while yanking on the reins to guide his mount out of the path of those raking horns. Flame, powder smoke, and lead ball spouted harmlessly over the bison's hump. The mare almost lost its footing, forcing Little Coyote to rein up to keep them both from tumbling to the ground.

Panther Burn was a blur of motion passing his friend at a dead gallop. The dark mane lashed his cheeks as he leaned forward, riding low and close to the mustang. The bison was fast. The sturdy little pinto was faster. But time was running out. The bull was leading Panther Burn toward a rock-strewn section of the meadow that would make pursuit even more treacherous. The pinto seemed to sense the urgency, and calling up a reserve of strength, pulled slowly forward, inching up until horse and rider were alongside the bull. Panther Burn raised his rifle, gripping the reins with his left hand, aiming the Hawken with his right. But he held his fire, waiting, daring a broken neck so as not to waste his shot. He had seen the animal's cunning and resisted the urge to fire. Suddenly the animal veered to the right, trying the same trick it had used on Little Coyote. Panther Burn yanked on the reins and the pinto veered in step with the buffalo. For a moment, stallion and bull were parallel, charging at breakneck speed across the mountain meadow. For a single moment, flashing hooves and slashing horn, sinew, flesh, and shaggy fur, horse and buffalo and man were a single entity, unstoppable and one, in wild and deadly flight upon the plain. Death or life in a matter of inches, in split-second timing, the difference between thought and instinct.

The Cheyenne sighted behind the shoulder, hesitated to allow the bull its stride as its hooves pounded forward, rib cage extended, leaving unprotected and vulnerable the bison's swiftly hammering heart.

Panther Burn fired.

*   *   *

Memories slither out from shadows, memories glare with serpent's eyes from the dreaming embers. Only the keening drums toll the notes of tragedy. Tap-tap-tapping like some beating heart in the throes of sleep, moving into endless sleep. *Let me walk the spirit trail with my friends, All-Father, hear me!* Panther Burn looked up at his mother. She might be real, or a phantom of the night come to trap him. He had been lured into a trap before.

"I bring living water." She spoke in a soft tone. She stared into her son's agonized gaze. His fault . . . his fault . . . his most grievous fault. She wanted to offer her solace, but knew there was no comfort for him and did not wish to humiliate him by trying. Crescent Moon bowed and stepped out of the tipi, leaving behind the clay jar she had carried up from Crazy Wolf Spring. Panther Burn crawled over to the jar and cupped a handful of water to his mouth, cupped another and washed his face, the icy-cold water bracing in its effect. It made him feel better. And feeling better returned his pride. What had he done save make war on the enemies of his village? What wrong had he committed? Was he not of the Morning Star people, the blood in his veins Cheyenne blood? Enough of torture. Let the elders decide his fate. He had done what must be done. He would not hang his head and walk the path of shame, not for his father or any other chief of the village. The drums continued, signaling that the elders were still in council. So be it. He stood. Sucking in a draft of air, he recognized the smell of cooked buffalo meat. Memories of the hunt returned, and more than the hunt . . . the ride back. He would never forget the ride back.

Around the flagging campfire, Knows His Gun leaped the flames, loosing an ear-splitting war whoop as he touched earth, leaped again over the cook fire. Landing, he stumbled so that the brown bottle of whisky he held slipped from his grasp. High Walker reacted with an agility that belied his squat, stocky frame. His hand shot out and snared the bottle in midair, and continuing in a single motion, swept up to tilt the bottle to his lips. He took three swallows as Knows His Gun recovered his balance and lurched toward his companion.

"You'll drink it all, thief!"

Little Coyote and Panther Burn glanced up from the travois they had built to haul the meat to the village. They watched as Knows His Gun leaped for the whisky, as High Walker knocked him back and stole another mouthful of the raw, throat-scorching brew.

"It seems the trader who visited our village during the last moon brought more than blankets and gunpowder," Panther Burn muttered.

"Knows His Gun will have visions in the morning." Little Coyote chuckled.

"Just so long as they are visions of him doing his share of the work." Panther Burn finished tying off the leather fastenings that bound the lodgepoles into the woven pattern of a frame and glanced up at the black cliffs overhead, great brooding battlements of wind-gouged granite blotting out half the sky.

"At least the light of our fire is hidden from half the hills."

"You are like the *ve-ho-e* trader who weighs his gunpowder, his grain, the glass beads which the women prize so. My friend, you weigh your thoughts and trade them for trouble, only trouble, always trouble."

"We have seen Crow sign these days," Panther Burn replied. "In the presence of his enemies, only a fool says, 'I am safe, there is nothing that can harm me.'" He glanced at Little Coyote, wondering if his friend had taken offense. The words had been spoken with unintended harshness. It was not Little Coyote's fault that Yellow Eagle had ordered them out on the hunt. The two men continued in silence to stare into the light of the campfire where High Walker and Knows His Gun were locked in desperate struggle over the remnants of the whisky. Knows His Gun was astride High Walker's chest, both hands locked on the bottle that High Walker refused to release, laughing all the while. Panther Burn reached down and wrested the bottle from them both. He threw the bottle beyond the circle of light, sending it crashing among the rocky debris at the base of the cliff.

"Ahhhh!" Knows His Gun staggered to his feet and stumbled toward the edge of the circle, then looked back at Panther Burn. "You had no right."

High Walker tried to stand but his own brother shoved him back, shook his head in warning. Knows His Gun wiped a forearm across his features. His hair hung unbraided and clung in sweaty strands to his cheeks. He wore a breechcloth and nothing more. His nakedness wreaked of spilled whisky. Knows His Gun blinked to clear his vision as Panther Burn knelt by his own blankets and began arranging his Hawken rifle, shirt, and other gear. Knows His Gun straightened, his small but muscular physique swelled with false courage.

"I am no woman to be ordered about. I am not your slave. You had no right to take my whisky." He cleared his throat and spat on the ground, almost losing his balance. He steadied himself. "We have never walked in the same path, you and I, so you taunt me, you insult me."

"We have never walked in the same path." Panther Burn nodded without looking at the smaller man. "But I threw the white man's crazy water from camp because you had had enough. You and High Walker, both. And we are not safe among the lodges of our people on this night."

"Liar. Black liar. I say you seek to shame me." Knows His Gun slipped a knife free from its scabbard at the small of his back. Neither Little Coyote nor High Walker made a move; each was loath to precipitate violence against one of their own. Knows His Gun moved forward, the knife blade extended from his fist. "I am Knows His Gun ... swift as the hawk, strong as the silvertip ... a scourge to those who would be my enemy ... come, I am not afraid of you, come and kill me if you can."

"It will hurt," said Panther Burn, his black eyes

deep and merciless. His voice was soft, spoken for the man with the knife, a gentle voice that cut through the whisky-fed bravado and sowed the seeds of fear, more deadly than a knife. Knows His Gun could not withstand the bleakness in those dark eyes, the bitter truth in the quiet, solemn voice. It would hurt...a lot. And then he would be dead. The knife blade wavered, and lowered at last. Knows His Gun turned and walked back to his bedroll and slumped down upon his blankets. He closed his eyes, groaned, and passed out, his last thought that it was better to sleep in shame than die.

High Walker sighed and stretched back out on the ground. Little Coyote continued to his own blankets, where he checked his rifle before reclining. Warmth radiated from the glowing coals of the campfire, the sky overhead was clear and ablaze with stars, his belly was full—it had been a good hunt. He looked over at Panther Burn, who sat staring at the coals.

"Knows His Gun was drunk with whisky," Little Coyote said. "Do not let it trouble you." He folded his hands behind his head. "It is my way to brood over such things, not yours. Tomorrow we start home; the hunt is over. *E-peva-e*, it is good."

"The song to welcome us to our village has yet to be sung," Panther Burn replied. He continued to stare at the blood-red coals. Panther Burn's uncle had looked into such a fire as this and found the name for his newborn nephew amid the dancing flames, had been given a vision of a mountain cat watching him from the livid coals, a panther burning...burning in the night.

"What are you telling me?" Panther Burn challenged the pulsing coals, the voice of his thoughts, soundless as starlight, unnoticed by his companions.

TERRY C. JOHNSTON

Winner of the prestigious Western Writer's award, Terry C. Johnston brings you his award-winning saga of mountain men Josiah Paddock and Titus Bass who strive together to meet the challenges of the western wilderness in the 1830's.

☐ 25572-X **CARRY THE WIND–Vol. I** $5.50

☐ 26224-6 **BORDERLORDS–Vol. II** $5.50

☐ 28139-9 **ONE-EYED DREAM–Vol. III** $4.95

The final volume in the trilogy begun with *Carry the Wind* and *Borderlords*, ONE-EYED DREAM is a rich, textured tale of an 1830's trapper and his protegé, told at the height of the American fur trade.

Following a harrowing pursuit by vengeful Arapaho warriors, mountain man Titus "Scratch" Bass and his apprentice Josiah Paddock must travel south to old Taos. But their journey is cut short when they learn they must return to St. Louis...and old enemies.

Look for these books wherever Bantam books are sold, or use this handy coupon for ordering: